CHAIN REACTION

C.J. PETERSON

COPYRIGHT

Copyright © 2022 C.J. Peterson
ISBN 978-1-952041-65-5 (paperback)
ISBN 978-1-952041-66-2 (ebook)

All rights reserved. No part of this publication may be reproduced, stored in a retrieval system, or transmitted in any form or by any means, electronic, mechanical, recording or otherwise, without the prior written permission of the author.

Published by Texas Sisters Press, LLC.
Lufkin, TX U.S.A.

The story, all names, characters and incidents portrayed, and the names herein are fictitious. No identification with actual persons (living or deceased), places, buildings, and products are intended or should be inferred.

Texas Sisters Press, LLC
2022

✽ Created with Vellum

DEDICATION

This book is dedicated to my loving husband and dear family who love and support me. You all mean more to me than you will ever know. Thank you! I love you!

A portion of the proceeds from this book goes to:
Love Ministries (Dallas, TX)
Our Mission: To build, mentor, and educate at-risk children and teenagers who have incarcerated parents or are products of single-parent families. To be instrumental in juvenile development through Christ-centered teaching that develops good character and ethics in young people. To train teenagers in good work ethics for the job market. Assist young people in preparing for college. Provide parenting and marriage workshops and conferences. Provide assistance for the hungry and homeless.
http://www.loveministriesbuilds.org/index.htm

To learn more about C.J. Peterson, you can find her online at:
https://cjpetersonwrites.com
'While the stories are fiction, the journey is real!'

YouTube Book Trailer:
https://youtu.be/hzljKO_205g

SUMMARY

Tori St. James woke to her worst nightmare – framed for the murder of her best friend. She and her family's past did not help her case in court. She was found guilty, thanks to testimony from someone she thought was a friend. Her life as she knew it was over.

On the day of her sentencing, her world was turned upside down by her...great-great-great-grandson? Traveling back from the future in hopes of changing his family history, Tripp St. Claire went to the one relative he thought would be the best to help him on his mission.

With most of their ancestors living questionable lives or dying too soon due to tragic choices or circumstances, it was their mission to change their past in order to save their future. Would the changes they make achieve their goal, or will history continue to repeat itself? When you mess with the past, even in small ways, it could change the outcome of future generations. Will Tripp and Tori change so much that they cease to exist? What would you do to save the future generations of your family?

Ecclesiastes 3:11 – "He has made everything beautiful in its time. He has also set eternity in the human heart; yet no one can fathom what God has done from beginning to end."

CHAPTER ONE

19MAR2021: A Time To Die

Tori's eyes fluttered open while visions of the party the night before crashed into her mind one after the other – dancing, drinking, Chet hitting on her. The smell of vomit, alcohol, and smoke immediately assaulted her senses. She slowly inhaled and exhaled in an attempt to keep her body under control. That's when the bright light of the morning sun invaded the room with a vengeance causing Tori to close her eyes once again with a groan.

"Why do I do this to myself?" she mumbled. "That's it. I'm too old to keep this up. That was my last party – I don't care what Chrissy says."

She slowly sat up letting her brain catch up to the rest of her body. Taking a few more deep, cleansing breaths, she waited for the dizziness to subside. When she opened her eyes again and got a good look around, her jaw dropped. Chrissy's apartment looked like there was a brutal attack. Her entire apartment was trashed. Her couch and the cushions were slashed. Cups, plates, napkins, beer cans, and all sorts of trash were strewn through the apartment. Tables were tossed, and lamps were broken or shattered. Even Chrissy's favorite vase she had gotten from her mother when her mother went to

China was smashed and scattered in tiny pieces all over the ground. The flowers that were in it the previous night were a trampled mess.

Tori let out a low whistle. "That was some party!"

Tori slowly got up. As soon as she stood up straight, she made a mad dash to the bathroom. She barely made it before the acidic cascade projected from her mouth. Everything she ate yesterday came out in a matter of moments. Groaning again, she dropped her head onto her arm on the side of the toilet seat breathing heavily.

"Seriously!" she said, flushing the toilet. "Never again!"

Going to the sink, she held her long black hair with one hand, and with the other, she rinsed her mouth several times in an attempt to get the sour tang out of her mouth. "Where's the mouthwash?" Tori asked aloud. Looking under the sink, she found the precious bottle and smiled. "It's not toothpaste, but it'll do."

After Tori rinsed her mouth and gargled a few times with the mouthwash for good measure, she looked in the mirror for the first time. What she saw looked like a nightmare version of herself. Her dark-brown eyes were bloodshot. Her mascara was a mess. It looked like she had been crying. Her eye shadow was long gone. She was pretty sure her lipstick found other homes either on boys, cups, or bottles. Her hair, which normally hung to the middle of her back in waves, was a disastrous mess with portions of it sticking up while others were caked with food.

She shuddered. "Gross!"

Tori found Chrissy's brush and yanked it through the tangled mess in an attempt to at least not terrify Chrissy when she found her. Then she washed her face, removing any remaining makeup. Finally looking decent, she went in search of her friend.

Opening the bedroom door, she was met with a sight that would forever be seared into her memory. Her friend lay sprawled out on the bed in only part of her clothing. She and the bed were coated in blood. "C-C-Chrissy?" she stammered. When

Chrissy did not move, Tori took cautious steps to her bed, mind reeling.

Chrissy lay motionless, eyes open, staring at the window. Feeling like she was moving in a fog, Tori's trembling hands reached for Chrissy's neck to check for a pulse. She rested her other hand on Chrissy's back to brace herself. "Chrissy?" she asked again, lightly jostling her.

Feeling the sticky slime on her fingers, Tori pulled her hand away and rubbed her blood-covered fingers together. "I-I...I don't..." Tori could not form a complete thought as she shook her head. What little remained in her stomach threatened to emerge – BOOM! The door splintered, coming off its hinges. She spun toward the bedroom door. Four police charged into the apartment. She gasped as one pointed a gun at her. Heart racing, still unable to breathe clearly, she threw her blood-soaked hands in the air.

"Freeze!" the officer shouted. "I found two in here. One alive and one dead."

The officer pushed Tori to the ground on her stomach, his knee on her back. He snapped the handcuffs around her wrists, tightening them until they bit into her skin. "You have the right to remain silent. Anything you say can, and will be used against you in a court of law. You have the right to an attorney. If you cannot afford an attorney, one will be appointed to you. Do you understand the rights I have just read to you?"

Tori's head spun. *What was happening? What happened to Chrissy? Why do the police think I had anything to do with it? Chrissy is – was – my best friend!*

"I said, do you understand the rights I have just read to you?" he repeated louder.

Tori's head spun even faster. Her breathing was erratic. Her mind went into overload as a black cloud took over, and she gratefully passed out. She hoped with every fiber of her being it was a nightmare, and that she would wake up with Chrissy giggling and talking about the previous night.

03MAR2022

Nearly a year later, and Tori still needed to remind herself that it had not been a nightmare. This was her new reality. Her days now consisted of wearing a pair of orange scrubs, a white tank top, and what she called shower shoes. The orange canvas slip-on shoes were not her fashion choice by any stretch of the imagination. In fact, the entire scenario was completely out of her control from the get-go.

The police did not listen to her when she told them she was drunk and passed out. Before she passed out, Chrissy was alive. They claimed Tori killed Chrissy in a drunken rage because Chrissy slept with Tori's date that night. As far as Tori was concerned, Chrissy could have him. She had absolutely no attachment except friendship with her plus-one – Brett.

However, Brett told a different story in court. He said Tori was furious, throwing Chrissy's belongings everywhere. At one point, Tori supposedly grabbed a knife, waving it around. Tori knew he was full of it because there was absolutely no way she would ever do anything like that, especially to Chrissy!

As Tori stood in the courtroom with her hands folded in front of her, she jumped when the judge dropped his gavel and said, "May God have mercy on your soul."

Tori shook her head and wiped the tears from her eyes. One night of partying and her life turned into a complete nightmare. Her sentence was twenty years with the possibility of parole with good behavior in ten years.

"We'll appeal," the lawyer promised, as an officer once again placed her in handcuffs.

With her family's history, and even her own few stints in

juvenile detention for theft, assault, and breaking and entering, the judge said it was a pattern and it ended there.

Tori sat on her bed in her cell. Wrapping her arms around her legs, tears poured down her cheeks. She replayed the afternoon's events over and over in her mind. She looked toward the sky, shaking her head. "Please let me wake up from this nightmare!"

"We're all in this nightmare together, sweetheart!" chided the woman in the cell next to her.

"Leave Tori alone, Sharice," the woman across from her snapped. "Don't you remember the day of your sentencing?"

"Which time?" Sharice quipped.

Laughter rang out around the cell block while Tori silently wiped her tears.

"Let the princess cry it out," said another woman two cells down from her.

The lights systematically turned off around the cell block. "Light's out!" the officer shouted.

Tori lay down hugging her pillow. Someday, she hoped new evidence would prove her innocence. Until that day, this was her new life. As far as she was concerned, her life was over.

A flash of light in her cell woke Tori with a start. At first, she covered her head with the pillow hoping to shut out the rest of the world. Then she felt a hand touch her arm. She gasped and sat straight up in bed.

When she did, someone covered her mouth. She sat face-to-face with a man she had never seen. Heart racing, she stared at him.

"Shh," he whispered, his finger in front of his lips.

Tori's pulse throbbed in her ears. That was about all she *could* hear. *Who is this person? What does he want? What is he doing in my cell? How did he get into my cell with the door still locked? Is he going to kill me?*

Crouched in front of her, the man whispered, "I'm going to take my hand off your mouth. Don't scream. Okay?"

She nodded in response.

When he released her mouth, he leaned in so he was close enough for her to hear him but not invading too much of her personal space.

"Are you Victoria Elizabeth St. James?"

"Y-y-yes," she stammered. "Who-who are you? Why are you here?"

"Can you do me a favor and close your eyes for a moment?"

She narrowed her eyes.

"It's a good thing. I promise. I want to go somewhere we can speak normally."

She furrowed her brow but complied. Sighing, she closed her eyes. He clutched her hands. She gasped as it felt like she was flung from her bed. It took her breath away. Falling, she struggled to fill her lungs with air.

She felt the cool wet grass under her hands but did not believe it. She opened her eyes and looked at her surroundings, the moonlight as her only source of light. Unfortunately, the moon was in its crescent phase, so it was limited at best. Tall trees cast shadows around them. Tori shuddered.

"Very good," the man said. "I'm proud of you. Sometimes nausea is a side effect of sliding. I threw up on my first one."

"Sliding?" Tori asked.

"We slid back in time. We only went back a few years so the police aren't looking for you."

"Who *are* you?" Tori demanded. "Where are we? What are we doing here? How did we get out of jail? Are you going to kill me? What are –"

"So many questions," the man said, shaking his head and crossing his arms. Reaching down, he helped her off the ground. "Do you want the truth? Can you handle it?"

Tori rolled her eyes and brushed the dirt and grass off her clothes. "Yes," she huffed. "I can handle any reality that gets me out of that cell."

He chuckled. "They told me you were feisty, but I didn't believe them. When you meet your great-great-great-grandmother, you don't expect her to be quite so real."

She narrowed her eyes. "Your...*what?*"

"My name is Sebastian Tripp St. Claire. My friends and family call me Tripp."

"Tripp? What kind of name is that?"

"It's the nickname of my great-great-grandfather, also known as your son. His nickname was Tripp, as in Sebastian Connor Hayden, the third – Tripp."

Tori rubbed her temples as she processed his words. "Let me see if I'm following you. You're telling me I'm going to marry some guy named Sebastian Connor Hayden?"

"No. Not really. You never married him."

"A one-night stand?"

"No. It was more of a semi-long-term thing, but you two never made it to the altar."

"Great! So, you're telling me my entire life was a screw-up."

"Yes...and no. See, I know you didn't kill Christine Bell."

"Chrissy," Tori corrected.

"Right."

"Do you know who did?"

"Chet Matthews."

"I *knew* it! He was super creepy. He kept hitting on me that night! Ooo!" She balled her fists against her sides. "Oh! Wait! We're before she was killed, right? I can warn her!"

"No. Well, yes, but –"

"Which is it? Yes or no?"

"Victoria, I-I mean Great-great-great-grandma, I mean –"

"Oh, for Pete's sake! Just call me Tori."

"Okay. And you can call me Tripp."

"Yeah. Got that."

Tripp rubbed his chin. "So, let me see if I'm following this. You're not the least bit fazed by the fact that I'm your great-great-great-grandson. You don't seem to care that we've jumped through time, either. You're more concerned with where we are in time and how you can help your friend. I would think time travel itself or that I could be lying would be the bigger concerns."

"You know I'm innocent, right?"

"Yes."

"You are the first person in an entire year who actually thinks I might be innocent. I'm pretty sure my attorney and my parents think I did it too."

"I *know* you didn't do it."

"Right. You also know *who* did."

"Yes."

"Then, let's go save my best friend!"

"No."

"No?"

"No," he said, his face stern.

"Look, I'm not fazed because you say you came from the future. We were sitting in jail one moment, and now we're not. When there is no other reasonable explanation, it's a pretty good rule of thumb to accept the somewhat plausible explanation until something else changes your mind."

"Okay. I'm following you."

"Besides, you look a bit like me. You are a few inches taller, maybe around six-foot?"

"Six-foot-one," he corrected.

"Okay. My hair is black and wavy, and yours is more of a dark brown, close to black, but still wavy like mine. Our eye color is the same dark brown. You look like you could be my son by your features. So, sure. I believe it. However, if we're not here to save my friend, and it doesn't sound like you're going to let me, what are we doing here?"

"C'mere," he said, gesturing to a boulder overlooking an open field at the edge of the forest.

She slowly followed him, more curious than anything. If he could get her out of jail, then she would hear him out. Sitting on the rock she turned toward him and asked, "What are we doing here?"

"We need to save our family."

"What do you mean?"

"I've done a lot of research. If we could get a few of our relatives to change some crucial decisions, our family may not have had the tragic past that it does."

"You mean our short life spans and unfortunate incarcerations due to our family legacy of crime that has spanned generations?" She raised an eyebrow. "You're not proud of your family tree?"

"Well..." His voice faded, and his cheeks flushed. He shrugged. "It's not a family history I'm proud to tote around. However, that's not why I'm doing this."

"Why *are* you doing this?"

"The sins of the father tend to be passed down through the generations. In our case, there were a few who deviated from the family tendency, while everyone else either died very young or found their death through the judicial system. I want to change that. I want to help our family make wise choices. Just like the sins of the father can be passed down, so can a legacy we can be proud of if we do it right."

Narrowing her eyes, she studied him. "Isn't that the exact opposite of what we're supposed to do? If we change our history, either you or I might cease to exist."

He bore his eyes into her. She felt like he was looking into her soul.

"Tori, what would you do to save our family?" he asked. "Would you give up your future?"

Tori considered his words for a moment.

"If we don't do something drastic, our family line may end."

"You're here."

"Barely."

"Do I want to know?"

"Maybe later," he said, looking out over the field. He sighed. "Look. Our family's past is plagued with crime, danger, and early death. As it is, they actually figured out who killed Christine after four years. When they did, they let you out. You found my great-great-great-grandfather only a few days out of jail. He was the detective who helped figure out who framed you. You wanted revenge. Chet was in jail, so you went after Brett since he lied in court. You also found out some other information and killed another person as well."

"Who?"

"I can't tell you."

"Why not?"

"Please don't make me."

"If you want to change this then tell me!"

Tripp sighed. "You killed my great-great-great-grandfather."

"I – *what*? Why?"

"He tried to stop you from killing Brett. It was an accident, but you had the gun. You shot him and then killed Brett out of pure rage. You were eight months pregnant at the time. It threw you into early labor, and my great-great-grandfather was born. Your mother raised him because you were arrested as soon as you were released from the hospital."

Tori let out a low whistle. "Wow," she said, shaking her head. "That's a lot."

"I know. You were so heartbroken. You named the baby after my great-great-great-grandfather so his name would continue."

She got off the boulder and paced. Stopping for a moment, she considered his words. Glancing at him, she paced once again. Seeing him sitting on the rock, watching her intently with his hands locked in front of him, she stopped. "Okay." She nodded. "I've got nothing to lose. So, how do we fix this hot mess of a family?"

He clapped his hands, looking like he was about to burst from excitement. "You'll do it?"

"I don't know how wise it is to intentionally mess with the timeline. Everything I've ever heard about time travel says we're not supposed to mess with the past. We won't know what kind of damage this could do in the interim."

Tripp waved her off. "I know about the whole butterfly effect theory. They have proven it wrong by my generation."

"Did you have to get permission from someone to do this?"

"No. I'm an inventor. I'm considered the odd duck of the family."

"I see."

"It's been my life mission to save this family. I have been searching genealogies, any records I could get my hands on, history in general, along with possible timeline effects and outcomes since I was a child."

"How far back are we going?"

"Possibly all the way to the eighteen-hundreds."

"How do you have any records or information from back then?"

"Well," he chuckled, "while our family had a sorted past, there were a few other odd ducks who were fascinated by our family's history. They kept meticulous genealogy records as they dove into our past. There was some sort of program that came out in the early nineteen-eighties regarding genealogy research, DNA, and past family histories that helped people store this information as well. That filled in a lot of the gaps."

"That is true. I know a lot of people who used those genealogy programs. They were able to go back hundreds of years into their family's past."

"Well, it seems those rogue family members who did not follow our family, shall we say *careers*, were great at research. They continued to pass down as much as they could about our family history."

"So, what's the plan?"

"It's sort of a flexible plan."

She narrowed her eyes. "We're messing with time. I would think we would need a lot more of a solid plan than *flexibility*."

"Part of this is watching the chain reactions that happen as we change a choice here or there and make a plan as we go."

"And how do we do that? You are acting like it's no big deal to change history or to get someone to change their mind."

He pulled a hand-held device from his front pocket. "This is critical. We can*not* lose this."

"I don't even know what *it* is."

"Watch," he said. He typed a few things into the keyboard. Once something populated on the screen, he took two fingers and swiped them up. The machine projected what he was looking at about three feet in front of them. It hung in the air but was slightly transparent.

Cocking her head to the side, she stood in front of the projection. She ran her fingers through the laser lights, but it stayed a firm picture. "What is it?"

"These are our family records. If we make a change to it, it will change on this screen. We should be able to literally watch the domino effect the choices make to our timeline."

"Okay," she turned toward him, her arms crossed, "how do we do this? I'm not exactly dressed for the eighteen-hundreds. Also, how does this time thingy work?"

"Well, we can find clothes to fix one issue. We may have difficulty regarding money and food. As for the time-sliding, I have this," he said, holding up his wrist. There was a silver band with a tiny screen on his forearm. He tapped the screen once, and the band lit up. "We dial in the date, time, and location we want, and then we join hands and it sends us through time."

"That sounds a bit too easy. Why isn't this regulated?"

"How do you regulate something that doesn't exist?"

"What do you mean?"

"I told you I was an odd duck. I do a lot of tinkering and inventing. No one knows about this technology."

"How do you know it works?"

"Because I've tested it. I wanted to make sure it worked before I went into a prison to get you."

"How did you know it would work with two of us?"

"I didn't. I mean, I've time jumped with my cat before. She's the one who kept throwing up."

Her jaw dropped. "What do you mean you didn't know it would work? I'm not a cat! What were you thinking?"

Shrugging, he simply said, "Experimental technology.""How do you know this will work if we go back in time? What if we drain the battery?"

"It's solar. I'm not concerned. The further back we go, the sun will be younger and stronger. It should charge without a problem."

"*Should?*" She placed her hands on her hips as she raised an eyebrow. "What happens if we get stuck?"

He shrugged. "We just wait until it's fully charged."

"You're very lackadaisical about this."

"I invented it. Since you're traveling with the inventor of the technology, it will be no problem. I'll fix it."

"Do you have a tool belt of some kind?"

"I do."

"And a backup battery?"

"It's solar," he reiterated.

"What if we drain the battery mid-trip?"

"Ooo! That's a good question!"

"I ought to slap that stubble off your face!" she growled. "You are messing with not only my future but also our family's future. This is a gamble at best."

"What are you willing to risk to save our family?"

She threw her hands in the air. "You act like this will just be a walk in the park!"

"Would you rather go back and sit in jail, hoping I get it right?"

"Why me?"

"Because in searching through our family history, as strange as it sounds, you are the most practical and level-headed. Despite the incidents, our family has a lot of respect for you and your memory. If you weren't accused of killing your friend, you probably would have turned out okay."

"But, according to you, I killed two people within at least nine months of getting out of jail. How is that sound thinking?"

"With the brainchildren in our family, trust me, you are the most grounded."

She scoffed. "This family is in trouble."

"Well, there were a few who ran illegal operations very well, but I did not want to take criminals back in time. There's no telling if they would turn on me. So, how about it? Are we going to fix our family together?"

She debated for a few minutes before she cautioned, "You *do* understand once we make our choices, we cannot change them. If we mess with the past, it will impact the future. I mean, what would happen if we stopped someone from killing someone, and they turned around and killed the guy who killed Hitler before he had a chance to do it? The things we do can drastically change our futures as well as impact the future of the entire world."

"That's why I want you with me. I have all of our family's history here," he said holding up the hand-held device.

"What *is* that thing?"

"I call it C.A.I.T., which stands for Computer-generated Artificial Intelligence by Tripp."

"That's conceited."

"No. If I were conceited, I would have named it directly after me. I thought CAIT made a cute acronym and name." He shrugged. "Either way, it's mine. I made it, so I get to name it. If you create something, you can choose its name for yourself."

She sighed. "Fair enough. Okay. How do we do this?"

"First, we need to figure out where and when we need to

start. We also need to figure out who we need to talk to when we get there."

"How far back do you want to go?"

"That's the primary question. Do we want to go far back and work our way forward, or do we want to start sooner and work our way back?"

"I would think if we went back to the eighteen-hundreds when our ancestors first came to the States, we could see how things fall into place. Then we can make corrections through the remaining timeline."

"That makes sense. If we start sooner, we could keep messing up what we fix."

"Agreed," she said. "Now, where do we start?"

They studied Tripp's ancestry records. "I think we should go back to Pennsylvania in October of 1813."

"Why?"

"Our ancestor killed Oliver Hazzard Perry before the battle of Lake Erie," Tripp said. "It's also called The Battle of Put-In-Bay."

"Why is this battle important?"

"In studying history, I believe if Perry lives, he may be able to turn the battle. Because he was killed, America lost the battle for the Great Lakes. If we change that, then Perry defeats the British on Lake Erie, and things may shake out differently."

"So, are we shaping our history or our country's history?"

"Our relative got sentenced to death for killing Perry. If we stop him from killing Perry, we may be able to kill two birds with one stone so to speak. We may not have had to battle with Britain for so long. I mean, we eventually won, but still... If our ancestor didn't kill Perry, it might have happened sooner. Also, our ancestor would not have been shot for treason."

"I see your point. Okay. So, we're heading back to 1813 dressed like this?" She gestured to her orange apparel, and then to his clothing that was a white and silver jumpsuit.

"Is there a costume place near here anywhere?"

"Where is here?" she asked. "Last I knew, I was in the Lyncher State Jail in Humble, Texas."

"Oh! We're in a town called Lufkin, Texas," he said, studying his map on CAIT.

"Okay. Yes. There is. It's there. It's obviously closed right now, but –"

"Not a problem. Be right back," he said.

Tori watched as he was flesh and blood one moment, and then he went progressively transparent until he completely disappeared into a cascading shimmering wave of light. She rubbed her eyes to make sure she was seeing what she thought she saw. When she opened her eyes, she was still standing by herself next to the boulder on the edge of a forest. "All righty then," she said aloud. "I guess that's what we'll look like."

He was back a few minutes later, already changed into clothing from that time period. His other clothes were folded in a leather backpack, while he held another brown leather back-pack and a big bag with her new clothing.

"Um, isn't that breaking and entering? And theft?" she asked.

"Actually, it won't be by the time we're done with things."

Tori rolled her eyes and sighed. "Semantics."

"Well, when you're messing with the timeline, there are a lot of gray areas."

"Fine," she huffed. "I have to change."

She went into the forest behind the biggest tree she could find. After getting undressed down to her underwear, she looked through the bag. Slipping on the chemise, she looked at it. "Not too bad," she said to herself. The shift or chemise was a short-sleeve cotton undergarment that went down to her ankles. "How did you know my size?"

"I guessed."

"Good guessing! This is comfortable!" she said with a smile, coming from behind the tree.

"You're not done yet. Keep looking."

"Oh. Okay." She went back to the bag and pulled out a pair of flannel pantalets. "I have a slip on. Why do I need these?"

"Um," he said, nervously clearing his throat. "It gets cold there, and they didn't exactly have underwear."

"Oh," she said and slipped them on under the chemise. "Could help in the cold weather." She reached into the bag and picked up a weird looking object. "What is this thing?"

"It's a corset. I got one that was thin-boned for better comfort for you. You may need a hand with that."

"Are you serious?"

"When in Rome..."

"Okay, fine. Come help me."

While she adjusted where it needed to be in the front, he put it together in the back and laced it up. Once laced, he tugged on it to get it tight.

"What form of torture was this thing?" she grunted as he yanked on it to tighten it. "How did women get this stuff on them when they were alone? Hey! Not too tight or I may pass out on you.""Oh! Sorry," he said and loosened it, allowing her to breathe. "Okay. The rest is up to you," he said and returned to the boulder.

She pulled the petticoat out of the bag. "Big," she remarked, sliding it on over her chemise. When she pulled out the dress, she examined it in the moonlight. "Pretty."

"Blue is your favorite color, right?"

"You've done your homework," she said, slipping the blue calico dress over everything. "It's considerably lighter than I thought it would be."

"I put a couple pairs of knee socks in there, a pair of boots, along with –"

"An apron," she said putting it on after buttoning up the front of her dress. "I got it." She pulled out a knitted shawl and wrapped it around her torso. There was also a gray wool cloak with an attached hood inside the bag as well.

When she finished putting on her socks and boots, she

wrapped the cloak around herself, securing it under her chin. "This is warmer than I thought," she said. Once she had everything on, she spun around in a circle. "I like it!"

Lastly, she pulled out a brush and brushed her hair before braiding it in a low braid. She twisted the braid around to create a bun at her nape, securing it with a hair pin that was in the bottom of the bag. She shoved it through the braided bun to hold it in place. When she finished, she folded her clothes and placed them in the leather backpack. She also rolled up the bag and put it in the backpack in case they needed it at some point.

"How's this?" she asked, coming around the tree.

"Looks great!" he said. "Now, we look about the same age, so maybe we should tell people we're brother and sister instead of four generations apart? I think they might question us if I told them you were my great-great-great-grandmother."

"Good point," she agreed. "How old are you?"

"Twenty-eight."

"I'm twenty-five so we can pull this off."

"Does that mean since I'm older that I get the final say?"

"Don't get ahead of yourself, junior. I'm more than a hundred years your senior."

"Semantics." He shrugged. "So, what's our backstory? We should probably be on the same page in case we get separated."

"Okay." She tossed a few ideas around in her mind. "What if our parents died and we live with our aunt in Boston?"

"Well thought out," Tripp agreed. "And we can use it through the timeline. What's our aunt's name?"

"Beth Graham."

"Where did that name come from? You came up with it awfully fast."

"She was a friend of mine in kindergarten."

"Got it. So, are you ready?"

"Who are we looking for?"

"Our relative who needs to make a wise choice is Frederick Collins."

"What does he do? Do we know what he looks like?" she asked.

"This is what he looks like," he said, showing her a picture on CAIT. "He actually killed Oliver Hazard Perry the day before the Battle of Lake Erie started. So, let's go back the day before the battle when he's in port and talk to him. Hopefully, we can convince him not to kill him."

"He's going to think we've lost our minds."

"Not if we can tell him things."

"Like what things?"

"Like who his family is, and what they do?"

"He'll think we're spying on him," she pointed out.

"Okay. How do you propose we talk to him about this?"

"Hmm," she said, rubbing her chin. "What can that computer thing do?"

"It can project pictures," he offered.

"Do you have any of him and/or his family?"

"Yes."

"What about the battle? Do you have any of those?"

"I do. Here," he said, pulling them up. He projected them in front of him about three feet.

Tori went over to the images and studied them. "Kind of neat how you can make a 3-D picture of them without ever seeing them before."

"CAIT is brilliant! She can do a lot!"

"Okay. What if we act like we're magicians and show him these?"

"He'll think you're a witch. The Salem Witch Trials would be long over by then, but that doesn't mean they've forgotten about them. He'll think you're a witch and they'll hang you."

"Okay, Einstein! How do we do this?"

He shrugged. "Just play it by ear. Maybe I'll take him on a trip to the past or forward a few years like I did with you?"

"That's not a bad idea. I kind of like it. Keep the idea of

moving forward or backward in the back of your mind and we'll take it from there."

"Okay. So, it looks like we're going to South Bass Island near Put-In-Bay on say, the 9th of September in 1883," he said, dialing it into the computer on his wrist. "Sound about right?"

"Remember, times were different back then. Women's words did not hold much clout. You're going to have to do a lot of the talking," she reminded him.

"Right. Well, are you ready?"

She slid her backpack onto her back. "What about food?"

"It's in my backpack."

"Water?"

"My backpack. Trust me. I have us covered."

"What about money?"

"Well," he said hesitantly, "that may be a different story. We'll have to see what we can do."

"Fair enough," she said looping her arm through his. "Let's go."

"Hold on tight!" he said and then activated the device on his arm.

CHAPTER TWO

09SEP1813 (AM): A Time To Gather Stones

At first, Tori felt like there was a cool, shimmering waterfall dropping all over her, and she shuddered. Then, she felt a thrust forward, and her body felt like it was being pulled limb-from-limb. Just when she thought she would explode, she dropped to the ground in the middle of the night with a THUD!

She lay on the ground with the wind knocked out of her. Pulling her hands up to her sides, she took a few deep breaths. She closed her eyes, waiting for her world to catch up to her. The air felt cleaner yet extremely moist. The waves lapped against the shore from the bay, and the musty, earthy scent of the lake water was a constant, while it mixed with the smell of burnt wood. She could hear loud voices, but she could not discern what they were saying or where they were coming from. She shook her head and opened her eyes.

Wide-eyed and jaw-dropped, she looked around in awe. The island was not settled at all. She expected buildings and people, but there were none. She saw several large ships in the bay. In the moonlight she could make out the name of one of them. It was the *USS Lawrence*. There were make-shift tents all over the place, with small fires periodically lit in pits around the campground.

"I-I don't…" she shook her head.

Tripp was immediately at her side. "It's okay. Just breathe. I'm sincerely impressed you haven't thrown up yet."

"I'm in too much pain!" she growled. "Why aren't you in pain?"

"I have a buffer built into my arm device."

She narrowed her eyes at him. "Why didn't you think to get me one as well?"

"We may jump forward if this is too rough for you and get one, but for right now we have a job to do. While we technically could go back and try again, it's not advised," he cautioned. "We could run into ourselves."

"So, this is a one-and-done type situation?"

"Yes."

"Why didn't you say that earlier?"

"Would it have changed your mind?"

"No. Not really. However, it would have been nice to have a head's up," she said, slowly sitting up. "What time is it?"

He looked at the device on his arm. "It's three o'clock in the morning here."

"So, we can pick the date and the place, but the device picks the actual time?" she asked.

"No. We have some control over that. I picked the middle of the night to get you out of jail, as well as coming here so no one would see us. Could you imagine if someone saw us suddenly appear out of nowhere?"

"So, when we jump, we should probably make sure it's the middle of the night each time."

"Agreed."

"Any more of these rules or guidelines I need to know about?"

He shrugged. "Guess we'll figure them out as we go."

"Lingo."

"What?"

"We need to watch our lingo and slang. This is a different

time. We need to make sure we're speaking the same way they are. We'll have to listen for context and try to blend in. Maybe we should go to the local place to eat in the morning and just listen?" she suggested.

"With what money?"

She groaned. "Oh yeah."

"We can still listen. In fact, maybe you should get a job as a waitress, and I can find one doing something else?"

"Like?"

"I don't know. I'm a tech and inventor guy, not an 1800's guy. I don't have a clue on how to operate anything here. I mean, with time and tinkering, I'm sure I can figure it out. However, farming and soldiering are not in my list of skills. What about you? You can be a waitress."

"Where am I supposed to be a waitress? Tent city over there?"

"Good point."

"You said we had snacks, right?" she asked

"Yes."

"Please give me some water and snacks? I'm hungry and thinking on an empty stomach isn't helping."

"Here you go," he said, reaching into his backpack, while she kept a lookout. He handed her a water bottle and an energy bar.

"How did you get these?"

"There was a grocery store across the street from the costume shop."

"You *stole* these?"

"Technically, not yet."

She rolled her eyes. "Semantics."

"Do you have money?"

"No."

"Then..." he gestured. "Eat."

She nibbled on her energy bar while she took in the area. The ground was damp, but not too damp that it soaked through her cloak. There was a slight layer of dew on the ground and trees around them. She let the sound of the waves penetrate into her soul, bringing her peace while she looked around. The voices she heard were deep, so her guess was there were all men in the tent camp. She could make out a few of them walking around. They looked like they were drinking something from a cup, while they had guns over their shoulders.

When she finished her energy bar, she handed the wrapper to him to put in his bag. "We cannot let anyone see any of this stuff we brought from the future."

"Agreed," he said, shoving it to the bottom of his backpack.

She stood up and guzzled her water so he could get the bottle quickly into his bag. When they both finished eating and drinking, she asked, "What do we do now? We have a few hours before anyone is up."

"We could look around," he suggested. "Get familiar with the island."

The early morning breeze brushed around her in whisps. She enjoyed the peaceful scene before her as they sat lazily on a few rocks, deep in thought. Tori could have sat there all day, but she only had to wait a few hours before the sun began its rise over the massive great lake. The peach and light blue gave way to stunning colors of gold, red, and orange right before her eyes.

"Who are you? And what, pray tell, are you doing here?" a man's voice demanded from behind them.

Both Tori and Tripp jumped. They immediately stood, facing the man. He was slightly taller than Tori, with dark hair and eyes. His clothing told Tori that he was someone important in the Naval Fleet. He scrupulously looked them over. Tori did not care for the way he looked at either of them.

"I asked, who you are and what you are doing here?" he boomed louder. "Are you spying for the British?

"No, sir. We're not spies. I'm Tripp St. Claire, and this is my sister, Tori," Tripp started, sticking his hand out to shake his hand. When the man did not reciprocate, Tripp pulled his hand back and shoved it in his pocket.

"What are you doing here? Do not make me ask again," the man said firmly.

"Not really sure. We just stumbled onto this island," Tripp admitted, rubbing the back of his neck.

The man crossed his arms. "Why do I not believe you?"

"I honestly don't know what to tell you," Tripp said. "We don't have any money. We found our way here while looking for work or a food source."

"You're looking for work? Where are you from?"

"Boston."

"Well, you're a strapping, young lad," the man said, circling them as he looked them over. "How are you on a ship?"

"Never been."

"What about you?" he asked Tori. "What do you do?"

"I can cook," she offered.

"Well, having a woman on a ship is not good form," the man said, still sizing them up while he debated in his mind.

"I can have things cooking here on the island?" she suggested. "If you have food, I can cook it."

"That is a possibility. What about you?" he asked Tripp.

"I'm a fast learner," Tripp said. "I pick up things quickly."

"I can offer you a slot on the *Niagara* if you wish, but she will have to stay on shore. You may start on the *Lawrence* so you can work on both ships."

Tripp grinned. "That would be great!"

"I will pair you up with one of my men who can show you what to do. My name is Commodore Oliver Perry. The *Lawrence* is my ship. I need to warn you that we may be going to battle in the next few days."

"I understand, sir. I have to take care of my sister. I will do whatever it takes," Tripp promised.

"Fair enough. Report to the *Lawrence* post-haste. You, young lady, start working on a fire pit and gathering wood for cooking."

"Yes, sir," she agreed.

"Come," he said to Tripp.

"Sir, may I have a word with my sister before I follow you?"

"Make it quick!" he said and left.

As soon as he was out of earshot, Tripp thrust his backpack toward her. "Keep this with you at all times."

Tori nodded as she wrapped her arms around it. "Okay."

"I mean it," he said, taking off the wrist computer. "If something goes wrong, get back to your time immediately."

He took a few moments to show her how to operate both CAIT and the wrist computer before shoving them into his backpack. "This will buffer travel for you. I'm going into war. I may not come back. If I don't, get out of here as soon as you can. Understand? I will do my best to find Fredrick Collins. Hopefully he's aboard the *Lawrence* or the *Niagara*."

"Be careful and extremely alert," she warned as she gave him a hug.

"I will. I'll be back as soon as possible."

With that, he left, following the same path the commodore took toward the ships looming in the distance.

Tori sighed. "Okay," she said to herself, panic rising at being left alone in a time period she was not familiar with, "how do I do this?"

She secured the one computer to her wrist under her clothing. Then she took her stuff out of her backpack and shoved it all into his since his was larger. After rolling her backpack, she crammed it into his and then slung his backpack onto her back.

"Time to make a fire pit," she said and began to search for big rocks to build into a circle.

Tripp could not believe his eyes. The pictures of the ships from this time period did not do the gun-brig ship justice. It was about a hundred and eighteen feet long and made of oak. There were nine short-range cannons on each side and two long-range twelve-pound guns for the ship. The two masts were toward the middle of the ship with its sails rolled up, and there were men crawling all over it.

"Welcome, young Tripp," the commodore said with a grin when Tripp got on deck. "Collins! Take young Tripp under your wing!"

"Yes, sir!" a man yelled from the other side of the deck.

Tripp gulped.

"What?" Collins asked, walking up to him. "Are you okay?"

"Are-are you...I'm sorry," Tripp said, sticking his hand out. "I'm Tripp St. Claire."

"Fred Collins," the man said, shaking his hand. He had the unmistakable dark-brown hair and brown eyes of their family. He and Tripp were about the same height. Cocking his head to the side, Fred asked, "Do I know you? You look familiar."

"No, sir," Tripp said. "I apologize. I have only seen these ships from the shore."

"You will get your sea legs in no time," Fred assured him, resting his hand on Tripp's shoulder. "Now, normally I work on the *Niagara*. However, the commodore asked me to get this ship in shape. We will only be on this ship today. We will be on the *Niagara* starting tomorrow."

"Fair enough," Tripp agreed. "Where do we start?"

Tori stacked multiple rocks into a wide circle. Then, she piled a stack of wood in the center.

"Are you Tori?" a man called out to Tori from down the path.

Tori spun around, startled. "I-yes. I am."

When he caught up to her, he stopped and stared at her.

Tori's heart rate picked up. "I'm-I'm sorry. Is there something wrong with my clothes?" she asked, looking over her clothing. "My hair?" she asked, patting her hair down. She could not imagine the moisture from the lake helped her hair at all.

"No. No. Not at all. It's all perfectly fine," the young man said with an ear-to-ear grin. He reached out toward her to shake her hand, "I'm Patrick St. James."

"St. James?" Tori asked, surprised. "Your last name is St. James?"

"Yes. Why?"

"I've just known other people with that last name. Sorry. I'm Tori St. Claire," Tori said, remembering Tripp had introduced her as his sister after giving the commodore the last name St. Claire.

"The commodore sent me to help you gather for cooking."

Tori tucked a portion of her hair behind her ear that slid out of the braid. "Are you the cook?"

"According to the commodore, you are," he said. "C'mon, let's go to the icehouse for the food storage."

He led her down the path. As they walked, they talked.

"Are you married?" Patrick asked, running his fingers through his blond hair.

"No," she said, shaking her head. "You?"

"No. I have not found my true love yet."

"How old *are* you?" she asked. "I thought most married young."

"Says the young lady who is also not married yet," he pointed out.

"I'm only twenty-four."

"I'm only twenty-five."

"I thought most married in their teens," she said.

"Again, says the woman who is also not yet married," he said with a smirk.

She smiled as she blushed. "You have a point."

He chuckled. When he smiled, her grin could not help but become larger. His blue eyes sparkled, and she liked the freckles scattered across the bridge of his nose.

"The icehouse is over here," Patrick said, gesturing toward a building that was built into the side of a hill. He went over and flipped the latch, opening the door.

"Ooo! It's really cool in here," she said, rubbing her arms. It was like walking into a cooler of a restaurant. What hit her was the potency of the meat and the dirt that permeated the icehouse. While the meat was fine, it was coated in salt, creating an almost metallic scent. The vegetables either hung on a rope or were stored in pots with dirt.

He raised an eyebrow. "Have you never been in an icehouse?"

"No. My family did not own one. We went to the market for our daily food."

"I see. My family was the same for a while. However, now with the farm, we are no longer short on food. What we do not readily have, we have to get at the market fresh. For our over-stock, to keep things cool, we have a root cellar."

"Do you have any brothers or sisters?" she asked.

"As far as I know, my two older and two younger brothers, along with my three younger sisters, are still alive."

"Wow! That's a large family!"

"Many hands make light work," he said with a chuckle. "As I said, my family owns a farm. As we get older and leave, my parents have to hire people to work for them."

"I see. They are probably missing you."

"Yes." He nodded. "They mention that in their letters many times. So, take a look around. What do you want to cook for lunch?"

She glanced through the myriad of meat and vegetable options. "How many am I cooking for?"

"Last count was around fifty or sixty men."

Her eyes widened as the color drained from her face.

Patrick burst out in a fit of laughter.

She gulped while her heart raced. "That's a *lot* of men to feed!"

"Just make a lot. Trust me. They will eat it."

"Okay," she said and then took a deep breath. "Do they like stew and bread?"

"If it is hearty, they will eat it."

"Okay, then," she said and started piling food into Patrick's waiting apron he held out.

"I am assigned to help you in cooking. Whatever you need."

"What about pots?"

"Pots and the tripods to put over the fire are over there." He nodded toward the cast-iron tripod stands. There were numerous pots that could hang from it over the fire.

"I may need to make two pots in order to cook for all of them," she said, thinking aloud. "Probably need to make another firepit for that, as well as another to cook bread over."

"We need another to boil water," Patrick pointed out.

"Hmm, looks like I need to make three more fire pit circles."

"You make a list of what food you want," Patrick said, "and I'll bring it all to you. In the meantime, you can build three more fire pits."

"Agreed," she said and left him with a list of items she would need.

She ran back to their spot and built three more rock circles. She then gathered the sticks needed to start the fire. Looking around to make sure no one would see her; Tori pulled the lighter from her backpack and quickly lit the fires so they could get going. Just as she closed her bag from retuning the lighter to its spot in the bottom of the bag, and the backpack on her back, Patrick walked up with the food.

"Well done!" Patrick said, impressed. "You are a master fire maker as well, I see!"

"Well," she shrugged as her face flushed, "I can hold my own."

"Here is all the food. We will have to make multiple trips for the tripods. They are really heavy."

"Okay. Put the food on this big rock so I can start cutting

the vegetables. Can you get the stands and pots by yourself?" she asked.

"It *is* a long walk. However, the men will be looking for food soon. Yeah. I can get them. I'll get the pots first."

"Thank you. When you get them here, if you can set them up that would be helpful. Also, please fill the pots about half-full of water?"

"I can do that," he said, and they got to work.

CHAPTER THREE

09SEP1813 (PM): A Time To Speak

Tori finished a mid-afternoon meal just as the men came back to shore. The heavenly scent of fresh baked rolls and beef stew swirled all around them. Tori even heard a few stomachs growl as the men got in line.

"We start early in the morning," Commodore Perry said as they got in line for Tori and Patrick to serve them. "We have a huge battle coming and I want us to be ready. They have beat us in other battles, but this one is ours to win."

"Sir, I do not mean to be negative," Fred Collins spoke up, "but with so many losses, *can* we win?"

"Who said that?" Perry demanded.

"Collins, sir."

"Collins, step forward," he ordered.

Fred stepped out of line beside Tripp so the commodore could see him.

"Young man, we need to enter this battle with a strong mindset. We *must* make this a decisive Naval victory!" He paced while he spoke. "When my former captain, Captain Lawrence, died, his last words to us were, *Don't give up the ship.'* On that day, we did lose the *Chesapeake*. The Officers for this upcoming battle know what they need to do this time. We *will not* give up the ship! We *will* win!"

When he said that, there were several cheers heard through the crowd.

"Yes, sir," Collins said.

"I cannot hear you!" Perry shouted at him.

"Yes, sir!" Collins shouted back.

"I still cannot hear you!"

"Yes, sir!" all of the men yelled at the same time, much to Collins's embarrassment.

"Good! Now, let us partake of this meal created for us by young Tripp's sister and young Patrick," Perry said and got back in line.

"I hate it when he does that," Fred grumbled, taking his spot back in line in front of Tripp.

"Does what?" Tripp asked.

"I hate it when he makes an example of a person. It makes us feel less than. He needs to be taught a lesson," he said with fire in his eyes.

"Fred," Tripp said quietly, "he's commander of this Naval fleet."

"I get it, but no one knows who pulls the trigger in a battle."

Tripp gulped. "You can't mean that."

"I most certainly do!" Fred hissed. "This is not the first time I have been made an example of by him!"

The line inched forward as the two spoke in hushed whispers that only the pair could hear.

"He trusted you with my training," Tripp pointed out. "He must think highly of you. Maybe he feels you are strong enough to handle being made an example?"

"No." Fred shook his head. "I have a plan."

"Can we talk more as we eat?" Tripp asked, knowing their turn was coming up.

"Agreed. I will need help," he said, stepping up to Tori. "Thank you for this fine food," he said to her.

"My pleasure. I hope it's good." She ladled a spoonful into his bowl. "Patrick also has bread over there to go with the stew."

"Much obliged," Fred said, moving over to Patrick, while Tori scooped some into Tripp's bowl. "It smells wonderful! Much better than anything Patrick has dished us lately."

"That wasn't nice," Tori said, as Patrick stood there, face flushed.

"My food was okay. It just needed a woman's touch," Patrick said.

"Agreed," Fred said, and continued to the drink line.

"He's not happy," Tripp said quietly.

"Who is that? Perry said his name is Collins. Is that Frederick Collins?" Tori whispered.

"The one and only. Perry paired me with him. I'm going to talk to him. Don't think I'm ignoring you."

"You do what you need to," Tori said sternly. "The battle is tomorrow. That's supposedly when he kills Perry. Stop him. This is the first step in saving our family."

"Trust me. I get it," Tripp whispered.

"We are all hungry," the man behind Tripp insisted. "I get that she is pretty, but how about letting us eat before you take up with the young lady."

"The young lady is my sister, in case you missed Commodore Perry's announcement," Tripp corrected him.

"C'mon, Tripp," Fred encouraged.

"Gotta go. Be careful," Tripp whispered before he left with Fred.

Tripp got his bread and water to eat with his stew before he and Fred went off by themselves so no one would hear them talking.

"Adam can be mean if you are not careful. He was being nice when he said that, but there is no telling how long he would be nice if you slowed him getting food in his stomach," Fred pointed out. "He is one you want on your side."

"Agreed. He *is* of considerable size," Tripp said, eyeing the man who was behind him in line.

Fred chuckled. "That's a clever way of wording it."

"However, your mind could meet his any day," Tripp countered.

"Agreed," Fred said. "Now, for tomorrow. I do not know what time the battle will begin, but the commodore has been following their movements, so I am certain he knows."

"We are supposed to be on the *Niagara* tomorrow. How do you plan on hurting him? Elliot is our captain on that vessel, not Perry."

"I may get myself on the *Lawrence*."

"Please stay with me?" Tripp asked. "I do not know anyone else here."

"You will do fine," Fred encouraged. "You did an excellent job today!"

"Thank you. I feel a brotherly bond with you," Tripp said.

"And I you," Fred agreed. "That is why I trust you with this plan."

"Do you have any family?" Tripp asked.

"Yes. I have a wife and three young ones. My wife's name is Emma. Then my oldest son is Daniel. My second oldest son is Mark. And we also have a little girl named Victoria."

"Oh! Like my sister," Tripp said with a smile.

"We call her Victoria. Why do you call her Tori?"

"Tripp and Tori are our nicknames. Her real name is Victoria Elizabeth, and mine is Sebastian Tripp. Our parents called us Tripp and Tori. Always have. The names stuck." Tripp shrugged, sopping up some stew with his roll.

"Where are your parents?"

"They are dead. We came over from England several years ago. They said it was to give us a better life. While we were here, they both got sick and died a few months apart. I have been looking out for her by myself ever since."

"I see. She is a beautiful young lady. I am surprised she is not yet married," he said, glancing over at her. She was laughing at a few of the men who were teasing her.

"I am very protective of her. If the right man comes along, I will consider it."

"I can understand that. When Victoria comes of age, I will be in the same mindset," Fred said and then took a drink of his water.

"You cannot do that if you are dead or in jail," Tripp pointed out.

Fred furrowed his brow. "What do you mean?"

"If you let what Perry said get to you, and you go forward with your plan, you will not be alive to see her get older. You will either be shot upon return to solid ground or even possibly on the water. If not, I'm sure there will be a trial, and you will either get hanged or sent before a firing squad. If any of these scenarios occur, there is no way you can teach your boys to be men, nor will you be there to make sure Victoria is married to a good young man."

Fred took a large bite of his stew. He glared at Tripp as he chewed. Finally swallowing, he grudgingly admitted, "You have some fine points, Tripp. I will consider them."

"What is said now or in battle may not matter tomorrow. Is not returning to your family more important?"

"It is."

"Then, come with me to the *Niagara* tomorrow. Do not go on the *Lawrence*. If there is some distance between you, there will be less temptation."

"I will sleep on this and let you know in the morning."

"Fair enough. That is all I ask," Tripp agreed.

"You are very pretty," one of the boys said to Tori.

Tori blushed. "Thank you."

"Are you married?" another one asked.

"No."

"Do you have a beau?" another asked.

"No."

"Why not?" another asked. Then he leaned forward and quietly whispered, "Do you not like men?"

"Oh!" Tori smiled. "I do. My brother and I move around a lot. I am sure if I find the right man, I will be happy to have him as my beau."

"Well, ma'am, my name's Charles," he said, taking off his hat. Nervously twisting his hat with his hands, he continued, "I would love to chat with you if you have some time later."

"She is helping me with the dishes," Patrick spoke up. "You men need your sleep."

"Stuff it, boy!" one of the men snapped.

"Do not be mean to him," Tori snapped back. "He makes the food that fills your stomachs! If you are mean, what is to stop him from making it horrible?"

"He has to eat it, too," another one spoke up.

"I can make it bad after she and I eat," Patrick responded with a grin. "Want to test me?"

"No," he admitted.

"Good. Now, get your food and eat. You men have to be rested, for the morning may bring war with it," Patrick warned. "You leave this to us."

"Thank you," Charles said, accepting his bowl of stew, bread, and a cup of water.

After the men filed through, Tori said, "Thank you for standing up for me. While I do not think he would have done or said anything untoward, I also do not believe my brother would have approved."

"This is your first day here. Tomorrow may be scary. I want

you to be able to rest. There is no telling how long the battle will last," Patrick pointed out. "And while we may want to watch –"

"Watch?" Tori asked, taken aback. "Why would I want to watch?"

"To make sure you know the fate of your brother," Patrick said, removing the pot from the fire.

"Oh. Good point." Tori considered his words. "I did not think about that."

"Well, you also have to be thinking about food...all day. You will need to have food ready at a moment's notice the entire day. If they get time to eat, they will not have much time. We must also have water boiled and bandages ready. We are not only cooking, but also providing medical."

Tori gasped. "Wait! What? I do not know the first thing about medicine."

"I have been doing it for a while. I will tell you what to do," Patrick assured her. "You will help me on the medical side, and I will help you in cooking."

"Agreed," Tori said, thrusting her hand forward. As they shook hands, she added, "Deal!"

"Okay. We need to clean this up, gather wood, and start boiling water."

"When will we sleep?"

"We will not sleep until we're ready," Patrick said. "We can set up for men coming in over by that willow tree over there. That will give us an unobstructed view of the bay to see what's coming."

Tori looked from the willow tree, out into the bay, and then back to Patrick. "It's going to be a long few days, isn't it?"

"Yes. I am afraid it is. Much will depend on how tomorrow goes."

"Then, let us get started," Tori said on a sigh. "Maybe we can get at least a few hours of sleep before it starts."

"Agreed," Patrick said, and they replaced the cooking pots with pots of water to boil. The more they had, the better off they would be. If they needed to make a tea or boil anything, it would be better to have it already boiled once.

Tripp and Fred were lying on the ground, using their jackets as pillows. They were gazing at the stars.

"They're beautiful," Tripp said.

"Enjoy the beauty while you can. While these stars will still be there tomorrow night, we may not."

Tripp sighed. Then, glancing over at Tori and Patrick, who were working on setting up for the next day, he asked, "Is Tori going to get any sleep?"

"The only reason we are to get any sleep is because we have prepared over the last few weeks," Fred pointed out. "Patrick has medicine and bandages. Now they must prepare regarding food and medical."

Tripp turned his head toward Fred. "Medical? My sister is not a nurse."

"She will be tomorrow. Do not concern yourself. Patrick will teach her."

"I'm sure he will," Tripp said, rolling his eyes.

Fred quietly chuckled so as not to wake the others. "Patrick is a good man," he assured Tripp. "If they come together, he is one I would trust my daughter to had she been of age."

"Really?" Tripp asked.

"Yes. He comes from a strong, Christian family. They are farmers. His mother taught him to use the plants around the home for medicine. His father taught him to hunt and to work with wood. They are a large family. Good stock."

"I see," Tripp said, now eyeing Patrick and Tori. He knew nothing could happen between the pair. Patrick had another life. When messing with the timeline, they had to be careful not to affect too many other portions of the timeline. *They had to focus on their own family line. Yes, they were messing a bit with the general timeline by not letting Fred kill Perry, but what the outcome would ultimately show, they would have to wait and see. Would saving Perry's life help America win this battle? If so, would it help America win sooner?*

"Do not concern yourself with the two of them. They will be too busy," Fred said. "Once the battle starts, there will be no time for talking."

"She will tell me what happens when I return."

"*If* you return," Fred corrected him. "You may not have been in battle yet, but you need to know the battles have not been kind to us."

"I am choosing to think positive."

"Shh," Fred hushed him. "The commodore is speaking to his officers. Listen."

Perry stood and faced his officers. "Keep as near the *Lawrence* as possible. Engage your designated adversary, in close action, at half cable's length. We must work together to win this battle. I want a decisive victory. I want no doubt in their mind who won."

"Well," Fred said, impressed, "I must give him credit where it is due."

"Do you think he will stand by his words?" Tripp asked.

"He will do everything in his power to win tomorrow," Fred assured him.

Tripp leaned closer and whispered, "He cannot do that if he is dead."

Fred looked over at him and nodded in understanding. "I will be with you on the *Niagara* tomorrow. I will not let my temper take me from my children. I will not go down by my own hand. I give you my word."

"Thank you. I do not want to have to find your wife and children to explain the situation we talked about earlier."

"Thank you. We will make sure both of us survive tomorrow."

"That would be appreciated," Tripp agreed.

"Have you noticed the men we have here?" Fred asked after a few moments of silence.

"What do you mean?" Tripp asked.

Fred glanced around the area to make sure no one heard him, "The men in this group brought in by Elliot are not exactly of the highest caliber. I am adding myself to the list. We are not the best soldiers. Elliot took the best of the worst, of which I will own, and put us all on his ship – the *Niagara*, leaving the rest for Perry to sort out."

"What kind of sound military decision was that?" Tripp asked, eyes bulging as he froze. Knowing he was with the worst the Navy had to offer terrified him more than anything at that moment!

"He did not know he was coming with us," Fred said and then chuckled. "He thought he was sending us to die. When he realized the potentially fatal choice he made in his selections, he took the best of us for the *Niagara*. Perry was not happy when he realized everything either. However, he is doing the best he can."

"Now you are defending Perry?" Tripp asked.

"If we are all to make it through this, we will need to work together. While this group may not be the best the Navy has, we are a feisty group. We are the ones who get in fights. We argue with each other all of the time. That is one of the reasons why Perry makes examples of us. He is trying to get us in line, but it is not working."

"Well, we had better *all* get in line if we are going to survive tomorrow," Tripp said, slightly panicked. "I thought I was with military men."

"You are."

"Just not the best."

"I am sorry, but no."

"Good to know. Then, you watch my back, and I will watch yours?" Tripp asked.

"Agreed," Fred said. "Let us get some sleep while the men

decide the best course of action for tomorrow. Rest well, my friend," Fred said and rolled over. "We are going to need it."

"You as well," Tripp said and slowly drifted off to sleep, looking at the thousands of stars above him. They were more than he had ever seen. Amazed to be in this place at this time, he had a difficult time shutting his brain down enough to sleep.

However, Tripp understood that Tori would not be sleeping this night, so he had to get enough sleep for the both of them. After the battle was over, and Fred made it through without killing Perry, they were going to disappear.

CHAPTER FOUR

10SEP1813 (AM/PM): A Time To Kill

Tripp was woken by the yelling and rushing around of men as they scrambled to get up, get breakfast, and get out to the ships.

"Get up!" Fred said, jostling Tripp. "The battle may be upon us at any moment. We must be ready."

"Y-yes, sir," Tripp stammered as he struggled to wake up. He got in line for breakfast.

"Morning, sleepyhead," Tori said when he got to her.

"Morning. What's for breakfast? It smells like last night's dinner. Not saying it wasn't good, but I don't smell eggs or bacon."

"It's bread and stew again," she responded. "We figured better give y'all something to hold you over, not knowing when you would return."

Glancing around the area and the set-up, he asked, "Did you get *any* sleep?"

"Not really," she said, ladling stew into a bowl for him. "We have been setting up all night for today. We have teas ready and cooled. We have bandages boiled and cleaned. We also have plenty of water boiled and tools sterilized. We have blankets set up to lay the wounded on while we work, and the medicine at the ready. He said we will let the dead sit until we are finished. I have to tell you I'm nervous."

"You should be!" Tripp said to her astonishment. "This is not the cream of the crop when it comes to the Navy," he said so only she could hear.

"For real?" Tori asked.

"Yeah. Just found out last night. I talked Fred into coming onto the *Niagara* with me. That will keep him from Perry. He's on the *Lawrence*. The *Niagara* supposedly has the best of the worst on it. Fred and I will keep an eye on each other in hopes of all of us making it through."

Tori gulped.

"I will do my best to bring all of us out of this alive," Tripp promised.

"At least you. While I can operate CAIT, I would rather you were with me."

"That is my intention. Now, keep yourself focused on this matter and not on Patrick," he teased.

"I'm not!" She blushed. "He's a nice guy, but there is way too much to do."

"Agreed."

"Besides, it's not like we'll be here that long, right?" she asked.

"No. As soon as we get Fred through this point, we're out of here."

"Good. Now, go eat. I see ships in the distance," Tori pointed out. "There's no telling how long you'll have to eat before you're called to the –"

"All hands! All hands to the ships!" Multiple people yelled. "All hands! All hands to the ships!"

"See?" Tori said. "Here." She fished into her backpack and pulled out a few energy bars and shoved them toward him. "I wish I could give you water."

"No. I cannot take these either. If any are found, we could be in trouble and mess with the timeline," he said, handing them back. "Besides, you may need them."

"Wherever we land next, we'll have to make sure to eat and drink plenty so we don't dehydrate," Tori said on a sigh.

"*If* we make it out of here," Tripp said and disappeared with the others.

"I hope they do well," Patrick said, watching them all run to the ships. "Lord, please be with them during this battle."

Tori furrowed her brow. "What does the Lord have to do with them coming back? He has only been with the British so far during this war."

"We are to remain faithful, even during trying times," Patrick said. "Do you believe in God?"

"I believe there is some higher source."

"Do you believe in Jesus Christ?" Patrick asked.

"No. I'm sure there was some nice guy named Jesus far back in time. However, as for Him being the Son of God?" Tori shook her head. "I highly doubt it. Why would the God of all creation give His Son for our lives? That's just stupid."

"I am sorry you feel that way. I will pray for you," Patrick said. "Jesus is central in my life. He is a relationship that has carried me through when I felt otherwise completely alone. Now, we must ready ourselves. The battle may begin at any time."

As the ships pulled away, Tori looked toward the *Lawrence* to see Perry hold up a flag that said, '*Don't Give Up The Ship!*' Cheers rang out from those aboard the ships. The cheers were loud enough for even Tori to hear.

"This is a battle for the waterways," Tori said quietly. "I know how this will end."

"How do you know such things?" Patrick asked. "Are you a witch?"

"Me? No." She shook her head. "I just know history."

"History refers to the past, not the present. You speak as if it is already destined."

As they talked, they cleaned up breakfast and then headed over to the medical area to prepare.

"It may be a doomed battle."

"Then," Patrick said, "let us pray it is doomed for the British this time and not for us."

"As you wish," Tori said.

"Keep faith in mind. Hebrews 11:1 says, *'Now faith is the confidence in what we hope for and assurance about what we do not see.'* This battle is the Lord's."

"Whatever you say," Tori said with a shrug.

She looked out at the water to see the boats pulling away from the shore. Then, she glanced over at the British ships, seeing them near their area. She shook her head. She knew her history. Her hope was that Tripp and Fred may somehow be able to change what history recorded as a bloody loss to the American side into a victory.

When Patrick was not looking, she got into her backpack and pulled CAIT to the top, yet out of sight of anyone watching. She glanced at the time as the first shot rang. At 11:45, the Battle of Put-In-Bay began.

T ripp and Fred worked on the *Niagara*. It was a bigger ship than the *Lawrence*. For that, Tripp was grateful. He was also grateful Perry and Fred were on two different ships. If he could keep them apart, it may be just enough to make a difference.

After a few hours, Tripp noticed something. "Why is it we continue to not be near the *Lawrence?*" Tripp whispered to Fred. "Did Perry not say to stay close to them?"

Fred looked up noticing what Tripp had seen. "Captain?" he called out.

"Yes?" Captain Elliot answered.

"Why, sir, are we not joining closer to the battle?"

"What is wrong with you?" one of the other sailors growled. "He's keeping us safe!"

"At the expense of the others in our fleet!" Fred countered.

"We will continue to –"

"Captain, the *Lawrence* is going down!" another called out.

Perry was aboard a smaller ship, heading their way. When they arrived, Perry met Elliot on the deck. Elliot asked, "How is the day going?"

Perry shook his head. "Badly."

"I can take your boat and rally the remaining schooners?" Elliot offered.

"I think that would be best. I will take command of the *Niagara*," Perry acquiesced.

Tripp looked at Fred, concern written all over his face.

"He is now in charge of our ship," Fred hissed, glaring at Perry. "How am I supposed to get back to my family if the devil continues to put this man before me?"

"Stay by me," Tripp said. "I will keep you out of trouble."

"As you say," Fred agreed.

"Gather your courage, men!" Perry shouted. "Let us join the battle! We will not give up this ship! Fight! Leave it all on the line! Our country needs us!"

"Yes, sir!" the crew responded in unison.

Tripp watched as Elliot sailed away from the *Niagara*. He shook his head. To him, Elliot was a coward and a traitor. When he could not destroy the mission with a poor caliber of men, he chose to leave the battle.

"We got this!" Tripp whispered as they loaded a cannon.

"What does that mean?" Fred asked.

"It means we will give everything we have. We *must* win this battle!" Tripp said. He plugged his ears as their cannon went off, suffocating them with the ongoing scent of metal and sulfur from the gunfire. His eyes watered. Coughing, he searched for the next cannon ball to load. He would continue to fight as long as there was life in him.

After another hour or so, in the midst of heavy cannon fire, Perry snapped at Fred.

"Sir!" Fred snapped back. "We are doing the best we can!"

"Do better! We must win!" Perry roared.

When Perry went to walk off, Fred went to jump him. Tripp wrapped his arms around Fred's waist to stop him. Fred was shouting at Perry, so Tripp covered his mouth. Fortunately, Perry could not hear him over the cannon and gunfire.

"You *must* make it back to your family!" Tripp hissed in Fred's ear. "Calm yourself!"

Fred shook Tripp off and sulked back to the cannon. "Bloody Captain!" he snarled.

"Focus, man!" Tripp yelled. "Win this for your wife and children!"

Fred simply nodded in response, resolve taking over his emotions.

Tori took a piece of cloth and used it to wrap around her head to keep her hair out of her face. It worked for the most part, but as she bandaged another sailor's arm, a piece of her hair fell into her face. She knew better than to move it out of the way without washing her hands first.

"You will be fine," Tori said as she secured the bandage.

She then went over and washed her hands in the water. It was not clean by any stretch of the imagination, but it got the blood out of her fingernails. Only then did she tuck her hair behind her ear.

"Tori! Come quick!" Patrick called out.

Tori ran over to him. "Yes?"

"Put pressure on this wound," he ordered.

Wide-eyed, she gasped. Blood squirted from the sailor's carotid artery. Horrified, she froze.

"Tori!" Patrick snapped. "Now!"

Tori grabbed a cloth, but not before getting blood all over her apron. She thrust the cloth over the area and held it down. The cloth was soaked in a matter of seconds, with blood running over her fingers. Staring down at her fingers, she rubbed two together as a flashback shot through her mind of when she found Chrissy. She fought deep inside to keep control of her emotions. The the watery-iron scent of blood was everywhere. Multiple times, she thought she would vomit as the horrific smells of what was going on near them on the lake combined with the blood and waste around her. "P-Patrick?" Tori stammered. Doing her best to take deep, cleansing breaths, she closed her eyes. "Patrick?"

"Tori!" Patrick yelled at her. "Calm down! I need you to work with me here!"

"Patrick, help!" a man shouted from a distance.

Tori looked and saw two men carrying another man. They each had one of the man's arms over their shoulders. What horrified Tori was that the man's right leg was missing at his knee.

"Good Lord!" Tori exclaimed.

"There will be more," Patrick said quietly. "Keep pressure on his neck. I'll take care of that one."

While he was working, and Tori was holding the man's neck, Tori looked up to see Charles stumbling up the shore, holding his left arm to his body. As he got closer, she saw how pale his face was and his body shook. What took her aback was how much blood coated his clothing. His hand was missing from his left arm. He dropped to the ground on his knees about twenty feet from the tent.

"We got him!" one of the two men who carried the man with no leg said. They ran over and dragged Charles over to the area. "What do you want us to do?"

Patrick gave them instructions. As they were working, Tori looked down at the face of the man she was holding the cloth to his neck. "P-Pat-Patrick," she stammered.

The faraway look in his eyes was unmistakable. Her hands trembled as she lifted the cloth. No more blood flowed from the wound.

Patrick ran over. He put his fingers on the man's neck. Shaking his head, he covered the man. "Go help Charles," Patrick ordered. "There's nothing more you can do for him."

"Yes, sir," she said and went over to Charles.

"Hold him down," one of the men said.

"Hold him...what?" she asked, stunned.

The man went over to the fire and pulled out a red-hot rod with a towel wrapped around his hand to protect him from the heat. He walked it over to them. "Hold him firm," the man ordered.

"I —" Tori shook her head as Charles struggled in her arms. "I can't!"

"Do it!" the man shouted. "Do it, or we'll lose him!"

In the distance, cannon and gunfire combined with yelling and shouting. To Tori, it was almost deafening!

Tori shook her head. "This is not okay!"

"Hold him!" the man snarled.

Tori and the other man held down the squirming Charles. When he saw what was coming, Charles fought harder. Tori cringed and shuddered as she heard the unmistakable sound of searing flesh when the man pressed it onto the end of Charles's wrist to cauterize the arm. She fought back more vomit at the smell of his flesh smoldering. She was grateful when Charles's screeches and screams stopped, and he passed out.

Tori released Charles. She rested her hands on her knees as she surveyed the area. Wiping her face, she said aloud, "I cannot do this anymore. This is barbaric."

"Barbaric is not trying to save these men!" Patrick countered. "It is our job to do our best. We have help with these two, who are...?" He asked the two men.

"My name's Samuel," one man said.

"And my name is Andrew," the other responded.

"Well, Andrew and Samuel, you are now part of our crew. You are not going back out."

"We would be much obliged," Andrew said. "Things are questionable at best out there."

Patrick shook his head. "I can only imagine." Turning toward Tori, he asked, "Are you going to help us save the lives of these men, or are you going to continue to fight me?"

Tori looked out at the battle, and then around her in the tent. She stood, straightened her shoulders, and said with determination, "I will help."

"Good. Stich that man up over there," he nodded toward a man who was holding his own wound with a cloth.

Together, the four of them worked until there was silence in the bay. Tori guessed by the sun that it was around three o'clock in the afternoon. The men on the Niagara and other ships were cheering.

Patrick, Samuel, and Andrew let out cheers as they hugged each other.

"Finally!" Patrick said, relieved. "We finally won! Perry is a hero!"

"The Hero of Lake Erie!" Andrew added.

Tori looked around the medical tent, shaking her head. They

won, but the cost of this battle broke her heart. The men who were alive in the area looked horrific. Some were missing limbs. Some got away only with broken bones. Others lay unconscious. All were bruised and battered in some fashion. Then, there were those who did not make it through. "Lord, if you are listening, I hope this is worth it. Please allow this battle to turn the tide of this war. Please allow it to count for something."

Over the next several hours, Tori, Patrick, Andrew, and Samuel continued to nurse the wounded. Meanwhile, before the men came back in, they buried the soldiers at sea who died during the battle. Afterward, they collected the dead and took them out to bury those who died at the medical tent. They buried twenty-seven Americans lost and forty-one British – all but six were buried at sea. Three officers from each side lost their lives as well. When they returned to the island, they buried all six officers under the willow tree near the medical tent. They put them on the side of the willow tree facing the bay, giving them the honor and respect they deserved as officers. It was a single willow tree in an open field. Putting them under the willow tugged at Tori's heart. She always knew them as weeping willows. While the Americans won the waterways, it took many lives. The symbolism of the weeping willow did not escape Tori.

As they buried the officers, Tori watched Fred and Tripp dig one of the graves. She knew at that moment both she and Tripp were forever changed. While this was an idea to save their family, they were able to also influence the War of 1812. Stopping Fred from killing Perry allowed Perry to win the Battle of Put-In-Bay. This also allowed the Americans to win the battle sooner, allowing for less loss of life. There would be fall-out from the actions of some of the men, including Elliot.

"Tori, when you're done with him, take a break and eat," Patrick ordered as Tori nursed a soldier.

"Not right now."

"Yes, right now. Also, you may need to cook some more. Pretty sure by the lines that food is running low."

"I doubt it. While some are eating, they're not eating a whole lot," Tori pointed out.

"Are you finished with him?" Patrick asked, watching her tie off the bandage on the man's arm.

"Yes."

"C'mon." He waved her over. "Andrew, Samuel, you reckon you can handle this for now?"

"Yes, sir," both men said in unison.

"We are going to take a break and cook some more."

"Take your time, sir," Andrew said as he and Samuel worked on another soldier.

"We can handle this," Samuel assured him.

Making their way across the field to check the food, Patrick asked, "So, you've really never done anything medical?"

"Nope."

"You're really good. A natural, even. You may want to consider being a nurse."

"Not sure if I fit in the medical field."

"What is it you normally do?"

"Honestly?" Tori asked.

"Always be honest."

"I have not really thought about it. I mean, I have had ideas, but I generally just hang out with my friends."

"Hang out? What does that mean?"

"Oh!" Tori's heart skipped a beat. She had become so comfortable around Patrick that she forgot to keep the slang terms from her vocabulary. "Sorry. I mean, my friends and I like to go to the pond and swim, have picnics...that sort of thing."

"Oh. I understand. Even with the state of the country?"

"Well, the females. I do miss my male friends, though."

"Do you have any interest in any of those male friends?"

She shook her head. "Not right now."

Patrick looked into the pots. "You're right. They are not eating a lot. Come. Let us take a walk," he suggested.

Tori and Patrick wandered away from camp toward the water. They sat down on a good-sized boulder they found.

Hearing the moaning and groaning from the soldiers in the medical tent and the other men who were talking about their day or helping their friends who were injured, Tori focused on the sound the water made coming and going on the shoreline in hopes of tuning out the horrific events of the day. She relished in the sound the waves made on the shore, but not the stench emitting from the water. It smelled of death and destruction. "It's so peaceful. Hard to believe there was a brutal battle here just a few hours ago."

Patrick raised an eyebrow. "You mean outside of the men moaning and the literal blood in the water?"

"I'm trying to focus on the good," Tori said on a sigh. "That was a lot to think through today."

"You did very well."

"Thank you. As did you."

"I am in training. I will be going to medical school after the war to be a doctor."

"That is very admirable!" Tori remarked.

"My parents want my oldest brother to take over the farm, and he has been training with them to do so. I feel better helping others, so I chose to become a doctor."

"I think you will make a great doctor!"

"I could really use a great nurse to help me?" he hinted.

Tori shook her head. She could not help the smile that came to her face or the rush of blood to her cheeks. "I am sure there is another young lady you have an interest in?" Tori suggested.

"No. I want a woman who I know can handle herself in situations like this."

"I did not do very well at times."

"This is the first time you have ever done this. After those first few, you not only handled it well, but you were also able to do a lot of the tricky ones on your own." He nudged her with his elbow. "I watched the resolve take over, and you did incredible after that. I must say I am very impressed with you. You also cooked for these men as if you were doing this all your life."

"I am certain there are ladies out there who you will take a shine to, and they to you."

Patrick furrowed his brow. "Do you not like me?"

Seeing the hurt in his eyes, she assured him, "Oh, yes! Unfortunately, I know we will probably be moving on tomorrow."

"What are you searching for?"

"What do you mean?"

"Why do you two continue on?" he asked.

"Well, we have kin who need our help," she explained. "We're trying to get to them."

"Will you come back?" he asked.

"I honestly do not know."

"I would love for you to come back. How will I know how to find you?"

"You may want to set your eyes on another," Tori said. "I do not think we will be back."

He turned, taking both of her hands into his. "What if I do not want to? What if *you* are the one I want to set my eyes on?"

She shook her head. "You just met me. How can you say that?"

"I have seen all I need to in order to make the right choice. You are different than other girls."

"Oh yeah!" Tori laughed. "You can say that again."

"Why would I want to say that again?"

"Never mind." She shook her head. "Look, there are many differences between us."

"Such as?"

"I am not a Christian," she said.

"Why not?"

"I guess after losing so much, I have a difficult time justifying there is a God out there. Why did He not stop everything from happening?" she asked.

"Your parents," he said in understanding.

"Also, the wars, *and* I had a friend named Chrissy who was murdered a little over a year ago. I was in the house with her when it happened, but I was sleeping."

"Praise God you are still here!" Patrick said, eyes wide. "What happened?"

"It is a long story. The short version is that I lost my best friend."

"After losing your ma and pa," Patrick said, recovering from the shock. "I can see how you would be angry. There is much loss in this wild country. Many battles. Much death."

"See? That's the thing. Why does God not stop it?"

"I cannot answer that. I do know He gives us free will to make our own choices. Sometimes those choices are not good ones, and they hurt others. Sometimes we make a choice to stand up for something we do not think is right, and we end up in battles like we are now." He gestured toward the lake. "I do know that I trust Him and His ways. I trust He knows all of the angles, while I do not. He sees all and knows all. And for that, I am grateful."

"Why? Why do you follow someone you cannot see? How do you know He is really there?"

"Well, you are here. You are alive. You and your brother came in time to help us through this battle. Your brother is not a soldier, but he fights like one. Why do we fight for freedom? It is something we cannot see. Why do we fight for love? It is also something we cannot see. There are many things we believe in that we cannot see. We also cannot see the wind, but I do know it is there."

"I can feel the wind."

"So can I. I can also feel the Lord. I feel tingles when I know He is working. I see evidence of His creations as the birds fly and feed every day. The fish have a home in the water and are fed each day as well. What I am saying is there is much out there we cannot explain. For example, we trusted this rock would not break when we sat on it," he said, knocking on the boulder with his knuckles. "We have never sat on it before, but we trusted it to hold both of us."

"That's pretty deep."

"It is also true, is it not?"

"It is."

"Just because you cannot see something does not mean it is not there. Just because you have not tested it does not mean you cannot trust it. I do hope this makes sense."

"It does." She nodded. Then she asked, "You said something about Jesus earlier."

"Yes."

"I mean, I know He was some guy who lived a while ago, right?

"Sort of. Jesus is the Son of God," Patrick explained. "He came a long time ago and lived on this planet as a man. He also died on the cross for our sins."

"What do you mean by that?"

"For the sake of time, this is the short version. A long time ago, sin entered the world," he started. "When that happened, God and man had a separation. In order for God to forgive people's sins, He had them make burnt offerings. Jesus came to earth to be that perfect sacrifice for man. He died on the cross to be the ultimate sacrifice. Not only that, but He also rose from the dead three days later. He beat death, so we can have eternity with Him."

"Interesting," Tori said, thinking through his words.

"He wants to be more than worshipped. He wants a relationship with us. He has been through this and wants us to know He understands us. God wants to help us to live our best life. Then, there's the Spirit, the third part of the God-head. He is our guide."

"Third part?"

"Think of it this way: an egg has three parts. There is the shell, the yolk, and the egg white. All three parts are the egg. Right?"

"Right."

"The God-head has three parts: God the Father; God the Son; and God the Holy Spirit. They all work together."

"That makes sense."

"I would love to talk to you more, but I know we do not have time."

"I need time to process this anyway."

"Fair enough. May I request that you keep an open mind and search to see where you can see God working?"

"I will consider it with an open mind," she agreed.

"Thank you. Now, if I wished to court you, to whom would I speak?"

"Patrick," she shook her head, "we are moving on. I do not want you to waste your time waiting for someone who is not coming back. We may get killed on the way to our kin. Please, just move forward, looking for that special lady God created just for you."

"What if it is you?"

"I really doubt that. While I like you, our paths may never cross again. Please do not talk to anyone about me."

"As you wish," he said somberly. "Even though you are everything I have been looking for."

"I am sure there will be others to fit what you are looking for. Other ladies who are considerably younger and who have a heart's desire to follow you into the medical field."

"You speak as if you are not worthy to work in the medical field."

"I am painfully aware of how men consider women in these times. If I wanted to be a doctor, I know that would not be possible right now."

"Out west they may allow it," Patrick suggested. "In a small town."

"That is not comforting. I also know how women are viewed. I promise you that I will get in a lot of trouble because of my outspoken ways. The only reason I took orders these last few days is because it was not only my life on the line but others as well."

"So, you do not listen at all?"

"I choose to whom I listen," she countered. "There are times where it is necessary. I also listen to Tripp. I respect him. I trust him. I know he is doing his best to protect me."

"Do you not feel your husband would do the same?"

"I am twenty-four years old. I am considered an old maid."

"Do you not want to marry?"

"Of course I do! Some day."

"How will you know if you can trust him and respect him?"

"Time."

"Do you not feel in time you could come to trust and respect me?"

"I do trust you. You have not done anything to break that trust. I also have mad respect for you."

"Mad respect?" Patrick cocked his head to the side. "You say strange words. Where are you from again?"

"Mad respect means crazy respect."

Patrick shook his head. "I am not crazy."

"No. I mean. I have the utmost respect for you and a lot of it."

"Okay. I think I understand."

"Look. I like you. There is a definite attraction between us. However, I do not know what my future holds, and I do not want you waiting for me. If I find out otherwise, I will be upset with you."

Patrick smiled. "What if you hear of me and choose to come back to me?"

"I do not know what my future holds."

"God does," Patrick assured her. "He will let us know if we are meant to be together."

"In the meantime, do not stop looking for the young lady to be your bride," Tori added.

"More like, in the meantime, we have some more cleaning up to do. We have taken a long enough break," Patrick said, hopping down from the boulder. He put his hands on Tori's waist and helped her down. When she stood right in front of him, he warned, "Whenever you do leave, please be cautious and alert. This country is volatile. Without this war, the Indian territory is dangerous. With this war, any traveling is deadly."

"I will be careful," Tori promised.

Looking around to make sure no one saw them, Patrick leaned down and kissed her cheek. "Be safe. May God lead your steps."

"Be safe as well. Just because you are in a medical tent, it does not guarantee safety."

"Agreed," he said, and they walked back to the camp.

CHAPTER FIVE

11SEP1813 (AM): A Time To Mend

In the early morning hours, after dinner and cleaning up, Tripp pulled Fred and Tori aside. "We need to talk," Tripp said quietly.

They went over to an area by themselves, drinking tea, while the others continued to celebrate, tend to the wounded, or sleep.

"Fred, we needed to speak with you in private," Tripp started.

"I get that, but there's a celebration we need to go to!" Fred grinned ear-to-ear. "We actually won!"

"We need to leave," Tripp explained. "Before we leave, we wanted to speak with you regarding your family."

Fred pursed his lips. "What does that mean?"

"You are important to your family," Tripp said. "Tempers run in your family, but you have an opportunity to change that."

"What do you mean?"

"They run in our family, too," Tori explained. "Tempers end up getting us in trouble and even killed at times. We do not want that for you. We want you to live a long life. We want your children to live long lives. In order to do that, you are going to have to change how you react to things."

"What right do you have to tell me how to live and act?" Fred growled.

Tripp turned to make sure no one was listening before he whispered, "We know how behavior can affect children and those children's children...far into many generations."

"How do you know?" Fred asked.

"I study history," Tori jumped in. "I have studied generational history. Have members of your ancestors lived long lives?"

"Not really," Fred admitted.

"What happened?" Tripp asked.

"They either died in wars, committed crimes, and other, um, let's just say activities."

"Is that the future you want for your children?" Tori asked.

Fred considered their words for a moment before he shook his head.

"You have a choice," Tripp said. "To have a different future, when you return to your family, you must behave differently. Just like I calmed you down so you did not hurt Perry, you can teach your boys to do the same."

"They *are* a bit short-tempered," Fred admitted.

"Then teach them to stand up for themselves, but not get in too deep," Tori said. "Teach them balance."

Fred sat back and crossed his arms. Neither Tori nor Tripp said anything as Fred considered their words.

Finally, after a few long, tense moments, Fred nodded. "How do I do this?"

"Teach them to take their frustrations out in other ways. Whether it's chopping wood," Tori suggested, "or teaching them a skill like woodworking or blacksmithing. Both are physical. Both would help them take out their aggression, yet appeal to their creative side."

Fred nodded. "All right. Fair enough. Agreed," he said, shaking their hands. "I think that would be a wise choice."

"Thank you," Tripp said. "Future generations of your family will thank you for making this change."

"Now," Tori stood, "there's something we need to take care of."

"It was a pleasure getting to know you," Tripp said, shaking Fred's hand. "Be kind to your family."

"I will. Thank you. Where are you going?"

"We have to take a look around the island for something," Tori said. "Blessings to you and your family."

Together, they left into the woods. Before they ducked into the tree line, Tori scanned the area for Patrick. She saw him by the fire talking with some men. One of them had just finished a story that had them all in fits of laughter. As soon as Tori saw him, he stopped laughing and looked toward the tree line, almost directly at her. They were connected. Tori could not deny that. She sighed as they turned and walked deeper into the woods. The further they went into the woods, the better they felt, knowing they were not followed.

"You're covered in blood," Tripp pointed out.

"I know," Tori grumbled. "What new time are we heading toward?"

"I don't know," Tripp said. "We have to go somewhere to look at CAIT."

"What if we do that slide thing?" Tori suggested. "Then we can look at CAIT without anyone seeing us."

"How will we know if we are sliding into someone's house or an Indian village?" Tripp asked.

"Are there any more deserted islands here we can slide to?" Tori asked.

"Yes," he said. "Actually, there are."

Tori handed him her backpack with his belongings in it. He knelt down and emptied everything onto the ground. As Tori put her stuff back in her own backpack, he filled his back up, making sure to leave CAIT and the wrist device out before slipping the backpack onto his back. Putting the wrist device on, he punched a date, time, and location into the device.

"Hold on," Tripp said.

Tori slipped her backpack on, then grabbed his arm. One

second, they were on the island; the next, they were an hour later, about two-thirty in the morning, on another island.

Tori was on her hands and knees, shaking. Tripp knelt next to her with his arm over her shoulder. "Are you okay? That wasn't too big of a slide."

"No. It *was* a shove, though. Remember, we haven't eaten much. Not that I could with all of that blood."

"Okay. Take a few deep breaths while I pull CAIT up."

Tripp sat on the ground beside Tori. He punched some information into CAIT before a projection appeared before them while she situated herself into a better position. They literally watched as there was a domino effect within their family tree. The names were either in white or black. It took a moment for all of the names to either switch or stay the same. There were some new names in Fred's family as well.

"The ones in white are where they died of natural causes or something non-criminal related," Tripp explained. "Looks like Fred and his family made the correct adjustments. It went okay through the eighteen-hundreds."

"Then what happened?" Tori asked. She pointed toward a few names in black. "Why are these still black?"

"While one is a fatality from World War One, the other is criminal activity," Tripp explained. "The parents are white. They died of natural causes. Looks like that whole family died way too early."

"Going to assume Anthony Williams is the World War One?" Tori asked. When he nodded, she asked, "Then, who is Margaret Williams? What did she do?"

"Well," Tripp cleared his throat, "seems she worked for the local speakeasy. She was part of the prohibition era. Being female, she was not watched as much as the males. She lost her brother, Anthony, in World War One on December 16, 1917. Remember, at that time there was no World War Two. It was known as The Great War back then. So, after her brother died, she took a job with her boyfriend, Warren Marshall. He delivered liquor to the speakeasies. He used Maggie, as she was called then, to do some of the running."

"I see," Tori said on a sigh.

"During one of those runs, she was stopped by the other local boss in the area. They figured out Warren was using her to run, and they decided to shoot the messenger...or in this case, Maggie."

"Okay, knowing that, when and where is our next stop?"

"Looks like we're heading to the 1920s. I'm going to jump forward and get some clothes and money. Do not ask where or how. You don't want to know the answers. Can you stay here for a few minutes while I get you something to wear? You can't wear that."

Tori looked down at her blood-soaked clothing. "Your clothes are not too much better."

"No, but I'm sneakier. Give me a few. Stay hidden."

He was standing there one moment, inputting information into his wrist device before he shimmered in the water effect and disappeared the next moment.

While she waited, she went to the edge of the trees of the island. An island over, in the distance, she could see a fire. She knew they were far enough that no one would have seen CAIT when he pulled it up. She also knew Patrick was over there. If there was one guy who stood out to her as her perfect match, it was Patrick. She could not think of anything negative to say about him. He was, however, almost two hundred years older than she. She sighed as she looked longingly at the fire.

Turning her attention toward the sky, the billions of stars amazed her. "God," she said, "if You're there, and You can hear me, please take special care of Patrick. Please bring a young lady to him that will allow him to forget about me. Also, if You're listening, please protect us and bless our efforts. I don't know if I really believe in You or not. If You are really there, please show me. Patrick believes in You. If You are real, I would like to get to know You. If You really sent Your son, please let me know that too. I don't know how You would do that, but I'm willing to keep an open mind."

Hearing someone clear their throat behind her, she jumped. Resting her hand on her chest, she had difficulty regulating her breathing. "Tripp! You scared me to death!"

"Sorry. I didn't want to interrupt you."

"It-it's fine. Did you get everything?"

"Yes. You're going to have to change out of those filthy clothes. Here are some new ones," he said, holding up a bag.

She got off the ground and brushed herself off. Getting a good look at him, she cocked her head to the side. She let out a low whistle as she circled him. "Nice! I approve."

"Oh, this old thing?" He shrugged with a dramatic flair. "Just something I threw on."

He wore a gray fedora with a black band and a gray wool coat. Under the coat, he had a suit that was a little broader at the top. It was a loose-fitted, double-breasted suit. Under his jacket, he had a nice dress shirt and high-waisted pants, with suspenders and a tie. The jacket and pants were black with gray stripes, along with a gray tie.

"I'm liking the 1920's look," she said, nodding in approval.

"Now for you," he said, gesturing toward the woods. "Go change. And yes, this time I got some money."

"Do I want to know?"

"No. Just go get ready."

"Yes, sir," she said and headed into the woods. Taking off her clothes, they almost felt like she had to peel them off with all of the blood. She was grateful for the clean clothing. She slipped on the underclothing, along with the new chemise, before picking up her dress. "Nice!" she whispered. The light-blue, low-waist dress was just her color. She slid it over her clothes. The sleeves went to mid-bicep, while the top part went to her waist with a darker shade of light blue for the ribbon. The dress itself was still to her ankles, draping at various lengths. She pulled out the pearl necklace, which hung to her mid-chest, along with the light-blue hair band that was the same color as the ribbon. She re-braided her hair, wrapping it in a bun again. While it did not look quite the "bob-style" of the times, she was not going to cut her hair off just to fit in for a week or so. She slid her new T-strap, blue shoes that matched the ribbon on her skirt as well.

"Tripp!" she whispered loudly. "Tripp!"

"What? Oh! You look great!"

"What do I do with this bloody clothing?"

He shrugged. "Burn it?"

"No. For real. What do I do with it?"

"Just leave it."

"What did you do with yours?"

"I put it in the trash."

"Can we just do that when we get there? I don't want someone to find this and think I was attacked and killed."

"Good idea. Put the coat on as well. I got you a hat if you wanted to wear it."

"I'll put the hair band away until later and just use the hat," she said, taking out the tan cloche hat that matched her coat. It was a long coat, with fake fur around the lapels. "Fancy!"

"The 1920s definitely had style. I got you a couple dresses in case you wanted to change," he said, handing her another bag. "Also, instead of backpacks, I got us side bags. We should put our backpacks in them, though. For most of the other timeline stops, backpacks will work."

"Fair enough," she said, shoving all of her belongings except the clothing from the current time into her bag. "It's a little full, but it will work."

"Okay. Maggie died on September 27, 1922. What if we travel to September 25th so you and I can have a few days to get to know her before she is killed? Maybe we can convince her not to go that night?"

"What if we go in a few more extra days early so we can get some rest?" Tori asked.

"Okay, then let's go in on the 20th?"

"That will work. I also have a question."

"What?"

"Well, if Anthony died in 1917, and she died in 1922, how did the family line continue?"

"Anthony got a young lady, Anna Edwards, pregnant prior to shipping out. The young lady had a daughter that she named Elizabeth Victoria Williams, after the father's family name."

"Then, should we not be looking more for Anna Edwards?"

"Maybe. Let's see if we can save Maggie first."

"Okay. Let's go," she said, taking his arm.

"It's a bit of a jump, so exhale now," he said, and hit the button on his wrist.

Tori felt the familiar feeling of ice-cold water while they shimmered. Then, the thrust took the rest of her breath away. Feeling her body want to pull apart, she gritted her teeth, praying the feeling would stop soon!

CHAPTER SIX

20SEP1922 (AM): A Time For Peace

Landing on her hands and knees, Tori gasped for air, hoping her head would stop spinning.

"It's okay. Just breathe," Tripp coaxed with his arm around her.

"Sure....easy for you to say...you have a buffer...I don't," she said in between breaths. "Not fair!"

"I know. That's why I do more of the sliding. Just relax and breathe. It will pass soon. You can do this."

"Where...are we?"

"Is she okay?" a man asked, walking down the street, seeing the pair in the alley.

"Maybe just a bit too much going on. It's okay," Tripp said.

"Ma'am, I would feel better hearing it from you."

"Such a gentleman. I'm fine. Thank you. My brother will help me get home safely," she responded.

"Okay. Have a good evening," the man said. He tipped his hat before he walked on.

"We need to get you off the ground. Are you okay?"

"Yeah. Here, put this stuff in the trash before someone sees it," she said, handing him her clothing from 1813.

"I will if you stand."

Tori slowly stood, using the wall to brace herself. She watched as he went further into the alley to a trash bin and shoved the clothing deep into the bin. When he returned, he said, "Done. Are you ready to find somewhere to sleep?"

Her eyebrows rose in surprise. "You mean actually in a bed?"

"You'll get an actual bed *and* an actual bath. You up for it?"

"Oh, good Lord, yes!"

"Okay. Let's go."

They went down the road to a hotel that was in a decent area and checked in. Tripp let Tori take the first bath. She scrubbed herself several times, washing her hair at least three times. By the time she finished, the tub was disgusting, so she drained the water and cleaned the tub for Tripp.

After she finished, she got in the chemise to sleep in, not really seeing anything else to wear to bed. She also braided her hair. She decided she would figure out how to style it in the morning.

"Your turn," she said, coming out of the bathroom.

"Did you leave me any hot water?"

"Well, the water wasn't overly hot to begin with, but it's clean. I also cleaned the tub for you."

"Thank you!"

"If you don't mind, I'm going to go ahead and go to sleep," she said, climbing into one of the two twin beds in the room.

"Go for it. You deserve it."

While he headed into the bathroom, Tori laid down on the bed. It was the first decent bed she had slept on in over a year. She did not consider the mattress in jail as a true bed. It was thin at best. The pillow and blanket were pathetic. Having said that, it was a little better than sleeping for those few hours on the ground she got before the Battle of Lake Erie.

She shook her head. It was difficult to comprehend that she was in 2022 three days ago, 1813 just a few hours ago, and was now in 1922. *Was this real or some elaborate dream? Would this really work? Can Tripp and I save their family? Will we make it through all the family shifting? Would we still exist after this was finished shaking out?*

There were so many questions and no answers. Only time would tell. She sighed. *Back to time again.* She closed her eyes. Amongst all that horror, she was able to have a bright spot – Patrick. His six-foot frame, with his blue eyes and bright smile continued to flash into her mind. His last name being the same as hers blew her mind! However, he was in the past. *She should forget about him...but could she?* She played their conversations in her mind until she gratefully drifted off to sleep.

Tori woke with a splitting headache. The stress of the last few days weighed heavily on her. She moaned when the smell of bacon, eggs, and toast hit her. She swallowed the bile that threatened to come up.

"Tori? Are you okay?" Tripp asked as he was eating his breakfast in bed, while reading the newspaper.

"No. I feel like I have a massive hangover," she groaned.

"It could be from all the traveling and stress. I can go pick up something for you at the drug store?"

"Please."

"Are you ready to eat? I got you something from room service." He gestured toward the cart with food. "I wasn't sure what you wanted, so I got you eggs, bacon, toast, and a fruit plate."

"Not yet. Aspirin first, please?"

"You got it!" he said and got up. He went into the bathroom to change before he left.

"We need to talk about how chipper he is in the morning," Tori grumbled on her way to the bathroom. After using the facilities, she washed her hands and face. Stopping by the cart on the way back to her bed, she picked up two pieces of toast. "Toast should be okay." She took them, along with the fresh-squeezed orange juice, back to her bed.

She was still nibbling on the toast when Tripp walked in. He handed her a bag.

"This is more than aspirin."

"Yes. I got you a nightgown, along with both of us each a toothbrush and toothpaste."

"Ooo! Good thinking!"

"Thank you. I do that once and a while." He smiled proudly. "So, what do you want to do today?"

"Maybe walk around and get used to the town?" she suggested.

"What if we go clothes shopping? We're here for at least seven days. You and I are both going to need more than just two outfits to last that long."

"Do we have the money for that?"

"Yes."

She furrowed her brow. "Exactly how much do we have?"

"I have what we need. I can get more if we need it."

"From where?"

"You don't want to know."

"Are you making us a modern-day Bonnie and Clyde?"

"Their spree doesn't start until 1932," Tripp pointed out. "So, technically, they would be a modern-day Tripp and Tori by the time they come along."

"Wow! You *are* a historian. I'm impressed."

"Thank you," he said and bowed before sitting on his bed. "How are you doing with all of this?"

"Honestly?"

"I would hope we're honest with each other. We're on this mission together. If we can't trust each other, then we're in trouble."

"True. It's a lot to take in. One night I was sentenced for supposedly killing my best friend, the next, I was in 1813. Then today, we're in 1922. I guess I'm wondering if this will really work?"

"Well, if it's any consolation, what we did in 1813 worked for our relatives, as well as for America. I was right that not killing Perry turned the war of 1812 for the Americans sooner."

"That's a lot of power."

"Not really. America won that war anyway. We just nudged the final battle to come a little sooner. We made that battle a little less bloody...literally."

"True. Did you know that Patrick's last name was St. James?"

"Really?"

"Yes. Is there a way to check out his family's history to see how he turned out?"

"That would be a lot of work that I don't have time for right now. We still need to fix our family."

"I've been thinking about that. Anthony's daughter would be at least five years old by now. Would Maggie know about her?"

"Unknown."

"If she did, would it change her mind about working with Warren?" Tori suggested.

Tripp nodded. "That's a definite possibility."

"We need to figure out which speakeasy she works at."

"It's a place called the *Charleston Confidential*."

"Charleston...as in Charleston, South Carolina?" Tori asked.

"Yep. That's where we are."

"Okay. That would have been some useful information to know."

"Don't worry. I know where we are. I wouldn't let you out and about without letting you know."

"*Charleston Confidential*, huh? Do we know how to get in or where it's at?"

"I know both," he said with a smile.

"How do we get in?"

"A password."

"Which is?"

"Clandestine clique."

"I like it. What do we wear there?"

"Let's go shopping. I know what we need."

"Fair enough," Tori said. She took the aspirin for her headache, then got dressed.

Tori was glad they took a few extra days to get to know the area and to rest. She knew she would need it. Sleeping in a bed was a luxury. She could have slept longer if it was not for her headache. Shopping allowed the two of them to get to know each other better, along with their taste in clothing.

"What do you think of this one?" Tori asked, coming out of the dressing room in a white drop-waist dress, that was sleeve-less. The skirt was a little shorter and pleated. It hung to her mid-calf.

"This would look great with that dress," the sales lady said, bringing over a headband that had a white feathery flower and a black band. "Maybe a pair of black shoes and white gloves to top the outfit?" she offered.

"Definitely!" Tripp agreed. "Next?"

She picked out four dresses. One white evening dress, another royal-blue evening dress, both used black as the offset color. Then, for the daytime, she picked out two more dress outfits. One was emerald green, and the other was red; again, both used black as the offset color. She did that so she would not have to buy multiple pairs of shoes for just seven days of activi-ties. Tripp also had her get a robe and three nightgowns to change out.

While they were in the store, one of the sales ladies showed Tori how she could keep her hair long but style it to look as if it were a bob cut. It required using gel, combing her hair into waves, and a fine hair net to keep it all in place, but it was doable.

During their shopping, Tripp also picked out four different suits to complete his wardrobe. He could wear them in various ways, including without the jacket or using suspenders if he wanted a more relaxed look. He also picked out a few more hats to complete his style.

"Very nice," Tori said when he came out of the changing room to show her.

"Yes. I approve," the salesman agreed. "I took the liberty of picking out three different ties to go with that outfit. Which do you like best?"

"Definitely this one," Tripp said, holding a navy blue and white striped tie to match his suit.

"It's the cat's meow!" the salesman remarked.

"I agree!" Tori said with a smile.

"Where, kind sir, would you recommend I take my sister for dinner?"

"Well," the man looked around to make sure no one heard him, "the Charleston Confidential is always an amazing place to go. It's swankier than the average. The owner, Warren Marshall, is the real McCoy. A regular Joe, you know? However, you did not hear about it from me."

"I know of the place."

"It's a real gin mill, but it's the bee's knees. Giggle water is always flowing, good food in abundance, and it's the place to be, especially for a young pair like yourselves. Keep an eye on her."

"Oh, I don't need to worry about her. My sister can handle herself quite well."

"I would still keep an eye on her. She's a looker," the man cautioned. "Do you know the entrance?"

"Yes. I know how to get in as well."

"Enjoy! And thank you for your patronage," the man said, handing them their hand-written receipt and bag of clothing.

As they walked down the street, Tori leaned into Tripp and

said, "I love the lingo during this time period. The southern drawl while using it is cracking me up. I'm trying not to giggle, but it's kind of like living in a bad retro book."

"Just go with it," Tripp encouraged. "We're here for the next week. It will take us a bit to get in good with Maggie and Warren. We're going to have to convince her not to be a runner."

"I still feel like we should try to find Anna Edwards to see about the baby. Children are a huge motivation to straighten yourself out," Tori suggested.

"I agree. Let's get ready to jump into this fascinating new world," Tripp said with a smirk. "I really love this time. The roaring twenties."

"Keep that thought in mind. Every decade has its pluses and minuses," Tori cautioned. "The 1920s are a bit more of a carefree time, but there's also a higher level of danger when it comes to territories and mafia bosses."

"Really? To me, it always seemed like an anything goes decade."

"No. As you said, they killed Maggie to get back at Warren. He is obviously encroaching on someone's territory and was being successful enough for them to take notice. They only take someone out when they feel threatened. Otherwise, it was a matter of dodging the coppers."

"Oh!" Tripp chuckled. "I see what you did there, tossing in a bit of the lingo."

"Keep that spirit up. We're going to need it," she said as they entered the hotel.

"Looks like you had a fine day of shopping," the concierge said when they walked in.

"Yes, sir," Tripp said. "We'll be taking in the local gin mill you recommended as well tonight."

"Please mention to Mr. Marshall that Clyde sent you. He likes it when we recommend his place."

"I definitely will," Tripp agreed as they went into the elevator.

"What floor please?" the elevator man asked as he closed the gate.

"Third. Thank you."

The elevator man cranked the lever to their floor number. "Looks like you had a profitable day of shopping," he commented.

"We did. Thank you!" Tori said as the elevator started its ascent.

"How are you finding Charleston so far?" he asked.

"It's a beautiful area," Tripp said. "The people are very friendly as well."

"It's that southern hospitality," the elevator man said with a grin. "If we didn't our mamas would make sure to let us know later. It's ingrained since we were young!"

Tripp and Tori chuckled.

"Here we are," the man announced, opening the gate to their floor.

Tripp handed the man a tip and said, "Thank you, sir."

"My pleasure. Have a good day."

"Thank you. You, too," Tori said to him.

When they got into their room, Tripp mentioned, "Looks like we're going to be giving Clyde a bit of a bonus as well."

"Gain favor where we can." Tori shrugged. "This is a really nice hotel."

"They were built to last in these days."

"Let's hope the people were made the same way."

CHAPTER SEVEN

20SEP1922 (PM): A Time To Plant

Dressing in her royal blue and black outfit with overcoat, and Tripp in his navy blue and white striped suit and trench coat, the pair walked into the local grocery store.

"Welcome," the store owner said with a smile. "Is there something in particular you're looking for?"

Tripp went over to the counter. In a low voice, he said what Clyde told him to tell the clerk, "Clyde told us about the Charleston Confidential. Do you happen to have a copy of it?"

"Of course! We tend to keep those in the back. Go on through the curtain and down the stairs. The room with the confidential papers is down there. Earnest can help you find what you are looking for."

"Thank you," Tripp said. Tori looped her arm through Tripp's as they headed through the curtains behind the counter. They went down a set of stairs with no lights.

"Obviously, safety is not high on their list. One could break an ankle down here," Tori commented.

"Just go with it, and be careful," Tripp said. "I'm really surprised you can't hear anything down here." He knocked on the door. When he did, a small window in the door slid open. "I was told Earnest can help me with some confidential papers?"

"Any papers in particular?" the man huffed.

"Clandestine clique," Tripp said.

The man did not say a word. He simply closed the window and opened the door.

What they walked into blew Tori's mind. She felt like she was walking into a ritzy movie set. There were multiple booths along the walls with plush, burgundy velvet. The tables running along the next row were four-seaters. The tables were small with the same burgundy seat cushions. Gold trim corresponded with the burgundy on everything. Even the bar area had burgundy leather, with gold beading. There were people talking, smoking, drinking, and having a good time all over the place. It was as if there was an entirely different world going on under the city.

On the stage was a young lady with black hair and dark-brown eyes. She looked to be only a few inches taller than Tori's five-eight. The woman's voice was smooth as she sang a jazz tune. She wore a gold dress similar to the style of Tori's dress, with gold gloves and shoes, and with a long string of pearls. The headband was gold with white feathers.

"Do you want to bet that's Maggie?" Tripp nodded toward her. "She looks like she could be your sister."

"Welcome! Welcome!" a man walked up to the pair. "Newcomers!"

"How do you know that?" Tripp asked, shaking his hand.

"I know everyone who frequents my establishment."

"Are you Warren Marshall?" Tripp asked. Before the man could respond, he added, "Clyde sent us."

"Good man! Good man! Yes. I'm Warren Marshall. He only sends the special guests here. Please follow me to a table for such a beautiful couple."

"We're actually brother and sister," Tori mentioned.

"Noted. Please have a seat here, and," he added to Tripp, "keep an eye on the young lady. With gams like that, the dodgers will hone in on her. We don't allow any funny business. We are a well-run establishment. However, there are a few cake-eaters in here looking for any dumb Dora they can find."

"She's a smart one," Tripp said. "I have confidence in her ability to defend herself."

While Tripp and Warren spoke for a few moments, Tori took in the room. Some people were dancing, and some were at tables, booths, or the bar. Everyone seemed to be enjoying themselves.

"Her voice is beautiful," Tori mentioned.

"What?" Tripp asked.

"I said her voice is beautiful. It's like an angel singing," she said.

"Maggie's my girl. I have to agree. She would appreciate hearing that. During her break, maybe we can come and chat with you two and give you an official welcome to the Charleston Confidential. Being new to the area, we would love to chat with you."

"Please do!" Tripp said. "It would be great to get an inside track on the town."

"How long are you here for?" Warren asked.

"Only about a week."

"What brings you to Charleston?"

"Vacation," Tori jumped into the conversation. "We've had a rough time of things lately and we're looking to take a break."

"Sorry to hear that. Don't worry about the coppers around here. They won't bother us. We have an understanding," Warren assured him. "Just relax and enjoy! I'll send Betty over here to take your order."

"Thank you," Tripp said. "We appreciate it and look forward to talking to you later."

When he was gone, Tori leaned over to Tripp and quietly said, "He doesn't seem that shady."

Tripp raised an eyebrow. "Shady?"

"Someone intertwined in crime," Tori explained.

"No. He seems really laid back, enjoying life."

"Let's hope we can help Maggie to enjoy life after the week is up," Tori said as the waitress made her way over to the table.

Through the night, they danced, enjoyed excellent food and drinks, and were able to relax and unwind. Whenever someone asked Tori to dance, she turned them down and danced with Tripp. She only danced with Tripp because she did not want to become attached to anyone during this time and potentially mess up any relationships that were supposed to form. She felt like she may have done that with Patrick and did not want to make the same mistake twice.

They danced dances that Tori absolutely loved! She learned them as they went. The dances included *the Charleston, The Fox Trot,* and *The Texas Tommy.*

"Whew!" Tori said, plopping down in their booth after a faster dance. "That was so fun!"

"I know! Now I understand why they call this the roaring twenties."

"Can I get you two something to eat or more to drink?" Betty asked, coming up to the table.

"Yes. Please," Tripp said and ordered food for both of them.

While they ate, they watched others around the room. To Tori, it was surreal knowing these people lived and died, most of them before she was born. In bouncing through time, she had a newfound respect for her ancestors. Actually, meeting some of them allowed her to step into their lives for a bit. To see what they saw. To feel what they felt. To see and understand them on a whole other level.

Around ten, the band and Maggie took a break while jazz music played in the background. Warren and Maggie came over to Tripp and Tori's table. "Maggie, I would like you to meet the siblings, Tripp and Tori St. Claire," Warren introduced them. "Tripp, Tori, this is my girl, Maggie Williams."

Tripp & Tori shook her hand, and the pair joined them in the booth.

"I have to admit I feel special getting to meet you on our first night here," Tori said to Maggie. "Your voice is absolutely stunning!"

"Thank you!" Maggie smiled. "It took Warren quite a while to convince me before I finally decided to get on stage."

"I tried to tell her that her voice was incredible, but she never believed me," Warren added.

"Well, I'm glad you finally gave in," Tori said. "It was beautiful. Even haunting in certain songs."

"That's on purpose," Maggie admitted. "Sometimes, we want people to slow down. It's nice to get a break, though."

Warren got up. "I'll go get our food."

"Want some help bringing it to the table?" Tripp asked.

"Thank you," Warren said, so Tripp followed him to the kitchen.

"Your brother seems nice," Maggie said.

"Yes. He's protective of me as well."

"That's not a bad thing in here," Maggie said. "There are nights where it gets a bit rough, but Warren's guys keep everything under control. That's their agreement with the coppers. They don't give us any guff as long as we keep the trouble out of here."

"Sounds wise. So, is this all you do? Or do you work outside of the club?"

"Keeping these hours, I don't do much during the day except sleep and shop," Maggie admitted. "Warren keeps me busy."

"What about your family?"

"My brother and I were orphaned due to a car accident in 1915. Then, I lost my brother in World War One."

"That's harsh!" Tori remarked. "I understand, though. We lost our parents as well."

"What happened?"

"Spanish Influenza for our mother, and The Great War for our father," Tori said as Tripp came back to the table with Warren.

"What are you ladies talking about?" Warren asked.

"Comparing depressing family history notes," Maggie said. "They lost their mom due to Spanish Influenza and their dad in The Great War."

"And she lost her parents in a car accident and her brother in the war," Tori filled Tripp in.

"A lot in common," Warren remarked. "I count myself blessed to still have my parents."

"His dad and brothers all dodged the draft," Maggie said.

"More like my dad took care of it," Warren admitted. "He didn't want to lose any of us."

"I don't blame him," Tripp said. "The war was brutal."

"How did you get out of it?" Warren asked. "You look old enough to have been drafted."

"I was stationed state-side," Tripp explained. "Administration."

"Well done," Warren congratulated him. "Few were able to get out of it. However, we don't talk about it to others because many were not as fortunate."

"I understand," Tripp said.

They talked until around eleven o'clock. Maggie had to go back on stage, but not before agreeing to meet Tori for lunch and a little shopping the next day.

Tripp and Tori finally left the Charleston Confidential around midnight. As they walked out onto the street, Tripp remarked, "It's wild that all that fun is going on, literally under this city."

"They kept that stuff quiet. There are also tunnels in case the cops caught wind of it. Prohibition caused a lot of *necessity is the mother of invention* ideas," Tori pointed out. "I am enjoying this time, but I will admit to missing Patrick."

"I saw that the two of you were getting close. Fred said he was a good guy."

"He was. I wish there was a way to figure out how he turned out. I would hope he found his lady, and they had a slew of children."

Tripp cringed.

Tori looked over at him. "What do you know?"

"I can't say."

"Why not? It's not like we can go back. You already said it was a one-and-done type situation."

"Tori, just focus on this time and Maggie. Forget about Patrick."

She looked forward as they walked. "I'm trying. Had I been born at that time; we would have been a perfect match."

"You said he was a Christian."

"Yes."

"And you're not. So, therefore, you are not perfect."

"He asked me to keep an open mind about God, and I agreed. He said to look and see where God worked in the upcoming days."

"I think he meant in 1813, not in 1922."

A pang of irritation shot through Tori. "He had no idea we were not from that time. I feel like we're being fake. I feel like we're manipulating people."

"We are," Tripp said. "We're doing it to save our family, though."

"I don't know how much that actually matters," Tori said. "We are lying to them."

"Only in our story. Everything we are talking to them about, everything we're sharing from our heart is real."

"I don't know." Tori shook her head. "I don't know how much longer we...*I* can keep doing this."

"Would you rather sit in a jail cell for the rest of your life?"

"Will anything we do change the outcome of that day?" Tori asked. "You said I can't go back and save her. What's going to stop Chrissy's death? What's going to stop me from being arrested and convicted of a murder I didn't do?"

"Tori, we may not even survive this," Tripp pointed out. "We're shifting people around. It may cause us not to even be born."

"That's my point! Why are we still doing this? At this point, we *do* still exist. We saw that in the family tree on CAIT. There are also more of us. What if we make a wrong choice? What if we take the wrong step? We could seriously mess things up!"

"We talked about this. We made a choice in 2022."

"I know. I'm just...I'm struggling. Everyone seems so nice, so normal."

"Everyone makes a choice," Tripp said. "Sometimes those choices end in a good way, and some have dire consequences. The problem is figuring out which ones will help and which will cause circumstances we may not be able to overcome."

"Like floating through time? Like messing with people's lives?"

"Like fixing our family line," Tripp countered.

Tori sighed. "Now that we have time to breathe, I guess I'm rethinking this."

"You can't," Tripp said, grabbing her arms and turning her toward him. "We are fixing our family."

"Some things cannot be fixed. Some things *should* not be fixed."

"Tori!" Tripp snapped. "We made a choice!"

"So did all of these other people! How do we know *we* are making the right choice?"

"We're making a choice to save our family!"

"Is it right?" Tori crossed her arms. "We're playing God. Is manipulating people to change their choices the right thing to do? They have a right to live their lives and make their own choices. They have a right to pick what they want to do and what they don't want to do. Maggie has no other family."

"She doesn't know about Elizabeth," Tripp said. "That little fact may make the difference."

"And how do you intend to explain we know that little fact?" Tori asked.

"We need to find her first," Tripp said. "That's my plan for tomorrow while you're meeting with Maggie."

"I'm not *meeting* with her. I'm going out to lunch with her. We're going to have fun, not go on some assignment." Tori took a step back so he let her go. "I'm going to get to know our relative."

"What are you saying?"

"You talked to Fred and then just popped out of his life. You didn't get to know him. You never found out who he truly was."

"Well," he huffed. "I'm sorry. I was in the middle of a war at the time. I'm sorry I didn't take the time to *get to know* him."

"We could have stayed a bit longer."

"Why? So, you could have gotten to know *Patrick* better?"

Tori furrowed her brow. "Where did *that* come from?"

"You're pining after someone you can never have! He's from a different time and place. You can't be laser-focused on him when the rest of *our* family line is at stake!"

"That's narrow-minded of you!"

"And it's selfish of you!" Tripp said, getting loud. "We're all making sacrifices here."

"What about you? What kind of sacrifice are *you* making? You're acting like this is all fun and games."

"It's not!"

"What are *you* sacrificing?"

"My family is dead, too. I am the last St. Claire *or* St. James," he admitted.

Tori's arms fell to her sides as her jaw dropped. "What do you mean?"

"The criminal background caught up with us. Our family line will die with me if I can't get this turned around. Only having one child here or there isn't working for our family line. It needs to be larger to survive the generations. We need to also stop dying so young! By the time the family line reaches my generation, I am the last one."

Tori's eyes widened. Words failed her. She understood the issue was important, but not desperate. *No wonder he was so adamant about fixing the family!* "Why didn't you tell me?"

"What? That I'm the last person in our family alive? That our line dies with me? That I have to survive if we're going to keep the entire family living on?"

"I-I don't..." Tori's voice faded as she shook her head. "I didn't know."

"And now that you do?" Tripp challenged. When she did not say anything, he pushed, "And now that you understand just how dire this situation is, what do you think?"

She shook her head. "I guess I understand why you're so desperate. I didn't know."

"You do now."

"How do we get them to understand without sounding like a couple of crazy people?" Tori asked.

"You work on Maggie. Stick to her like a sister. You have less than a week to get her to stop running for Warren."

"I can do that...I think."

"I'll work on Anna. If Maggie can see her brother's child, it may help her to know she has more family out there. If she knows there is something to live for, she may not be quite so reckless with her life."

"Okay," Tori agreed. "We'll keep going forward."

"Are you sure?" Tripp asked. "I don't want to have this conversation again. You either need to be all in or all out. If you're all out, I'll take you back to your own time and handle this myself."

Tori tossed it around in her mind for a moment before she nodded. "I'm in."

"Okay," Tripp said as he went back to her side.

She looped her arm through his while they finished their walk back to the hotel. A heavy silence hung between the pair.

Tori enjoyed this area, but there was an odor that hung around. It smelled musty, like swamp land. Tonight, there was a light fog that flowed through the streets. It reminded Tori of a spooky horror movie. Being so late at night, and the spooky ambiance, she was on edge until they reached the hotel.

When they were in their room and the door was closed, Tori turned to Tripp. "I'm sorry."

"So am I. We have a huge job to do. Fred's children's generation was large enough to carry the name into the 1920s. Maggie's generation needs to do the same."

"They're about to hit the great depression in seven years. How will she sustain a large family?"

"I can handle that," Tripp said. "I'll make sure she finds a tidy sum a year or so into the depression to carry her family through."

"How can you do that?"

"We get this going first. I'll take care of the second issue."

"Are you sure?"

"We're in this together," he assured her. "We're all family. This is extremely important."

"I understand."

"We need to get this generation through. Hopefully, this will be the last course correction."

"We'll find out," Tori said on a sigh.

With that, they got ready for bed, with Tori going first. While she lay in bed, and Tripp was still in the bathroom, her mind wandered back to Patrick again. She remembered him laughing with the men near the fire just before she ducked into the trees.

"I'll find out what happened to him," she said with determination. "There are libraries around. I'll find out."

CHAPTER EIGHT

21SEP1922 (PM): A Time To Search

Tori groaned as she rolled over. The sun streamed through the curtains, invading her dreams.

"This late-night and sleeping-in thing is not going to help us get the job done," Tripp pointed out as he ate his lunch from the room service he ordered.

"I'm not used to staying up so late," Tori said. "What time is it anyway?"

"About twelve-thirty."

She jumped out of bed. "I have to get up and get ready to meet Maggie."

"If you weren't up soon, I would have woken you up," Tripp assured her. "I have to get going as well. Are you going to be okay?"

"Yes. I got this. You find Anna. I think if you can find her, and somehow get Maggie to meet the two of them, it will help. Not sure how we'll do that."

"I think it's a solid plan." Tripp nodded. "I'll handle my end of it. Finding an Anna Edwards who has a daughter with a different name in this day and age shouldn't be too difficult."

Tori leaned against the doorframe of the bathroom, and asked, "You're going to use CAIT, aren't you?"

"There's a reason I have CAIT with us…several actually. This is one of them. So, yes, I'll be using CAIT. You use your sparkling personality and keep befriending Maggie."

"I can do that. Your job is more difficult than mine."

"Go get ready," Tripp said, shaking his head as he dug into his bag for CAIT.

"I cannot believe how much we have in common," Maggie said, as she and Tori were eating lunch on the patio at a local café called *Mike's*.

"Me too! It's weird."

"I agree. Sometimes you find your kindred spirit when you least expect it."

"Agreed. So, what all do you do at the, um, place?" Tori asked, looking around to make sure no one heard her.

"We'll call it CCs for short," Maggie said quietly.

"Good idea. So, do you only sing at CCs?"

"No. Sometimes I help him with his deliveries."

"Like food deliveries?"

"Nooo," she said, glancing at the only table occupied near them. Making sure they were not paying attention to her and Tori, Maggie leaned in and whispered, "Sometimes it's easier for a female to get away with carting prohibited material around. The coppers don't suspect a dame to be doing that sort of thing."

When Maggie said that, Tori took a sip of her drink. She choked down her sip of water, doing her best not to spit it out. It took her a few moments to recover from the coughing fit.

"It's okay. Sometimes things go down the wrong way. She's okay," Maggie said to the couple at the table who were now looking at Tori concerned while Maggie patted Tori's back.

"I'm…good…It's…it's okay…I'm okay," Tori said between

coughs. When she calmed, she said, "Thank you. I'm fine. Sorry to interrupt your lunch. Please continue." She then leaned forward and whispered, "Is that safe?"

"What do you mean?"

"Is it safe for you to drive that stuff around?"

Maggie shrugged. "I've got nothing to lose."

"What do you mean?"

"I have no family. Working and being with Warren is the only thing in this world I have. If I don't do what he asks, and he gets mad and fires me, I don't know what I'll do."

"Get another job."

"As what? A secretary for a guy who ogles me? A job in a factory, where I get paid half of what the men get? C'mon. You're a smart gal. Figure it out!"

"This can't be your only option."

"For a single woman, my options are limited."

"What if...what if I could help you find something else to do? Would you consider it?"

Maggie sat back in her chair and crossed her arms. "You're smart, but I don't think you got the connections to help me here."

"Give me a chance?"

Maggie leaned forward and interlaced her fingers together, studying Tori. "You really think you can do it?"

Tori squared her shoulders and sat straight in her chair. "I do."

Maggie eyed her for a few moments. "Okay. I'll let you try. We can't tell Warren, though."

"Agreed."

They enjoyed the rest of their lunch, talking about what Maggie may like to do. Tori got many ideas. Her next step would be to help find Maggie somewhere else to work. She had six days to save Maggie's life.

"**D**id you find her?" Tori asked, walking into their hotel room. Tripp was sitting at the desk.

"Actually, thanks to CAIT, I did."

"Have you met with her yet?"

"We're having lunch tomorrow."

"How'd you swing that?"

"I told her I had news of her daughter's family."

Tori raised an eyebrow. "How did you convince her?"

"I told her I was a private investigator hired by a private citizen."

Tori nodded in approval. "Good thinking."

"How did you and Maggie fair?"

"She's willing to look at another job if I can find her one."

"Well, Anna has a job. That's why I had to wait until tomorrow."

"What does she do?"

"She works as a telephone operator."

"Do you think she can get Maggie a job there?"

Tripp rubbed his chin. "It's possible. Let me handle that aspect. I know you told her you would, but I think you being with her is more important. I'll figure something out."

"Why would you be able to, and not me?"

"I was thinking we could do it together. I think if you're with me tomorrow when I meet with Anna, she should relax a bit more. Then, we can work in the conversation about Maggie, and then her current position."

"Let me think about it."

"Well, what if you think about it while you get ready to go to the Charleston Confidential?"

Tori giggled.

"What?"

"Maggie and I nicknamed it CCs for short."

"That sounds like a good idea. Do you want to go to CCs?"

"Sure. Give me some time to change."

"Sounds good. I'm going to do some legwork. I'll be back in about an hour or two. Would that give you some time to relax before dinner?"

"Sure."

"Okay." He got up, grabbed his coat and fedora, and then left the room.

"Hmm," she said to herself, "I wonder what that's about?"

Tori spent the first fifteen minutes getting changed into evening wear before she laid down on her bed. At first, she just relaxed. Then, her mind drifted toward Patrick again. *Why am I so hung up on him? We were only together for about a day and half. But ohhh, how those days stick in my mind!*

She glanced over at the nightstand. "If I remember correctly, Bibles in hotel rooms started around 1908. So, if that's true, then..." her voice faded as she opened the drawer. "Bingo!"

She pulled out the Bible. Not sure where to start, she began with the only Bible verse she knew. John 3:16. She added verse 17 too, *'For God so loved the world, that He gave His only begotten Son, that whosoever believeth in Him should not perish, but have everlasting life. For God sent not His Son into the world not to condemn the world; but that the world through Him might be saved.'*

"I've read the first one, but the second verse is new. What else does it say?"

"John 3:18 says, *'He that believeth on Him is not condemned: but He that believeth not is condemned already, because He hath not believed in the name of the only begotten Son of God. And this is the condemnation, that light is come into the world, and men loved darkness rather than light, because the deeds were evil. For everyone that doeth evil hateth light, neither cometh to the light, lest his deeds should be reproved. But he that doeth truth cometh to the light, that his deeds may be manifest, that they are wrought in God.'*

"Okay. Sort of makes sense, sort of not. Confusing."

She went downstairs to the front desk and asked, "Do you have a phone book?"

"A what?"

She shook her head. "A book with a list of addresses of businesses."

"Oh! A city directory. Yes, ma'am. Here," he said, passing it to her.

"May I take this up to my room for a bit? When my brother and I go out later, I'll bring it back down."

"Of course."

"Thank you," she said, and grabbed it before heading back upstairs. When she got there, she pulled some paper and a pencil from the desk drawer. "I don't have many things I have kept my word on, but I will keep my word to Patrick."

She flipped through the directory for several minutes before she found what she was looking for. She wrote four addresses down, and then closed the directory.

Glancing at the clock, she saw that Tripp could be another hour, so she left a note before leaving the room. "Here you go. Thank you," she said, dropping off the directory at the desk.

"My pleasure."

"If you see my brother, please let him know I left a note on the desk."

"Will do, Miss," he said with a curt nod.

Out in the afternoon sun, Tori looked at her list. She stopped a man on the street to get directions to the first address. Thankfully, it was not too far from the hotel.

Walking up the steps of the cathedral-like church, Tori's heart pounded. She pushed through her fears and put her hand on the doorknob. The door was not locked, so she went inside. The air felt strange to her. It felt heavy, and smelled of aged wood and vanilla. The high ceilings and stained-glass windows lent to the heavy ambiance of the church. Her heart pounded harder.

"May I help you?"

She looked forward and saw a young man putting hymnals in the pews. He had light-brown hair, blue eyes, and wore the clothing of a priest. She had seen enough movies to know what one looked like.

"I-I'm not sure," she stammered.

"Are you looking for someone?" he asked, walking up to her. "I'm Father Flannagan."

As she shook his hand, she said, "In a manner of speaking, I guess I am looking for someone. My name's Tori."

"Who are you looking for, Tori?" he asked, crossing his arms.

"God."

The priest cocked his head to the side. "What do you mean?"

"I had this friend. His name was Patrick. He asked me to look into God with an open heart. So, I read these verses in the Bible. They don't make sense, so I thought I would go to a church and ask."

"What verses are they?"

"May I?" she asked, gesturing toward the Bible in the pew next to the hymnal.

"By all means," he agreed, following her to the pew. He sat in the one in front of her.

She looked up the verses, and showed them to him.

"These are good verses to start." The priest nodded. "You see, we as humans like to hide our sin. When you hide something, you tend to like to keep people in the dark. Does that make sense?"

"Yes."

"And when someone shines a light on your sins in the darkness, you want to run and hide."

"True," she agreed.

"That's why we have confession," he said, gesturing toward the small, two-door room. "Confession clears the soul and brings light."

Tori nodded. "I see. Thank you. I appreciate your time."

When she stood, he asked, "Is there anything else I can help you with?"

"Not right now, but thank you."

"Are you sure there is there nothing you want to confess? When was your last confession?"

"Thank you, but I really need to go," she insisted.

"If you change your mind, I would be happy to take time to hear your confession."

"I appreciate it, but no," she said and left.

As she stood on the front steps, she looked at her list. She took her pencil and crossed off the first address. "I like his interpretation, but he only seemed to want me to confess to him. Not what I'm looking for. Next one," she said on a sigh, and headed for the next address.

Walking up to the building, this one was made of wood. It was quite a bit smaller, and had no steps to the church doors. She checked the handle, and it was locked, so she went to the next church on the list, which was also locked. She sighed.

She sighed. "Can't there be one that gives me the answers I'm looking for?"

She looked down at the last address on the list. She stood tall and pushed forward to the next church. She hesitated before touching the knob. *What if it's locked, too? Will I have to wait longer for answers? If it was unlocked, would the person there be able to give me the answers I'm seeking or will they just want a confession from me as well? Please don't let this be a waste of time!*

When she touched the knob, it opened, so she walked in. No one was there, so she called out, "Hello?"

"May I help you?" a young lady came out of the office.

"Is there a pastor or priest or someone I can talk to?" Tori asked. "I'm looking for someone, and I think he can help me."

The woman smiled gently. "In this church, it's Pastor John Phillips. I'll get him. You are welcome to wait in the sanctuary," she said, gesturing deeper inside the church.

"Thank you," Tori said, and went through the doors. This

church had a homey feel to it. There were no high ceilings or stained-glass windows. There were pews with hymnals and Bibles in them. The windows were glass and looked like they would slide open or closed easily to let fresh air in when they wanted.

She also noticed a rope hanging on the wall next to a door. She went over and looked up the rope. Through the small hole in the ceiling, she could see that it led to a bell tower. "Interesting," she said to herself.

"That helps us to ring the bell easier. Unfortunately, it is, at times, a bit of a temptation for the young who are a little mischievous."

Tori's face flushed. "Sorry. I just wondered what it was."

"Nothing wrong with a little curiosity. Dorothy mentioned you wanted to talk to me? I'm Pastor John," he said, extending his hand.

When she shook it, she said, "I'm Tori."

"Well, Tori, how can I help you?"

"May I?" she asked, pointing toward the Bible.

"Please do."

She looked up the verses again and showed them to him, not saying a word.

After he read them, he said, "These are good verses. Do you have any questions?"

"I do," Tori said cautiously. "You see, I'm looking for someone. I thought I may be able to find Him by reading this book. I read these verses, but they didn't make sense to me."

"Who are you looking for?"

"God."

"Well, this is a good place to start. Jesus is the Son of God. If you know the Son, you will know God, the Father. May I?" he asked, putting his hand out for the Bible.

She handed it to him, hoping he would have the answers she was looking for.

"This may take a bit, so bear with me, okay?"

"Yes, sir," she agreed.

"We'll start here in Romans 3:23. It says, *'For all have sinned, and fall short of the glory of God.'* This started back when Adam and Eve were in the Garden of Eden. God created the world. When it was created, He also created man – Adam. He and Adam had a strong friendship. God told Adam that he could eat of any fruit in the garden, except from the tree of the knowledge of good and evil."

"Why did God put that tree there if Adam couldn't have any? Why put that temptation there in the first place?"

"He wanted Adam to choose to obey Him. Instead of looking at the one thing he couldn't have, Adam should have been looking at everything he *did* have. Adam even had the opportunity to name every animal."

"Cool."

"Cool?" Pastor John furrowed his brow. "It's not cool in here."

"No. It means neat...great."

"Oh. Okay." He nodded. "Ready to keep going?"

"Sure."

"Well, while Adam was naming the animals, he started to notice something. There were male and female of almost all the animals. However, when he looked at himself, there was only one man. He started to get lonely. God noticed that, and had Adam fall asleep. He took a rib from Adam and fashioned a woman – Eve. She was to be Adam's helpmeet. It was Adam's responsibility to tell Eve the one rule, along with the guidelines."

"Bet that went over well."

Pastor John chuckled. "I'm sure it did. And, actually, for a little while, it did. Unfortunately, Satan decided to mess with the humans. He went to Eve in the form of a snake. He tempted her to eat the fruit from the forbidden tree. At first, she resisted. Then, the serpent convinced her to eat the fruit. When she did, she knew the difference between right and wrong, the concept of good and evil. She took the fruit to Adam, and gave it to him to eat as well. He chose to try it. That's when they realized they were naked, so they made clothing from the leaves. Now, each day, God went to the garden to talk to Adam. When He called for Adam, Adam did not answer at first. When Adam finally answered, God asked what took him so long. When Adam told God they were naked and ashamed, God knew they ate the fruit. He knew, but He wanted Adam and Eve to admit it. Adam blamed Eve, and Eve blamed the snake."

"So, despite them making the choice, they blamed someone or something else?"

"Yes. Now, due to them eating the fruit, sin entered the world. Adam and Eve knew more than they should have ever known, and then blamed someone else for their sin. God tossed them out of the garden, leaving angels with flaming swords to block the garden."

"Wow."

"Yeah. God also cursed men to work for their food. He cursed women to have pain during childbirth. Then, he also cursed the snake, to always slither around on its belly, underfoot of men. Now, because of that sin, the direct communication with God was broken. In order to ask God to forgive them for sin, they had to make an offering. It had to be a perfect animal – without any type of blemish."

"That would help them be closer to God?" Tori asked.

"It was a form of worship, yes. You see, the Christian life is about a relationship with God, through Jesus. Here, if you have time we can keep going."

"I'm getting answers. Please continue," Tori said.

"Okay, remember that sin I mentioned earlier, where they had to sacrifice to have God forgive them?"

"Yes."

"Well, here in Romans 6:23, it says, *'For the wages of sin is death; but the gift of God is eternal life through Jesus Christ our Lord.'* You see, Jesus is the Son of God. He and God wanted the communication fixed between humans and God, so they came up with a plan. This plan took a while to implement. All through the Old Testament – which is the first thirty-nine books of the Bible –

there were predictions of a Messiah coming to save the world. Finally, in Matthew, everything came together. John the Baptist went around and told people that Jesus, the Messiah, was coming. In Romans 5:8, is says, *'But God commendeth His love toward us, in that, while we were yet sinners, Christ died for us.'* Then, we're going to combine that with the first two verses you showed me, John 3:16-17 says, *'For God so loved the world, that He gave His only begotten Son, that whosoever believeth in Him should not perish, but have everlasting life. For God sent not His Son into the world to condemn the world; but that the world through Him might be saved.'* You said you were seeking God. You said the verses you read didn't make sense. You now know the beginning with Adam and Eve, and you know that God and Jesus had a plan. You also know that there had to be a sacrifice to make up for the sins they did back then, and that it had to be a sacrifice of a perfect animal, without spot or blemish. It had to cost."

"Right."

"The plan God and Jesus came up with was Jesus Himself. God sent Him to the earth by placing Him in a virgin named Mary. She carried that child and gave birth to Him."

"Wait a minute," Tori stopped him. "A child out of wedlock back then was worse than it is now."

"And to compound the situation, she was betrothed to a man named Joseph."

Wide-eyed, she asked, "What did *he* say about this?"

Pastor John smiled. "Well, first off, Mary was stunned. She knew she did not have sex with Joseph or any other man. An angel told her she would give birth to the Son of God. I cannot imagine her reaction at first, but after the angel cleared things up, she said, *'behold, I am the handmaid of the Lord. May it be done to me according to your word.'* She knew she would be in trouble and have a lot of explaining to do, but she agreed.

"At first, Joseph was just going to send her away – which was merciful back then. Then, God sent an angel to Joseph to explain what was going on. He obeyed all the angel told him as well. They did not consummate the marriage until after Jesus was born. He helped raise a child he knew was not his. But he and Mary both knew what the angels told them and trusted God.

"Now, the day Jesus was born, there were many things going on. I'm going to save us a little time and jump to the portion that will help explain those verses. You see, Jesus grew up to be a man. He did many miracles. There were a lot of people following Him. He also helped train an inner circle of men, called apostles. These men carried on Jesus's work after He left this earth."

"Left the earth?"

"Yes. Remember verse 17?"

"Yeah. It said, *'For God sent not His Son into the world to condemn the world: but that the world through Him might be saved.'*"

"Yes. That sacrifice we talked about earlier?"

"Yes."

Pastor looked at her, waiting for her to make the connection. When her jaw dropped, he knew she connected the dots. "Yes. Jesus was the sacrifice. He was a man, but He was a man without sin. He was the Son of God. He was the only one who could make the sacrifice. He gave His life on the cross, fulfilling all those prophesies in the Old Testament regarding the Messiah. Despite Him fulfilling them, despite Him doing all the miracles He did, the priests in the temples were jealous of Jesus and called Him many names. They did their best to discredit Jesus, but time and time again, Jesus showed them up. They came up with a plan, but they needed one of His inner circle to betray Him."

"Would they?" Tori asked. "Wasn't Jesus their friend?"

"Not only their friend, but also their mentor."

"Who would do such a thing?"

"His name was Judas. He betrayed Jesus to the priests and the soldiers. He did it with a kiss."

Tori gasped. Covering her mouth, she shook her head. "Is that true?"

"Yes." Pastor nodded. "I'm afraid so. And back then, being

put to death was nowhere near as merciful as it is now. They dragged Him into court. Pilot tried to save His life by offering the swarms of people demanding that Jesus be crucified, a man who was a known murderer. He had the crowd choose who to release, and they chose the murderer."

"What? Why?"

"The priests stirred the crowd so much, they demanded Pilot crucify Jesus. So, Pilot washed his hands of the situation. The soldiers took Jesus, and beat him down to the bone with a cat o' nine tails."

"Horrific!"

"While that was going on, Peter, one of his inner circle, was in the courtyard trying to figure out what had become of His mentor and friend. There were three people who recognized Peter. However, Peter denied knowing Jesus. He did this three times, then the rooster crowed, just as Jesus was taken through the courtyard and made eye contact with Peter. You see, the night the Jesus was taken, they had what is coined as *the last supper*. During that time, Jesus told Peter that Peter would deny Him three times before the rooster crowed. Peter said there would be no way he would ever betray Him. However, this proved true, and Peter was distraught."

"I'll bet!" Tori said, caught up in the story. "Then what happened?"

"There were many things done to Jesus that night. These things also fulfilled more prophesies from the Old Testament. Then, the day arrived for His crucifixion. He was so beaten up He could not carry His own cross."

"Wait a minute," Tori stopped him. "They tortured Him, and then expected Him to carry a wooden cross?"

"The cross they were going to hang Him on at that."

Tori said let out a low whistle. "Brazen!"

"Well, they pulled a man from the crowd to carry Jesus's cross. When they got to the hill, they nailed Jesus's hands and feet to the cross with three-inch spikes, and then set the cross upright."

"What?" Tori asked, horrified.

"That's how they crucified people back then. In fact, there were other men on either side of Jesus on that day. One taunted Jesus, while the other rebuked the man. Jesus told the one who rebuked the man that he would be with Jesus in paradise on that day."

"Wow."

"Also, while He hung on the cross, He made sure that John would look after His mother. He even said to God, *'Father, forgive them, for they know not what they do.'*"

"So, even in the middle of all of this, Jesus still looked after others?"

"Yes. Then, at around three in the afternoon, Jesus finally died. He said, *'My God, my God, why have you forsaken me.'*"

"I'll bet He felt like He was alone," Tori said in understanding.

"He took on the sin of the world that day. There was so much, that God had to turn His back on Him for that time. I'm sure He did feel alone. Now, when He died, the clouds covered the area, the curtain in the temple tore in two, and Jesus's voice was heard to say, *'Father, into your hands I commend my spirit.'* He knew what was going to happen. He knew what they would do to Him."

"Then why did He do it?"

"Because He loves us...all of us. Even if it was just you, He still would have done it."

"So, He's dead?" Tori asked, frowning.

"No."

She narrowed her eyes at him. "No?"

"No."

"You just told me –"

"I know. All of that is true, but He's not dead. You see, the priests and generals got together and to make sure no one took

His body, they put a boulder in front of the tomb, along with guards. Jesus told people He would raise from the dead after three days, and He did it."

"What?"

"Three days after His death, the women went to His tomb to put spices and oils on His body so it wouldn't stink. They didn't do embalming like they do now, so that was customary. When they got there, the stone was rolled away, and the guards were unconscious. *And* there was an angel sitting there. The angel told them Jesus wasn't there, He had risen from the dead just as He said He would. Well, the women ran to tell the apostles."

"The apostles, including Judas?"

"No. Judas was so upset about what he did, he threw the thirty pieces of silver he got for betraying Jesus into the temple and hung himself."

"I'm not going to say what I'm thinking about Judas right now because we're in a church."

Pastor snickered. "You're not alone. Anyway, the woman ran to the apostles. Peter and John ran back to the tomb ahead of the women to see for themselves. They found it exactly as the women said. They didn't initially believe the women, though. They thought someone else had stolen the body. So, they went back and told the others. They then hid, thinking they were next. They knew people were looking for them, being that they were close to Jesus."

"They were probably on the top ten, or eleven in this case, most wanted."

"Yes." He smiled. "Here's where it gets interesting. You see, there were over five *hundred* people who saw Jesus *after* He rose from the dead. Despite the government trying to cover it up, people believed those witnesses. Things started happening. People started wanting to learn more about Jesus once the rumors circulated. However, Jesus could not stay indefinitely. He was there for a purpose. He had a few more things to take care of before He left. Can you think of one of them?"

"Peter?" Tori asked.

"Peter," Pastor John said, impressed she caught that. "He went to Peter and asked him three times if Peter loved Him. Three times, Peter said, *'You know I do.'* By asking three times, Jesus was showing Peter that He forgave him. He made sure to make things right for Peter's sake."

"That shows a lot of character. All of His actions seemed to be out of love," Tori pointed out.

"They were. He even gave His apostles one last gift before He left. He gave them the gift of the Holy Spirit. You see, when we accept Christ as our Savior, when we believe with all our heart, mind, and soul what He did for us, and that He is the go between for us with God. We also get the benefit of having the Holy Spirit in our lives. God is the King, the Father of all. Jesus is His Son. Jesus walks with us. He knows what it's like to be human. He understands. The Spirit helps guide and direct us. We have to learn what His voice sounds like. When we learn to hear Him, He helps us figure out the direction to take."

"That's really neat!" Tori grinned. "So, you said He isn't dead. You said before Jesus left. Where did He go?"

"He's sitting with God right now. He's preparing a place for us when it's our time."

"Time," Tori said, thinking through his words. "How do we know it's our time, or if there is a way to change things?"

"We're to live each day one minute at a time. If we live our lives with the mission He gave us, then you cannot help but know."

"What mission?"

"To tell others about Him just like I did with you. Here, allow me just a little more of your time?"

"By all means," she said, gesturing for him to keep going.

"In Romans 10:9, it says, *'That if thou shalt confess with thy mouth the Lord Jesus, and shalt believe in thine heart that God hath raised Him from the dead, thou shalt be saved.'* Over here in Romans 8:1, it says, *'There is therefore now no condemnation to them which are in Christ Jesus, who walk not after the flesh, but after the Spirit.'* Finally, here in Romans 8:38-39, it says, *'For I am persuaded, that neither death, nor life, nor angels, nor principalities, nor powers, nor things present, nor things to come, nor height, nor depth, nor any other creature, shall be able to separate us from the love of God, which is in Christ Jesus our Lord.'* You see here in First Peter 5:8," Pastor flipped through the Bible, showing her each verse as he read them, "it says, *'Be sober, be vigilant; because your adversary the devil, as a roaring lion, walketh about, seeing whom he may devour.'* You are being pursued by the devil."

"I'm *what?*" Tori asked.

"Remember when I said the devil went to Eve in the form of a serpent to tempt her?"

"Right."

"Satan was once an angel – a very powerful one."

"He was?"

"Yes. His name at the time was Lucifer. He thought he was more powerful than God Himself!"

"Traitor," Tori said.

"No, what was made him a traitor was when he convinced other angels to follow him while he tried to overthrow God."

"As in the Lord God?" Tori asked. Pastor nodded. "As in the One you just told me created the world?"

"Yes."

"That is actually more than treasonous! That is arrogant, pompous...and another whole string of words I cannot say because of where we are!"

"Well," he chuckled, "don't worry. God wasn't having it. He threw Lucifer, along with those angels who chose to follow him, out of Heaven. Satan knows he's doomed to hell for all eternity. He knows what his true fate is in Revelation. He knows this, and is trying to get as many people as he can to follow him."

"What if I don't want to follow either one?"

"You don't have that option. You *have* to choose one or the other."

"Why is this the first I'm hearing of this?"

"That I cannot answer. You should have. It's our job as Christians to tell the world. If you haven't heard it until now, then we need to be better at our job."

"Okay. So, you said we have to choose. What happens if we don't?" Tori asked.

"Remember way back when, when Adam and Eve sinned?"

"Yeah. That curse stuff, and they got thrown out of the garden."

"Right. Once that happened, people were born into sin. In other words, once people reach the age of accountability – which is a whole other conversation – they have to make the choice, or they are going to Hell. You see, because of that original sin, you start off on Satan's side. You actually have to choose to follow Christ before you die, or you're going to be with Satan for all eternity."

Tori froze. Her face went pale.

"This is where Jesus comes in. Remember Romans 10:9?"

She gulped. "Yes."

"Jesus gave His life for us, and in essence beat death, bursting back through the gates of Hell, He has made a way for us to go to Heaven instead of Hell. Because of His sacrifice, if we choose to follow Him, we will go to Heaven. Here," he said, flipping through the Bible once again. "In John 14:1-3, it says, *Let not your heart be troubled; ye believe in God, believe also in Me. In My Father's house are many mansions: if it were not so, I would have told you. I go to prepare a place for you. And if I go and prepare a place for you, I will come again, and receive you unto myself; that where I am, there ye may be also.'* Because of Jesus's sacrifice we can go to Heaven for eternity. Here's the key, we must choose to follow Him. Right now, you are walking in that darkness you read about in those other verses in John. Jesus is the light. He's trying to light the way to bring you out of that darkness."

"That actually makes sense. Thank you for helping me. So, how do I do this?"

"Romans 10:9 again," Pastor reminded her. "You have to pray and ask Him into your heart and life. He will come and bring with Him the Spirit to guide and direct you. Look, we're closing soon, but I would not be doing my job if I did not ask if you wanted to come back tomorrow to talk more?"

Tori tossed it around in her mind before she nodded. "Yeah. I want to learn more. What time?"

He glanced at his watch. "I should be available around 10:30 to answer more questions. In the meantime, I would recommend reading books like Romans, John, Hebrews, or Acts if you're looking for direction."

"Thank you. You've actually been very helpful. I will be back in the morning."

Pastor stood. "See you then, Miss Tori."

She followed him to the doors. "Thank you," she said, shaking his hand. "You've given me a lot to think about."

"Did you find who you were looking for?" the secretary asked.

"I believe I did, but I want to learn more before I take any action."

"Don't wait too long. You only have so much time," Pastor cautioned. "We will see you in the morning."

"Yes, sir. Thank you," she said, and left the church. She thought through Pastor's words as she walked back to the hotel.

With everything she learned, it's no wonder Patrick was so passionate about Jesus. What Pastor said made a lot of sense. He was clear in the path and the direction things took. It was the same idea Patrick had of Jesus. She was curious to learn more in the morning.

As she walked into the hotel room, Tripp was pacing. He stopped. "Where were you?" he asked.

"I told you I was out running an errand and I would be back. It's in the note."

"Tori, you've been gone for over two hours. The concierge told me when you left. He said you asked for a city directory. Where did you go?"

"To find someone."

"Who?"

"Someone who may be an important part of my life. I have to visit Him tomorrow morning at 10:30."

"You're going to be up before noon?" Tripp chuckled, shaking his head. "Good luck with that."

"I plan on leaving CCs around ten."

"That's right when Maggie takes her break. You have to stay focused on our mission."

"Fair enough," Tori agreed. "I'll stay until she goes back on. Agreed?"

"Agreed. Who were you looking for?"

"I'll tell you tomorrow if I find Him," she said with a sly smile.

CHAPTER NINE

22SEP1922 (AM): A Time To Scatter Stones

Tori got up early and went to the bathroom to get dressed and ready for the day around nine-thirty. When she walked our around ten, Tripp was on his bed, and asked, "So, what time are you coming back so we can go see Anna?"

"What time do you need me back here?"

"Ideally, you would not go today. However, I can see this is important to you, so if you could be back here by 12, that would be great. That will give us enough time to get to the diner to meet with Anna for lunch at 12:30."

"That'll work. Thank you," she said, and left the room.

On her way to the church, she thought through what Pastor John said the day prior. She knew this Jesus was important. He was important to Patrick, and He is important to Pastor John. The relationship aspect of what she was told fascinated her. The idea that a God cares enough about His followers to want a relationship with them was something new. The fact that both Patrick from 1813, and now Pastor John from 1922 had the same theory about God, Jesus, and the Spirit intrigued her. She was curious to know if the message of Jesus had not changed in a hundred years, would it change in fifty or a hundred more?

"Good morning," Pastor John said, standing from the chair he was sitting on in the foyer. "Right on time."

"I don't want to waste any time. Time is precious," Tori said. *Moreso than ever!*

"I agree. Time is not to be trifled with, especially when it comes to your eternal security. Come, let's talk," he said, opening the door to the sanctuary. "Have a seat," he gestured toward a pew, and then sat in the one in front of her. "Have you had a little time to think?"

"I have. I do have some questions."

"Well, let's get the questions answered first," he said with a kind smile.

"Well, I don't know how to say this without possible judgement from you."

"I assure you; I've heard it all before. I was clergy during The Great War. I was also a minister in a prison."

Tori nodded. She looked up at him. His eyes said he could be trusted. "My friend Chrissy was murdered, and I was accused, tried, and convicted of the murder. I didn't do it, though."

Pastor took a deep breath. It was not one of judgement. To Tori, it was one of him choosing his next words carefully. "What happened?"

"We were at a party, and I got overly drunk and passed out. When I woke up, I found her dead in her bed. Her throat was slashed. It was horrific. I −" She looked down. "I don't remember much of that night. She was my best friend." She looked up with tears brimming her eyes. "I could *never* hurt her, let alone kill her!"

Pastor nodded. "How did they convict you?"

"Turns out someone I thought was my friend lied. I found out later."

"I see. Well, you didn't do it."

"I didn't. My question is, if I actually did, would Jesus still want to be my friend?"

Pastor rubbed his chin. "Jesus loves you. He knows the

choices you are going to make. He would rather you did not kill. That's one of the ten commandments. Here's the thing some people miss: sin, is sin, is sin." When she raised an eyebrow, he chuckled. "Basically, what that means is to Jesus, it's all sin. When He paid the penalty for your sin with His life, He did it for *all* of your sins, not just the little ones. Imagine it this way: pretend we're standing in a courtroom."

"Okay," Tori said. "I can imagine that scene quite clearly."

"You're sitting at the defense table. Your lawyer isn't there yet, and you know the trial's about to start."

"Where is he?" Tori asked.

"Just wait." When she nodded, he continued, "The prosecuting attorney is a rather dashing young man. He's charismatic, and has quite a list of convictions on his résumé. The judge is sitting there waiting. Finally, he nods to the bailiff, who calls the court to order."

"But my defense attorney isn't present."

"Trust me. Just wait."

"Okay."

"The judge asks what the charges are, so the prosecuting attorney gets up with a sly smile. He's a smooth operator."

"Pretty sure I'm in trouble here."

"You are. The prosecuting attorney lists every single sin you ever committed. Everything from cheating on a test, to lying to your parents, to taking the Lord's name in vain. Then, he glances back at you and brings up the murder."

Tori dropped her head, shaking it.

"The judge looks sternly at you, and asks, '*How do you plea?*' You stood and gulped. Just as you opened your mouth, your defense attorney walks in, and says, '*Jesus Christ for the defense. I apologize for my tardiness. I was at another trial.*' The judge nods to the defense attorney to continue. The prosecuting attorney walks back to his seat, and quietly says, '*Good luck with that one. She's up for murder. That's a big one.*' Jesus shook His head. He looked up at the judge and said, '*Not guilty, your honor.*' Well, the prosecuting attorney jumped up from his seat objecting left and right. Jesus digs in His bag and pulls out a box. *'May I?'* He asks the judge. The judge nodded, so He took the box up to the bench and gave it to the judge. The judge opened it and flipped through the cards in the file box. When he finished, he set the box aside. He picked up his gavel, and said, *'Case dismissed!'* before pounding his gavel down. The prosecuting attorney jumped up from his desk objecting again, *'But your honor! She's guilty! I have the evidence!'* The judge looks at the prosecuting attorney and said again, *'Case dismissed. The penalty has been paid.'* *'Paid? By whom?'* the prosecuting attorney demanded. Jesus turned and looked him square in the eyes, and said, *'By Me. I already paid the penalty for all of her sins. She is one of mine. You cannot have her!'*"

Tori sat in her seat with goosebumps on her arms.

"When you are one of the Lord's, He protects you. As a child of The King, you get a clean slate. You get to start over. Just remember, every sin you have committed, or will commit is already taken care of by Him. Remember when He was beaten by the cat o' nine tails?"

"Yes."

"Imagine every lashing represents a sin of yours. Then, when He hung on the cross, He literally died for your freedom."

"Why?"

"Because He loves you."

"He doesn't know me."

"Oh, yes, He does! In Jeremiah 1:5, it says, *'Before I formed thee in the belly I knew thee; and before thou camest forth out of the womb I sanctified thee, and ordained thee a prophet unto the nations.'* He knew you. He knew you would be sitting right here in this very church, at this very time, asking the questions you're asking. He knew what I would say. He knew all of this before you were even born. He already made a plan for you. He has a purpose for your life. All you have to do is ask, and He'll show you. You have to have faith in Him. You have to trust Him."

"How do I do that? I've never seen Him."

"Honestly, you sitting here and not dead like your friend should tell you something. He wanted you to hear what I had to tell you today."

"How do you know He's real?"

"There are many verses that talk about faith and trust. Hebrews 11:1 says, *'Now faith is the confidence in what we hope for and assurance about what we do not see.'* Second Corinthians 5:7 says, *'For we live by faith, not by sight.'* One of my favorites is Romans 15:13. It says, *'May the God of hope fill you with all joy and peace as you trust in Him, so that you may overflow with hope by the power of the Holy Spirit.'* You see, they all work together. The Father, Son, and Holy Spirit all work together to protect and strengthen you. When you don't think you can stand, They will help you. In James 1:6, it says, *'But when you ask, you must believe and not doubt, because the one who doubts is like a wave of the sea, blown and tossed by the wind.'* Then, another favorite of mine is John 11:25-26, that says, *'Jesus said to her, "I am the resurrection and the life. The one who believes in Me will live, even though they die; and whoever lives by believing in Me will never die. Do you believe this?"'* Jesus is life. If you trust and have faith that He rose from the dead and is right now in Heaven pleading on your behalf, He will save you from eternal life in a literal hell."

Tori thought about Patrick. Even though he was dead by now, he was still alive in Christ according to that last verse. "So, if I believe in Jesus, and ask Him to be my savior from hell, that's it?"

"Yes...and no."

"What does that mean?"

"That means if you go out in those streets right now after praying to Jesus and accepting His gift of eternal life with Him, and you get hit by a car and die, yes, you will go to Heaven. However, if you go out there and continue to live for years, you have a job to do."

"What's that?"

"You have to tell others about Him. You are agreeing to have a relationship with Him. You are agreeing to trust your life to His plans for you. Life is crazy. Many of the men who were drafted or signed up for the war did not plan on going to war when they were teens. They did not plan to die at the hands of the enemy. You never know what life has in store for you." He thought for a moment before he said, "Allow me a few moments to tell you another story. One day I was in the hospital. A man was in his bed crying. So, I went over and asked if there was anything I could pray with him about. He said he had a best friend, Chris, since childhood. They both volunteered for the military just as they graduated. It was toward the middle of the war. They wanted to be able to stay together as much as possible, so they voluntarily signed up together. They succeeded. They went through bootcamp and then were assigned to the same regiment. They were sent to the front lines. The bombing, gunfire, and explosions were almost continuous. It was their turn to advance. As they were running, William tripped. Chris helped him up. They continued running. Suddenly, they both heard the shot. It was almost too late to react. Chris looked at William and jumped in front of him, taking the bullet."

Tori gasped, covering her mouth.

"William held the bleeding wound of his friend as gunfire continued around them. With tears in his eyes, he asked, *'Why? Why did you do that? It should have hit me!'* Chris smiled, and said, *'Because I know I will be with Jesus shortly. I also know you will not. If my sacrifice brings you to Jesus, then it's worth it. I love you, William. I want to be with my best friend in Heaven. Accept His gift of Heaven.'* William didn't understand. He didn't get it. I sat on a chair at the side of his bed and listened for hours of stories about the times William made fun of Chris for going to church. He teased him about all the Jesus talk Chris did. Every time Chris asked William to church, William would just laugh at him. Yet, Chris gave his life for William. He didn't have to. The bullet was headed for William, and both of them knew it. William was shot that same day, and he lived, but Chris died that day in the field."

"What happened to William?" Tori asked.

"It took him awhile to reconcile why Chris did that for him. Before I left his bedside that day, William accepted Christ as his Savior, and His new life in Christ began. I just got a letter from him the other day. He's now married and has two sons: William, jr, and Chris."

Tori smiled. "Nice."

"Some people don't understand why Chris did that when I tell them the story. Chris made a choice. Just like Chris gave his life for William, so William would have the chance to hear what I told him that day in the hospital, Jesus gave His life for you, so you could hear what I told you over these last few days. He wants you to come to Him."

"I know. I had a friend named Patrick. He told me about Jesus. He told me to keep an open mind when it came to God. He even mentioned the Holy Spirit. You went into more detail. Despite the difference in when I heard it, the basic message is the same. Jesus loves me and wants me to have a relationship with Him. I don't know how to do that, though. I get asking Him and trusting in Him. I even understand why. I just don't know how. And for you to just say *have a relationship* doesn't register to me. It doesn't make sense. I understand He will forgive me for my sin. I understand He paid the penalty. I get it."

"You get it here," he said, pointing toward his head, "but you don't get it here," he finished, pointing toward his heart. "That eighteen inches makes all the difference in the world. You have the knowledge in your head. It needs to reach your heart. Here, take this," he said, pulling a Bible from the pew. "This is now yours. Take it. Read Romans. Then, read Hebrews."

"I think I can do that," Tori agreed, accepting the Bible.

"If you want, we have a church service on Sunday morning. You can sneak in right at 10:30 and sit in the back. Pretty sure I'll be the only one who will notice. Then, you can sneak back out before church lets out. And if you want to come back and talk next week, I will be here at 10:30 available for questions. I'll be in the foyer whether you show up or not. This isn't something you're obliged to do. I'm just going to do it."

"I don't want to waste your time if you have other things to do."

"Your eternal security is the most important thing on this planet. I'll make time."

"Thank you. I have to go meet my brother for lunch soon," she said, glancing at the clock in the back of the church.

"I'll be looking toward the back of the church on Sunday, and will be here on Monday right where you found me today."

"Thank you," she said, clutching the Bible, while she shook hands with the pastor. "I appreciate your time."

"Seriously not a problem at all."

With that, she left the church. The pastor gave her some real-life applications to go with his words today. She imagined each story he told. She could almost see it in her mind. She shook her head. *Patrick would have given his life for her. He made sure, even with their limited time, to talk to her about Jesus. With more time, she wondered what else he would have said?*

"Just in time!" Tripp said with a smile when Tori walked in. "You're beginning to get this time thing."

"Shut up," Tori said with a smile. She placed the Bible on her bed. When she looked up, she saw Tripp looking at the Bible. "What?" she asked.

"Where were you?"

"Visiting a friend."

"Who?"

"Why?"

"Because I don't want you wasting our time."

"I didn't waste your time or mine. I don't consider my

errands any less than yours. I'm looking for someone. I needed the time to talk to a man before today."

"Why?"

"Because it's important to me."

Tripp put his hands in the air in surrender. "Okay. I give. Are you ready to go meet Anna?"

"What are you going to say?"

"I'll figure it out when we get there," he said with a shrug.

Tori sighed. "Okay. Let's hope she doesn't think we're a couple crazy stalkers."

Tripp laughed as they left the hotel.

"**M**r. St. Claire," Anna said, standing up as Tori and Tripp walked up to the table in the restaurant.

They both shook her hand, while Tripp said, "You can call me Tripp. This is my sister, Tori. Tori, this is Anna Edwards."

"Hi, Ms. Edwards," Tori greeted her while the trio sat down at the table.

"It's Miss," Anna said, "but you can call me Anna."

"Okay."

"Thank you for meeting with us today," Tripp said.

"You, um, said you had news of my daughter's family?" Anna asked. "How do you know about her? Who hired you? Why are they looking for me?"

"Maggie is Anthony's sister," Tripp started.

"I know that," Anna said matter-of-factly.

"He died in the war."

"You're still not telling me something I don't already know."

"Maggie needs you."

Anna narrowed her eyes at him. "What do you mean?"

"She doesn't have any other family. That little girl is her only blood family alive. You and your daughter are her only connection to family."

"I haven't spoken to her since Anthony's funeral," Anna explained. "Why is she suddenly looking for us now?"

"Did she know you were pregnant?"

"No. I was going to surprise Anthony when he came home," Anna admitted. "Then, when he died, she was my only part of him left on this planet. I don't want to give her up."

"Why would you have to give her up?" Tori asked. "She's *your* daughter."

"Maggie has a strong personality. I don't want her taking over, telling me how to raise her. I carried my daughter by myself. I gave birth to her with no one else in the room except the doctor and nurses. I mourned by myself when Anthony died. I cried for days. My little girl was the only thing that kept me sane. I don't know if I want to share her with Maggie."

"Maggie's in trouble," Tripp said.

Anna's eyes widened. "What do you mean?"

"She's working in a speakeasy. She's a singer. She's also doing some things that may cause her trouble," Tripp said. "She doesn't feel like she has anything to lose. Maybe, if you would be willing to let her meet you and your daughter, she may understand that there is more to life than what she's doing."

"Who hired you?" Anna pressed.

"I cannot say. They are choosing to remain anonymous. However, I promise you that no one is after you or your daughter. The person is only trying to look out for Maggie and show her she still has family."

Anna dropped her head in her hands. Tori almost said something, but she learned a long time ago that when there was a decision to be made, the first to talk loses, so she refrained.

Anna braced her chin on her hands. "What would this look like?"

"A nice casual lunch, just like this." Tripp gestured. "She has no idea we're here. She does not know any more than you do."

"Who is this generous soul?" Anna asked.

"Let's just say it's taken care of and leave it at that," Tripp reiterated. "My benefactor will remain nameless no matter how many times you ask."

"When?" Anna asked.

Tori's heart skipped a beat. "We'll see her tonight. When do you want to meet?"

Anna lightly ran her finger over her lips for a few moments. "What about Sunday afternoon...after church?"

"I think that would be a great idea," Tripp said. "What is a good time for you?"

"One-thirty?" Anna asked. "We normally go to my parents' house for a family meal, but we can skip it this week."

"Perfect!" Tripp agreed. "Now, what's good to eat here?" he asked, picking up the menu. "Our treat."

CHAPTER TEN

22SEP1922 (PM): A Time To Be Silent

That night, Tori and Tripp went once again to the Charleston Confidential. They sat at the table they had been sitting at for the past three nights.

"You two are becoming regulars," Warren said, coming over to the table as Maggie sung her last song before taking a break.

"What can we say. We like the ambiance," Tripp said with a grin. "Great people, great owner, excellent food, drinks, and music...you can't ask for more!"

"I agree. I must say," he said, sitting in the booth, "I'm glad you two are here. You have brought new life into Maggie and her music. She's been melancholy since her brother passed."

"We can only imagine. Losing our parents was bad enough," Tripp said. "I can't imagine losing Tori on top of it."

"And I can't imagine losing Tripp," Tori agreed.

Maggie plopped down in the seat next to Warren. "Whew!"

"You are on fire tonight!" Warren said, wrapping his arm around her shoulders, kissing her forehead. "Incredible!"

"I'm in a good mood," she said with a shrug.

"We're glad you two are together. Maggie, we wanted to talk to you about something, and we wanted Warren here with you when we did," Tripp started.

Maggie's forehead creased. "What is it?"

"This won't be easy to hear."

"What's going on?" Maggie demanded, as both she and Warren sat up in their seats.

"Anthony has a daughter," Tripp explained. "We were hired by a third-party to find her. We have talked to the mother, and she's willing to meet with you."

"What?" Maggie asked, jaw-dropped.

"What are you two playing at?" Warren snapped. "Her brother's been dead for five years!"

"And little Elizabeth Victoria is six years old," Tori explained.

"Who's her mom?" Maggie asked.

"Anna," Tori said. "She wants to know if you want to meet on Sunday at one-thirty? We will be there, too."

"Who hired you?" Warren asked.

"I cannot reveal that. It's a private third-party. Maggie, they wanted you to know you have more family out there. You're not alone," Tripp said.

Maggie shook her head. Almost breathless, she said, "Anthony had a daughter. Why didn't Anna tell me?"

"You can ask her on Sunday," Tori offered.

"I don't know if I'm comfortable with this. You also have a delivery to handle on Sunday," Warren pointed out.

"That's one you may need to do yourself," Maggie said. "This is important. This is my family."

"Where has she been for the last five years? I'm the one who picked you up and put you on the stage."

"She's family!" Maggie snapped.

"You owe me!" Warren growled.

Maggie's eyebrows rose. Then, she narrowed her eyes at Warren, and said, "Let me see if I understand what you are saying. Are you saying that I am to turn my back on the only family I have in this world? I didn't even know she existed until just now. But now that I do, that's *not* going to happen! It also sounds like you're saying I'm to make sure your business comes first because I supposedly owe you? I thought you loved me?"

"I do! That's why I did all this for you!"

"For me?" Maggie asked, chin held high as the muscles in her body tightened. "You are saying this club is here for me? Ha!" She turned to Tori and asked, "May I stay with you guys tonight? I don't feel like going to Warren's."

"It's *our* house!" Warren said, glaring at her with a coolness in his eyes Tori never saw before. He was usually light-hearted and happy.

"No. It's not," Maggie insisted. "It's obvious by your statements that you seem to think I'm your property, and that this is supposedly for me," she said, waving her arm, gesturing around the club. "You seem all happy when I do exactly what you want. You don't seem to care what is important to me! C'mon," she said to Tori and Tripp as she stood. "Let's go."

"You're not done here tonight!" Warren growled, nostrils flaring. "You still have to go back on that stage!"

"No. I don't." When she went to leave, Warren grabbed her arm. "Let me go!" she said in a low, threatening tone. "You are hurting me."

"We're not done! You're not done!"

"We *weren't* done until this very minute," Maggie said, all attention now on the four of them. "We *are* now!"

She shook loose, and then grabbed Tori's wrist, pulling her with her. Tripp sent an apologetic look to Warren before following the two of them out of the speakeasy, onto the street.

"Miss Maggie," one of the guards ran up to the trio. "Miss Maggie! Please stop a moment!" he called after them. He was a big man. Tori guessed he had to be at least six-foot-five, and around three-hundred pounds, but solid muscle.

"What do you want, Leo?" Maggie asked.

"Please? Just let me talk to you for a moment?"

"I will if you stay ten feet back," Maggie relented.

He put his hands in the air and took a step back. "Done."

Maggie crossed her arms. "What?"

"Miss Maggie, your voice is like an angel," he said. He looked around to make sure no one but the three of them heard him before he continued, "When I come to work, that is the one thing I look forward to listening to. I know I am not alone. Please come back?"

"As much as I want to, I just can't." Maggie shook her head. "He thinks his business is more important than me having family. I thought I was alone. I thought he was my only family. However, my brother had a daughter. He may not have even known it. I did not know it until tonight. I know it now. He tried to stop me. I want to see Anthony's little girl, and I want to see Anna."

"I understand." He frowned. Then he looked up and asked, "Will you come back after?"

"Leo, I don't know. I just don't know. I have some thinking to do."

He nodded. "Fair enough, Miss Maggie."

With that, he turned and headed back to the Charleston Confidential.

"He seems like a gentle giant," Tori observed.

"He is. He may be big, but he's like a giant teddy bear," Maggie said, watching him leave. When he reached the store front, he turned and looked at Maggie one more time before disappearing through the doorway. She sighed heavily. "There are some I will miss."

"Maggie, don't make any decisions right now. Rest tonight and tomorrow," Tripp encouraged. "Then, after you meet Anna, you will be able to make a knowledgeable choice since you'll have all the information."

"I think that's wise," she agreed.

The trio walked to Tori and Tripp's hotel. Tripp rented the room beside theirs. He gave the concierge a ten-dollar bill, and told him not to tell anyone which rooms they were in. Of course, he agreed, and left a note for the person coming in the next morning with the same instructions.

When they got upstairs, he gathered his things and moved rooms. "If you need anything, knock on the wall," Tripp instructed. "I'll be out of the bath in about fifteen minutes."

"Sounds good," Tori said, locking the door behind him as he left.

"I didn't mean to kick him out of the room," Maggie said, rubbing her arms. She shuddered.

"Here." Tori pulled a blanket off Tripp's bed and wrapped it around Maggie. "The adrenaline is making you chilly." As Maggie sat on the bed, Tori then dug in her bag and pulled out a clean nightgown. "You can use this nightgown for tonight. Why don't you go ahead and take a bath first? That way you can relax? I took one earlier. I'll just change and lay down until you're done."

"You sure?"

"Yes. You need to calm down and relax. I don't know if you're aware that you're shaking?"

Maggie shook her head.

"Go take a nice, hot bath."

"Thank you. I don't know what I would have done without you two there. I have so many questions."

"We can answer them tomorrow. Let's just rest our brains tonight. Fair enough?"

"I think that's wise."

When she left into the bathroom, Tori got changed and got into her bed. She pulled out the Bible Pastor John gave her. "Hmm," she said quietly to herself, "he said to read a couple different books. She opened the Bible to the first chapter of John, and read. There were a few pieces of paper on the desk, so she got up and grabbed them and a pen, and went back to the bed. As she read, she wrote down any questions or thoughts that came to mind.

What struck her was this "light" and "darkness" that was mentioned multiple times. She thought through the verses she first took to Pastor John. He mentioned the light and dark, and how Jesus was the light. She remembered he said people liked to hide their sin in darkness, and Jesus shined a light on it. It made her think of when she was younger, and she and her parents went on vacation to the ocean. There was a lighthouse. While they were there, a storm came in. She could still see the lighthouse's light shining, even in the darkness of the horrific storm.

She wrote the following, *'Is Jesus like the lighthouse? Does He continue to shine, even in the storms of life? Despite those storms swirling around us, does His light continue to show, giving us something else to focus on...letting us know we're not alone? The lighthouse is used to guide sailors to shore. It's a beacon, especially in storms. John 1 says Jesus is the light of the world. Verse 14 says, 'And the Word was made flesh, and dwelt among us, (and we beheld His glory, the glory of the only begotten Father,) full of grace and truth.' Pastor John said Jesus was a man, yet God, and lived among us. That makes Jesus 'the Word' in this verse? What does that mean?'*

When she finished, she set it aside on the nightstand between the two beds, and laid down on her pillow. She wanted to wait for Maggie to finish, but she could not keep her eyes open. She fell asleep thinking about Jesus being the Light of the world. Peace surrounded her in her sleep like it had never before. She drifted off to sleep, resting comfortably.

CHAPTER ELEVEN

23SEP1922 (AM): A Time To Uproot

Tori woke to see Maggie sitting on her bed reading the paper Tori wrote the previous night. She was eating her breakfast she ordered through room service while she read.

"Reading anything good?" Tori asked, sarcastically.

"It's actually a good question. I read John 1 in your Bible, too. It's interesting. Can you tell me more?"

"It's actually new to me as well. I'm working with a pastor at a local church. He waits for me at 10:30 in the morning, and I bring him my questions."

"Nice."

"Yep." Tori sat up in her bed. "I'm considering going to church on Sunday morning. Want to come with me?"

"Can I?" Maggie asked. "I'm curious now."

"You can honestly do whatever you want. Speaking of that — have you thought about CCs?"

"The bigger question is: *have I thought about Warren?*"

"Too true. Have you?"

She shrugged. "I don't want to be someone's possession to control. In case you couldn't tell, I'm a bit strong-willed. We just got the right to vote a couple years ago, but I've always been a bit ahead of my time. I joined in the marches. If I could, I would have signed up for the military. They want us to keep the fires burning at home. The men want the women to stay at home raising babies. It's just so frustrating."

"I know. I get it."

"And now Warren says I *owe him* for him taking me in? No." She shook her head. "I don't care for that. I'm not your normal woman. I can barely cook. I can't stand tea parties. I have very few friends who are women. To me, they're catty. There are some things I sincerely detest about females."

"Again, one-hundred percent agree," Tori said. Glancing at the room service cart, she asked, "Did you order anything for me?"

"There's some toast and fruit left if you're interested?" she offered.

"That will work." Tori got up and grabbed the fruit cup and toast. "So, what's the plan for today?"

"I need to get my stuff out of the house. I'll wait until CCs is open. If the doors are open, Warren's there. I can get in and out quickly. I'm only taking my clothes, and a box of pictures and family records I have. I never unpacked it, so it will be easy to grab."

"You don't want anything else?"

"No. Everything else was bought together. I don't want him thinking I stole something that wasn't mine."

"What's your plan here?" Tori asked. "Where are you going next?"

"I honestly don't know. I *do* know I can't go back to him."

"Okay. Sounds like you've made a choice."

"I have."

"What about CCs? Are you going to keep working there?"

"That's another interesting question. I don't know. I have a little money stashed away. It's in my box of records and pictures. He doesn't know about it. I hope to be able to use it to live on until I figure out what I am doing."

"Okay. What about your friend from last night?"

"I can't have contact with anyone there. If I do, I wouldn't feel like I could trust them. I would feel like they were spying on me."

"Okay. Well, are you ready for Tripp to come over?"

"Sure."

Tori leaned backward and knocked on the wall. She knocked three short knocks, then one, and then two long. He knocked back with three short knocks.

"He'll be over in a minute."

"How does he know we're not in trouble?" Maggie asked.

"Because I didn't pound on the wall."

"Must be nice to still have your brother," she remarked.

"It's different. I see all of these families torn apart by war. Then I see my brother still here. I know it's simply luck of assignment that he's here," Tori said in keeping with their story.

"Right. I know I look at Warren and his brothers, and there have been times where I couldn't help but feel resentful. However, they have been the family I've enjoyed for the last several years. I don't know. There's a lot of things I feel conflicted about in regard to Warren."

"You don't have to stay with him if you don't want to."

"I don't know if he'll let me leave. I've tried before. It was about a year ago. It didn't go well," she admitted.

"Why?"

"He has spies all over this city."

Tori's eyes widened.

"He found me."

"Maggie, does he, um, otherwise treat you right?"

"Well, he doesn't hit me. Yesterday was the first time he got physical. Pretty sure I pushed him to that one."

"No. He made the choice to forcefully grab you. The fact that you have bruises on your arm I can see, tells me it was way too tight."

"That was an unspoken warning. Sometimes he will pinch my lower back." She shook her head. "I've let him get away with a lot over the years. I thought he was protecting me, but I now wonder how much was control. He would always send me with one of the guys from the club if I went out."

Tori furrowed her brow. "There wasn't one when we went out."

"Yes. There was. I didn't want you to feel uncomfortable, so I told him to hang back and watch from a distance."

Tori shuddered.

"There's a lot I don't share."

"I can see why."

"I actually thought it was normal."

"No. It's not."

Just then, there was a knock on the door. Tori got up. When she saw it was Tripp, she opened the door, locking it when he was inside.

"Good morning, ladies," he said with a smile.

"Have you eaten yet?" Maggie asked.

"Oh," he waved her off, "I ate a couple hours ago."

"Unfortunately, brother here's a morning person. He's kind of like a pop tart."

"Pop tart?" Maggie asked.

"Yeah. He wakes up and pops out of bed all bright and sugary... meaning full of life and smiles. For someone like me who is *not* a morning person, it can get quite annoying." Then Tori turned to Tripp, and said, "Good thing you ate, because there's nothing left." She grabbed the bowl of fruit and ate a strawberry. "Mmm. So good!"

"Turkey!" Tripp teased. He pulled the chair closer to Tori's bed. When he sat down, he snagged one of the strawberries from the bowl and ate it.

Tori playfully shoved his shoulder. "Now who's the turkey?"

Maggie watched them with a smile. "I miss laughter."

"You shouldn't have to miss that," Tori said. "That tells me you're really lost."

"I kinda feel like I am. I feel like I'm in that storm you

described in your paper," Maggie said, nodding toward the piece of paper atop of the Bible on the nightstand.

"May I?" Tripp asked Tori. She nodded, so he got up to read the paper. Cocking his head, he asked, "Where's this coming from?"

"My heart. Why?"

"You've never mentioned Jesus before."

"Why does that bother you?" Tori asked.

He sat back down in his chair. "It doesn't. It's just new."

"Okay. So, what's the plan for today?" Tori asked.

"You'll need some clothes," Tripp said to Maggie. "Going to assume all of your clothes are at your house."

"That's Warren's house, and yes. Tori and I already talked about that. If we go when CCs is open, Warren won't be there," Maggie explained. "He'll be at CCs."

"But," Tripp held up his hand, "if I acted the way he did last night, I would have someone watching the house."

Maggie's eyes darted down. Tori could see the wheels turning in her mind as she nibbled on her fingernails. Finally, she looked up and said, "He would. What am I going to do? I have money, but the bank doesn't open until Monday."

"You have no clothes or even night clothes. We can either go shopping together, or you can tell me your size and favorite colors and I can shop for you," Tripp suggested.

"He's actually got great taste," Tori said. "That would also keep you out of sight of Warren's men."

Maggie bobbed her head side-to-side for a moment before she nodded. "Yeah. I think that's a good idea. Let's go with that plan. I guess my one concern about not going back are my records and pictures – especially those of my family."

"If I can get them, will you stay here?" Tripp asked.

Her eyebrows drew together. "How can you do that?"

"I'm a bit of an...umm..." Tripp's voice faded.

"He's a private investigator and a bit of a cat burglar when needed," Tori jumped in to help him. "Trust me. If he says he can do it, he will. He just needs to know where everything is."

"You promise not to get hurt?" Maggie asked. "I don't want anyone to get hurt because of me."

"Pictures of your family are important to you. They're the only memory you'll have of them," Tripp said. "Their memory will fade. The sound of their voices will even fade. Soon, you'll start to feel the loss, but won't be able to picture them in your mind. I know. I've been there. We don't want that to happen to you. It hurt to lose them the first time. It cut deeper to have to bury them. To know their memory is starting to fade, and to finally not remember them, is a fresh kind of pain I would not wish on anyone."

When he said that, Tori looked over at him. She saw the raw pain in his eyes. She knew he had a past, and if he was the last of the line, it was probably a brutal one. For him to literally go through time to change the outcome spoke of the desperation. But the pain she saw was a deeper pain than she ever felt. She had a new-found respect for him.

"You're right. If you can do it and not get hurt, then I will stay here."

"I'll stay with her," Tori promised. "We'll only order room service."

"Okay," Tripp agreed

After he got her sizes and the location of the box, he went to leave. Tori stopped him at the door. In a voice only he could hear, she asked, "Are you going to slide?"

"Yes. That's the only way to duck his guards," Tripp said just as quietly.

"Are you going to get money first?"

"Yes. I'll slide to a few weeks back to grab money and some clothes for her. Then, I'll slide back after CCs is supposed to be opened, and get the box today at seven. The club would have been open for over an hour by then and in the middle of the dinner rush."

"Sounds good. Please be careful," she said giving him a hug.

"Stay here a moment," he said, and disappeared. When he came back, he gave her his bag. "I don't want to leave this unguarded."

"CAIT?" Tori asked.

"CAIT," Tripp said. Then, he added, "If something happens to me, go to Put-In-Bay in 1880. I will leave something there for you. If you cannot get to 1880, I will leave another at the memorial for you in this time. The memorial will look like a stack of cannonballs in this time period. I'll do that after I get her clothes. Consider it a safety net."

Tori gulped.

"I don't know if he'll just have someone watching the house or literally inside."

"I understand," she said, looking down, processing his words.

Lifting her chin, he said, "You are my family. I will *always* look out for my family – whenever and wherever they are."

Tori nodded.

"Be back in a bit, ladies," he said loud enough to Maggie to hear, and then disappeared back into his own room.

Tori sighed as she closed the door and locked it.

"Okay," Maggie said to Tori, as Tori went over to her bed. "Tell me what you know about Jesus?"

CHAPTER TWELVE

23SEP1922 (PM): A Time To Seek

Tripp got the money and clothes without a problem. He would make slides back and forth to his room with the clothing from stores from a week ago. This allowed him to move in and out of time without too many ramifications.

The trick would be getting Maggie's box. He would have to sneak in and out without being caught by the guards he had no doubt were there.

After his last load, it was about six-thirty. He split the money he set aside for Tori into two different bags. He shimmered to Put-In-Bay for this time period. He took one of the bags, and tucked it under the cannon ball memorial. Then, he took the second back and disappeared into the shimmering light.

When he reappeared in 1880, he looked around to make sure no one saw him. He could hear a few people talking in the distance. The tiny island had grown into a small township. The church stood as the tallest building. There were a few homes and other buildings scattered around.

He slung the bag over his shoulder as he made his way to the willow tree. He rested his hand on it and whispered to the tree, "Looks like seventy-some years has done you some good in growing, old friend."

Noting that no one was near him, he quickly scaled the tree. Willow trees were great for climbing. They were sturdy and had massive arms. When he climbed in, he took a look around. The island was pretty quiet, as almost everyone was asleep. He chuckled to himself as he saw a few mischievous looking boys quietly made their way through town. He sighed, shaking his head. Then, he heard the waves coming in and out, and it reminded him of the night he and Tori sat on the shore before Commodore Perry found them. The scents were the same as that night. A lot was the same from that night so long ago, but not. Instead of a tent city, there were buildings and homes. Instead of ships in the water, there was a marina with small boats. The tree was different. It was considerably smaller then. He patted it. "Some things change and others grow. Help me out here, old friend. She'll need to get to it quickly," he said. That's when he saw it. Toward the top, there was a branch that created a nest inside a 'y' branch. He climbed up to it.

Setting the bag down, something caught the corner of his eye. In the lights from the other buildings, he could see something carved deeply into the tree trunk. He shook his head as he ran his fingers over the letters. "I don't know," he whispered, shaking his head.

He looked toward Heaven. Continuing to whisper so he could not be heard in case someone walked by, "If you really are there, Lord, why? Why are we going through all of this if this may be the result? With everything changing in our timeline, please say her past and present will change? I don't want to tell her this. Please, when we return, allow everything to have changed?"

With that, through his tears, he typed the date, time, and place to get back to the hotel. Once he returned, he took a deep breath and typed in the date, time, and location for Warren's home and disappeared.

When he reappeared, he was in Warren's living room. He listened intently. He only heard the pounding of his own heart beating in his ears. He typed the date, time, and location to get him back to the hotel room, so he would only have to hit the button and he would be gone.

He silently made his way to the bedroom, making sure to not get comfortable in the house. He found her box in the back of the closet under some other boxes. "She hid it," Tripp said, shaking his head.

Hearing something fall in the living room, he quickly hit the button with one hand, while he slid the box onto his lap with his other hand.

As he shimmered out of sight, a man ran into the room, gun drawn. He saw a flash of light in the closet. He gulped, and then made his way to the closet. He opened the door just as the shimmering stopped.

"I need to stop drinking on the job," he said, nervously chuckling to himself.

Tripp reappeared in the hotel room, crouched, with the box on his lap. Relief flooded his mind. He set the box down. One more mission.

He stood, and retyped the first date, time, and location before hitting the button on his wrist. He grabbed the bag from the cannonball memorial before typing in a new date and time. Then he disappeared from 1922.

When he reappeared in 1880 again, he was a little further from where he first appeared. He could still see the willow tree. Making sure everything was still quiet, he then made his way to the tree.

He looked around before climbing back to the top of the willow tree where his bag remained. He touched the tree again where the words were carved, *Patrick Shawn St. James March 15, 1788-September 14, 1813. A true man of God.*

"I'm sorry," he said and gulped. "I can't tell her. Her heart will be shattered."

He grabbed the bag and then hit the button on his wrist device. He heard someone exclaim as he shimmered out of sight. When he reappeared in the hotel, he crumpled to the floor in tears, heart hurting for Tori.

Patrick was a good man. He knew Patrick died in 1813. He left so quickly after the war was over because he did not want to see Tori's heart ripped out. He did not want her to have to watch him die. Through his records he found out there was a fight among the men. Patrick jumped in to stop it, and he was shot. Had it been closer to Tori's timeline, his life could have been saved. However, there was too much blood loss too quickly. He was also the medical person. He could not exactly save himself with surgery.

Tripp shook his head as he wiped off the tears from his cheeks. "She's been through too much. I cannot take her back to witness that too," he whispered, looking toward Heaven. "Please take the burden off her heart? Please don't make me show her the tree to convince her to forget about him?"

He sat in the middle of the floor with his head on his knees and his arms wrapped around his legs letting the tears fall. *Why were the good taken so quickly? Why would a God of love put a burden on their hearts for each other if he was to die a few days later?* He shook his head again.

After several minutes, he got himself under control. Going to the bathroom, he cleaned his face. When that did not do enough, he got in the shower for a bit to clear his mind. He did not want Tori to know he had been crying. She was sensitive to the feelings of others, and he did not want her to see or feel this one.

When he finished his shower, he got dressed. Locking the door behind him, he went next door to the girl's room and knocked.

Tori opened the door and pulled him inside. "Are you okay? Did anything happen?"

"I will say that I almost got caught, but I'm okay."

"And?" Maggie asked, holding her breath.

"Got it. Come next door. I have a lot to show you," he said opening the door.

When Tripp opened his door and turned on the lights in his room, both Tori and Maggie gasped.

"How did you afford several dresses?" Maggie asked, jaw-dropped. "And my box! You got my box! Thank you!" She threw her arms around Tripp's neck. "Thank you!"

"Can we see?" Tori asked, curiosity taking over. "We would love to see your family."

"Of course!"

"No!" Tripp said, shaking his head, knowing part of Maggie's family history. "No. I mean, not right now. We have a busy day tomorrow. Why don't I help you carry everything next door so you can get settled?"

Tori looked sideways at Tripp, her mind working on over-drive. "Why don't you go ahead and grab a load, Maggie? I'll grab the rest, and Tripp can get the box. We'll be over in a minute."

"Sure," she said, grabbing almost all of the dresses, while looking from Tori to Tripp. Tori's arms were crossed, and Tripp's hands were in his pockets while he looked down.

"We'll be over in a minute. Only open the door for us," Tori said, not taking her eyes off Tripp.

When she was gone, Tori walked over to Tripp. With her hands on her hips, she challenged, "Spill it!"

"Spill what?"

"Either tell me what's going on or I'm going to use CAIT...*in front of Maggie*."

"You can't!" Tripp said, his face going pale. "You'll pollute the timeline. She can't see that."

"Then?" Tori gestured for him to go on.

Tripp sighed, shaking his head. "Please don't make me tell you."

"Spill it!"

"I guess you'll figure it out anyway if you see the box. Fred went home. He had four more children: Elizabeth, Patrick, Shawn, and Sebastian."

"You're saying you don't want me to see that Fred had four more children?" Tori pressed. "And that he named them after us?"

"Us...and Patrick."

"I don't understand."

"He named two of his children after me and you...the other two were after a man who saved his life in a fight."

"What do you mean?"

"Patrick stopped a fight Fred got into a few days after we left. Obviously, Fred lived, and learned the value of not fighting," Tripp explained.

"That's a good thing. Why would you not share that with me?" She stared at him. Suddenly, a realization hit her. "Take me back!"

"No."

"Take me back to him!"

"I can't."

"Why not?"

"We have to finish our mission. Our family line is not yet fixed."

"Take me back to Patrick...*now*!"

"No!" he said, sternly. "We agreed to fix our family line. We agreed to fix the generations so I was not the last in the line. We have to do this to save our family. That woman next door is our family too, or have you forgotten that? You are so fixated on Patrick, that you are not focusing on the present. Patrick's already dead. He's gone. His life *and death* changed Fred. We cannot save him *and* our family. You are so concerned with a person who is no longer alive, that you are forgetting Maggie's right here in front of you."

"We *are* helping her. We're introducing her to Anna and Elizabeth tomorrow. Can we do it after that?"

"We'll see what that does to the timeline. Fair enough?" Tripp asked, not wanting to argue with her anymore.

"Fair enough," Tori agreed.

When they got back to the room Maggie and Tori were staying in, Tori brought the rest of Maggie's clothes and Tripp brought the box. He set the box on the desk, while Tori helped Maggie with her dresses.

"Thank you! I don't know how you did it, but this is amazing!" Maggie gushed. "You have phenomenal style!"

"Yeah. He's one cool cat," Tori added with a smirk.

"Can I admit something?" Maggie asked.

"Of course."

"I feel really comfortable with you two. I've only known you for a few days, but you've given me the confidence and bravery to start over. Whatever it will look like, I think I'll be okay knowing Anthony has a daughter, and I may be able to be a part of her life."

"I think you can be and do whatever you want," Tori said. "You're stronger than you think."

"I also have to say when I read your notes on John one, I was a little angry," Maggie admitted. "If this Jesus is supposed to be the Light of the world, why has He made my world black? I have a lot of questions for that pastor of yours. He may need to give *me* my own time slot, too." She smiled.

Tripp looked pointedly at Tori. "Too?"

Tori shrugged. "He's answering some questions for me."

"Interesting. And this all came from your conversation with Patrick?"

"Yes."

"Who's Patrick?" Maggie asked. "I haven't heard that name before."

"He was a guy I really liked, but we had to leave," Tori explained.

"If you really liked him, why did you leave him?"

"Because there are some things more important than a relationship," Tripp said, eyeing Tori.

"What's going on?" Maggie asked, watching them. "You know my secrets. What's this one with you two?"

Tripp sighed. Resting his hands on his hips, he explained, "I was hired to find your family for you. I was hired to connect you to Anna and Elizabeth."

"Elizabeth?" Maggie asked.

"Yes. Elizabeth Victoria Williams."

"I didn't connect it at CCs, but Victoria and Elizabeth are deep in our family roots," Maggie said. "Anna was honoring my brother and our family by naming her Elizabeth Victoria."

"I'm sure she took that into consideration," Tripp acknowledged.

"No. Really," Maggie said, going over to her box on the desk. She dug through until she pulled out an old journal. She carefully unwrapped the decaying leather strap that was around it and flipped through until she found the family tree. "See?"

Tori and Tripp looked over her shoulder. Until Maggie's generation, there was a Victoria or Elizabeth in every generation.

"Why is there not in your generation?" Tripp asked.

"There is," Maggie said. "My name is Margaret Elizabeth Williams. It's my middle name."

Tripp face palmed. "It never occurred to me to look for your middle name too."

"What?" Maggie asked.

"When we were, uh, given your name, it was just Maggie Williams," Tori quickly explained.

"Cannot imagine it was easy to find me that way."

Tripp blushed.

"Hey! Look! Sebastian is all through the family tree too!" Tori said, excited.

"Yes." Maggie smiled. "Anthony was Anthony Sebastian Williams."

"Wonder why those two names, well three names, are so strong in your family?" Tori asked.

"There's an old family legend of back when our clan was still in Ireland. One Christmas there were two people who came to our clan. They looked like angels, but said they were travelers."

"Travelers?" Tripp asked. "Traveling from where?"

"Well," Maggie said, sitting on the bed, as Tripp and Tori sat on Tori's bed. She crossed her legs, bracing her elbows on her knees. "They were *travelers*. As in travelers from another time and place."

Tori shook her head. "Time and place, as in from say Europe or the Americas?"

"No. This is why I said it was a legend. Supposedly, they were time travelers. They came to their time to talk to them. They said our family line would cease to exist if they did not make immediate changes. They said they went forward in time and corrected some things, but it had to start there."

"You're saying there were two people who came back in time to talk to your family?" Tripp asked.

"Yes. Their names were Sebastian and Victoria Elizabeth. Then, there was another instance back in 1813, when my great-great grandfather was in the Battle of Lake Erie, there was a Sebastian and Victoria Elizabeth who helped him over-come his temper to survive. He was so grateful for that, and then remem-bered the legend. He named his youngest children after them. However, from that first generation following the time travelers, we honored them by having those names passed down."

"So, you believe in time travelers?" Tripp asked.

Maggie went back to the box and pulled out another journal. This one looked immensely older than the one from her great-great-grandfather. She flipped through the pages until she found what she was looking for. When she did, she looked at it, then to Tori and Tripp. Looking back at the picture again, she looked back up at them and asked, "Is Tripp your real name?"

"Sort of," Tripp said cautiously.

Looking at Tori, she asked, "What's your real name?"

"My first name is Victoria – Tori for short."

Maggie walked over to them and handed them the journal. They were looking at drawings of the pair of them staring back at them. Then, she went back to her great-great grandfather's journal. She flipped to the back and pulled out a piece of paper. Opening the fragile page, the color drained from her face. "Who *are* you?"

They just stared at her.

She held up the piece of paper. They were looking at a picture of the two of them and Patrick. They were drawings from their shoulders up. Their faces were clear.

"Who *are* you?" Maggie demanded.

"I am Sebastian Tripp St. Claire."

"And you?" she asked Tori.

"Victoria Elizabeth St. James."

"According to this, you are Victoria Elizabeth St. Claire," Maggie pointed out.

"That's what we told Fred," Tripp said.

She took a step backward and almost fell onto the bed as she tried to sit. Meanwhile, Tripp and Tori just stared at her. "Wha... I don't...I don't know...how do you..." her voice faded.

"Anna had Anthony's baby," Tripp said. "We knew you needed your family. We came to help you find her."

"Why?" Maggie asked.

Tripp and Tori looked at each other, before Tori looked back to Maggie and said, "Because during one of your runs for

Warren, in four days, on the twenty-seventh of September, you are killed by a rival gang. We wanted you to know there was more to live for than driving alcohol for some guy whose dad is part of the mafia."

"His dad is head of the mafia in this area. Chances are, it *was* a rival gang," Maggie said quietly. "My head is spinning. I don't –" She shook her head. "You two...when were your born?"

"I was born on March 17, 1998," Tori said.

"I was born on August 12, 2156," Tripp said. "Tori is twenty-five, and I am twenty-eight. She is my great-great-great-grand-mother. She is *your* great-granddaughter."

"Whoa!" Maggie said, staring at them. "I don't know what to do with this."

"Nothing. We're here to help you connect with Anthony's daughter and Anna, and to live past the twenty-seventh of September," Tori explained. "There is nothing else that is of critical importance right now."

"So, if I leave Warren, am I safe? Are Anna and Elizabeth going to be safe?" Maggie asked. "Warren wants me back. If I connect with them, I could be putting them in danger."

"Do you think he would hurt them?" Tori asked.

"It's entirely possible. If he blames them for me being gone," Maggie said.

"Okay. New plan," Tripp said. He got up and paced the room. "We have to get you out of town. We also need to get Anna and Elizabeth to safety. Where do you want to live?"

"Together?" Maggie asked. "She doesn't know me well enough for that!"

"If your life is in danger, technically all of your lives, would it not be prudent to get you all under cover?"

"How?" Maggie asked.

"Where do you want to live?" Tripp asked again.

Maggie thought for a moment.

"If we get you to a safe place to live, and give you enough

money to last two months, that should give you enough time to get a job, right?" Tripp asked.

"Do we have that?" Tori asked Tripp.

"Yes," Tripp said. "I can get it. So," he turned back to Maggie, "where?"

Maggie took a deep breath and slowly let it out. "Anywhere?"

"Anywhere."

"What about something like Hawaii?" Maggie asked. "Is that far enough?"

"Okay," Tripp said.

"*Not* okay!" Tori said, horrified.

"Why not? There are military bases there," Tripp asked. "That should be safe for them."

"Hello?" Tori said. "Pearl Harbor? December 7, 1941 ring any bells?"

"Oh!" Tripp said wide-eyed. "Yeah. Not good."

"What about California?" Tori asked.

"I could handle California," Maggie agreed.

"Okay. Pack your bag," Tripp said. "I'm going to go take care of an errand. We leave with you in twenty minutes."

"Um, okay," Maggie agreed. She looked to Tori, and asked, "Will you help me?"

"Definitely!"

Tripp left, and returned a few minutes later with a suitcase for Maggie. "Go ahead and use this. I'll be back in a few minutes."

"Okay," Tori said, taking the suitcase.

After Tripp left, Tori set to helping Maggie pack her suitcase.

"I'm nervous," Maggie admitted.

"California at this date and time is good for females. When you get going, you may want to consider moving. Later, California isn't so good," Tori explained.

"Got it," she said, closing her suitcase. "I can't believe I'm doing this."

Tori put her hands on Maggie's shoulders. "You got this. You are a good person, with a good heart. You need to find a good man and raise many beautiful children. Bring our family line back into play."

"I can do that," Maggie agreed.

"And don't lose that box. Our family needs to know our history," Tori cautioned.

"Okay," Maggie agreed. She gave Tori a hug.

A split-second later, Tripp shimmered into the hotel room in front of Maggie.

"Is that what I'll look like?" Maggie asked, awe-struck.

"Yes," Tripp said. "Now, I've never taken three, so –"

"No. Just get her to safety. I'll stay here," Tori volunteered.

"What if he comes after you while we're gone?" Maggie asked.

"You need to go somewhere," Tripp said to Tori. "Stay here," he said to Maggie. "I'll be right back."

He grabbed Tori's hand. She quickly grabbed her bag and coat before she and Tripp disappeared.

When he returned, he grabbed the box, and Maggie grabbed her bag, and they disappeared.

09SEP1881

T ori was in the middle of the woods holding onto her bag, on her hands and knees. It took a few moments to catch her breath. One of these days she would get used to this time travel stuff! Until then, it took a lot out of her each time she did it. It was worse when it was through multiple decades.

Looking around as she stood, she saw it was dusk, but she could still see around her. "I can't believe he just dropped me and ran," Tori said quietly, rolling her eyes. Noticing the dress on the people, she whispered, "Now to figure out where…and *when* I am?"

Seeing the people in the distance, she wandered toward the voices, but not too far from where Tripp left her. She did not want him to have to search for her later.

As she was walking, something suddenly caught her eye, and she froze. Flashes of the battle sounded around her. It felt like her memories were swirling all around her. She could hear the moaning and smell the sulfur. She could see the men they repaired. She could see the ships on the lake. She could smell the stench of blood that assaulted her senses. She shuddered as she stared at the willow tree. Taking a deep breath, she saw the men digging the graves for the officers.

"That darn tree," she said on a sigh and shuddered. "I'm really beginning to hate willow trees. If I ever have one in a yard where I live, I swear, as God is my witness, I will cut that thing down!"

Despite herself, she walked over to the tree. Knowing six officers decayed bodies were below her feet, she shuddered again. She could still see the tent set up where she and Patrick worked. It was like it was right in front of her, but was a transparent, faded memory.

She leaned against the tree. In the dusk lighting, she saw a slight flash and ran toward it.

"You're back quickly," Tori remarked.

"It's amazing what you can do when you have a time machine on your wrist," Tripp said, holding his arm up. "There's not a lot of juice left. I made a couple other stops before coming back to you."

She looked around him to see his backpack on his back. "What did you do? Why is your stuff with you? When am I?"

"I have your stuff too. We're currently in 1881. I got Maggie settled in a nice hotel. Then I got Anna and Elizabeth. She took a little convincing, but knowing a mafia boss could take them out, she went with me. When Maggie explained everything,

Anna agreed that for their safety, they would stay with Maggie in California. Did I answer everything?"

"Do they have enough money?"

"I had to go back to Charleston to get some records and more money, but yes, they are set up well. I also warned them about the great depression. I told them that instead of spending frivolously during the upswing to save their money. They were going to need every penny they had."

"You didn't tell them where to invest or anything like that, right?" Tori asked.

"Not invest, per say," Tripp said slyly.

Tori crossed her arms. "What did you do?""Well, it's kind of like a trust," Tripp said. "I went forward in time while you were at one of your meetings with the pastor. I went ahead of the great depression to 1940. I slid in there just as World War Two started. I bought some shares in Elizabeth's name."

"Okay."

"I took them, and gave them to Maggie to put in the family box, and explained to both Maggie and Anna what would happen. I told them with their jobs, to make sure they had enough money to last from the stock market crash in 1929 until December 1941 when America joined World War Two. The economy was stimulated due to the war, and they would be good once that hit. I also made sure to tell them to stay away from Hawaii anywhere from 1940 through 1942."

"What did they say?"

"Maggie wrote it down in her journal. Turns out, she's one of those rare birds in our tree that was a record keeper."

"I was wondering why she was so insistent on getting that box."

"Yes. So, do you want to find out what our family tree looks like now?" he asked, wiggling his eyebrows.

"Sure. We should see about finding a hotel room somewhere first. I'm getting major flashbacks standing here."

"I didn't think about that. I'm sorry. Here." He put his arm out. "We don't have a lot of juice left, so let's just slide to Hawaii for now. It should be safe for a little while until we recuperate. We can get a hotel room, and then figure out our plan. We need at least one day of heavy sun to get it back to full."

"Good thinking," Tori said, taking his arm.

24SEP1922

One moment they were standing next to the willow tree, the next, they were standing in what looked like a rain forest! "Humid," Tori remarked. Then she groaned, grabbing her head. "This is giving me a headache."

"The humidity?"

"No. The traveling. I know this was an emergency, but can we limit travel for me for once a day, and then a day or so break? It takes a lot out of me."

"That sounds fair."

"I don't know how you did all the traveling you did today."

He held up his wrist. "Buffer. Remember? Now," he said, looking around, "we need to find a hotel. We're near Pearl Harbor. I needed a fixed place." Seeing that they were actually on the base, Tripp grabbed Tori's arm and slid them to Waikiki beach.

"Seriously! A little warning next time?" Tori asked, collapsing on the sand.

"We were on the base. That would not have been a good situation. Besides, that looks like a hotel. We just need to walk down the beach a little further."

"My head is pounding," Tori complained. "I feel like I'm going to throw up!"

"Come on," Tripp said, helping her off the ground. He took

her bag and carried it along with his, while he helped her with his other arm.

When they got to the Moana Hotel, they checked in. With no need for help with their bags, they headed to their room. Tori crawled into bed and went to sleep, but Tripp took a bath before he went to bed. It was an exhausting day. He was grateful all family members were finally safe!

CHAPTER THIRTEEN

24SEP1922 (AM): A Time To Sew

When Tori woke the next morning, she felt like she had a massive hangover. Running to the bathroom, she barely made it before throwing up into the toilet.

Tripp lightly knocked on the door. "You okay?"

"My head is pounding," Tori moaned.

"I have an idea on how to fix this. Get some rest while I charge the computer."

"I'm not planning on going anywhere."

Tripp sighed. Placing the wrist computer on the windowsill to soak up the Hawaiian sunshine, he let out a low whistle at the picture in front of him. The sunrise was stunning! The light blue, pink, and peach quickly gave way to the golden clouds that speckled across the sky as the sun came up over the hillside. While he watched, it occurred to him that he never realized how quickly the sun rose and set once it decided it was time.

Time. Time is ultimately the only consistent thing in this world. It comes and goes with no regard for what happened on that day. It was no different on the day of the Battle of Lake Erie, and it was no different today. The sun will still rise. It will still make its crawl across the day, and then set at the end of the day. What would time bring to the pair? Only time would tell.

24SEP1922 (PM)

As Tori slept, Tripp went around town. The heat made him stop by and pick up a lighter outfit for himself. He enjoyed the sun, the beach, and the laid-back nature of the people of the island. He did not enjoy the prices, but knew it was due to him not being a local. Anytime he visited the island, as he had through several trips, the beauty never ceased to amaze him.

Around five that night, he returned to the hotel room. Tori was still sleeping, so he quietly grabbed the wrist computer off the windowsill. "Fully charged. Perfect!" he whispered.

He snuck into the bathroom, put in the date, time, and location before hitting the button. As he shimmered, he saw Tori stumbling into the bathroom. He barely got out, "I'll be back," before he disappeared.

Tori groaned at the flash of light, but continued into the bathroom as if it were just another day.

03MAR2184

Tripp reappeared in his lab in his time. "Perfect!" He said, looking around. "Undisturbed."

He went over to the computer and punched in the family tree. "Hmm. Maggie married, and had four children," he said, searching the tree. "Anna's daughter had six. Looks like they fared the Great Depression pretty well. Good! And they're all colored white, along with their children. Well done Maggie and Elizabeth!"

His orange and white tabby cat jumped on the table to greet him. She purred as she rubbed against his arm.

"Hi, Philly!" Tripp said, petting his cat. He named her Philly, after the Philadelphia Experiment conducted on October 28, 1943. The project and its details fascinated Tripp, and actually motivated him, giving him the idea on how to fix his family line. "You need some food? You know I've only been gone for a few hours. You make it seem like I've been gone for weeks. Come on," he said, picking Philly up. He carried her to the kitchen and fed her some food. As she happily ate, her purring was louder than when he arrived. "Okay. Now that you're happy, I need to go figure this out. Enjoy," he said, and headed back to his lab.

Once there, he hit a key on his keyboard, and his family tree popped up on the screen. In looking through the tree, he furrowed his brow. "Hmm. Looks like Elizabeth and Maggie's kids did well. That generation boomed despite the depression. The next generation was still good, despite the sixties. Ooo! What happened here?" he asked, looking at the family tree in 1987. "The dates are the exact same for an entire family?"

He quickly tapped away on his keyboard. Several different windows popped open. Scanning the information, he found the one he wanted and sent it up in front of him. He got up from his desk and walked over to the laser screen in front of him and tapped the file. The headline for the Detroit Free Press for August 17, 1987 caught his attention. It said, *'Metro crash kills 161,'* with a byline of, *'Northwest jet slams under I-94 overpass; fiery crash is Michigan's worst air disaster.'*

"Whoa!" Tripp's eyes widened. "There was only one survivor in the crash? A four-year-old? That means..." he stroked his chin, "a branch of an entire family of seven was killed in this crash. I think 1987 is our next stop."

He wrote down what they would need to know. Then, he went

to work on a wrist computer for Tori. Sliding was literally making her sick. He wondered about possible radiation poisoning. Before it became problematic, he decided to create a buffer for her. He researched ways to counteract the effects of radiation. The best way would be to give her Iodine tablets and hydrate her. That would help eliminate the symptoms she was currently suffering.

Having everything he needed in the lab, it took him a few days to build her a buffer. This gave his wrist computer time to recharge while he worked. Once finished, he folded the paper with the information and put it in his pocket. Then he put on his own wrist computer and grabbed Tori's before disappearing back into the room in Hawaii in 1922, reappearing just a few minutes after he left.

24SEP1922

"Seriously?" Tori groaned. "Your sparkling personality is painful enough without the bright flashes of light that are coming with it today."

He chuckled at her sarcasm. "I brought you a present," he offered.

"Make it stop!"

Tripp laughed. "What?"

"If karma doesn't hit you, I will!" she snapped. "Migraine ring any bells?"

He blushed. "Sorry. For me, it's been a few days."

"I don't...don't do this to me right now. Seriously in pain here. And you're dangerously close to experiencing that karma action," she threatened.

"Here," he presented her with her own wrist computer. "Want to know what I named them?"

Tori raised an eyebrow. "They have names?"

"Well, you remember C.A.I.T. is: Computer-generated, Artificial, Intelligence, by Tripp."

"Right."

"Well, I'm calling these T.O.R.I., which stands for: Traveling, Over, Range, Indicated," he said, proudly.

Tori smiled for the first time that day. "Thank you. That's sweet."

He crouched beside her. Resting his hand on her shoulder. "We're in this together. Fixing our family is something we are doing together. I want it to be remembered."

"According to Maggie, it is."

"I mean in future generations, not just the past. What we're doing is big."

"I get that. I'm sorry I snapped."

He shook his head. "I should have known better. Are you feeling any better?"

"A little."

"Well, let's get you some hydration. Have you drunk anything today?"

"I've mostly been sleeping," she admitted.

Knowing the signs of possible radiation poisoning, and knowing it was more than likely a small dose, he said, "I'll get us some food. Most importantly, we need to get you hydrated. I'll go to the store to grab Iodine tablets for purifying your water. I'll also grab you some aspirin."

"Do I need the Iodine tablets? That's gross."

"I think for this particular time period we should. I'll have them in mine, too," he said, not wanting to alarm her.

"Okay. Thank you. I just hope I can keep it all down."

"You should be fine in a little time."

"Time is not our problem. This sliding thing is getting to me. I'm super thankful for my own TORI. Hopefully, that should ease the effects of sliding."

"I agree. I'll be right back with some food and medicine. While you eat, we can talk."

Tori nodded in response, so Tripp left, hearing her throw up again.

"This is much better," Tori said, finishing her water. She poured herself another glass of water from the water pitcher. "This doesn't taste the best, but it's helping."

"That's the Iodine. I'm sorry we have to drink it, but it will help tremendously."

She sat back on the bed after grabbing another piece of toast. "This is what I needed. Thank you."

"Happy to help. Now, we both also have fully-charged TORIs."

"Right."

"We need to figure out our next plan." He got up and closed the curtains so no light would seep out from CAIT. Then he pulled CAIT out, typed in the file name with the family tree, and pushed the file up with his fingers so it cast before them.

Tori got up and looked at the picture of the family tree. She had her glass of water in one hand and her toast in the other. As she scanned the family tree, this was the first time she saw all the Sebastian's, Victoria's, and Elizabeth's in the family tree.

"Were these three names this prevalent the other times I looked or did I just scan too quickly?"

"May have scanned them too fast," Tripp said with a shrug. "Your name being both was just confirmation that you were the family member I needed to bring with me. Well, add that to the other list of reasons. I don't regret coming to get you and bringing you on this mission."

"What happened here?" she asked, pointing to the seventeenth of August, 1987. "This looks like it took out an entire family of seven. What could happen to take out the entire family in one day? That generation must have been devastated."

"They were," Tripp said. "While there are still three other siblings with children in that generation, the loss hit them hard. There was a plane crash. Here," he said, typing into CAIT.

When the picture of the Detroit newspaper popped up in front of her, Tori used her two pointer fingers to enlarge the actual article enough to read it. When she reached a specific point in reading, she just about spit out the water she had in her mouth. Swallowing hard, she turned to Tripp, and asked, "The entire family died in this plane crash?"

"Yes. All seven of them."

"What, um..." She swallowed again. "How can we stop this?"

"We'll have to figure it out when we go to Detroit in 1987," Tripp said with a shrug.

"*Can* we stop this?"

"Depends on how creative we are. We first need to find out why they were going to Phoenix, Arizona."

"CAIT can't tell us?"

"No. This will take some leg-work."

"Then, we'll need to go back about a week or so before this happens. Make it kind of like when we helped Maggie."

"That's my thoughts. I'll do some research to find out where the parents work, and where the kids are. That may direct me as to why they got on the plane that day."

"Good idea." Tori nodded. "So, 1987?"

"Yes. But let's get you back up to health. I cannot imagine you'll complain if we take a few days to relax in Hawaii, go to the beach, enjoy a luau...you know, have some fun? If we have a few days of fun and relaxation, that should get you feeling better?"

Tori grinned. "Yep! That should do it!"

CHAPTER FOURTEEN

10AUG1987 (AM): A Time To Build

"We may want to consider coming a little bit later than this three in the morning stuff," Tori pointed out. She was dressed in a long-sleeve, light-purple, button-down shirt, with a white and a dark-purple tank top underneath. Her shirt was untucked, and she had it buttoned-up mid-way, with a belt on the outside around her waist. She also had on a pair of jeans, with the legs pegged at the bottom. She had on two pairs of slouch socks (one white, and the other dark-purple to match her tank tops), along with a pair of high-top sneakers. She wore a jean jacket to top the outfit. Her hair was long, so she wore a white scrunchy in her hair. When they arrived, she took off her jean jacket and tucked it into the gym bag Tripp got for her. It contained a few more outfits, along with her backpack from the other trips, some snacks, and a few water bottles.

Tripp wore a pair of stone-wash jeans that were long enough to drag a bit on his high-top tennis shoes. He wore a blue polo shirt, and a medium-length leather jacket, which he also put in his bag when they stopped.

"Is it better with your TORI?" Tripp asked.

"Very much so. Thank you!"

"So, this is Detroit in 1987?" Tripp asked, looking around.

"Not the cleanest. Jumping from 1813 to 1922 was weird. This is a massive difference as well."

"Well, the first jump was a hundred years. This one was through a massive transition in technology that may have seemed like a hundred years. Now imagine jumping from 1987 to just 2012. That may only be twenty-five years, but the technology difference is insane! Before our minds get completely blown, let's find a hotel. You got the money, right?"

"Yep. Well, I have half and you have half. Your half is in your bag."

"Good. That way if we get separated, we're still okay."

They walked for about an hour until they found a better part of town. Once there, they checked into a hotel room.

"Very eighties," Tripp snickered as he looked around the room. "Look at the bright colors."

"It's so bright, you gotta wear shades," Tori said, tongue-in-cheek.

There were two queen beds in the room. While Tori appreciated the bigger bed, the colors were brighter than expected for a hotel. The light blue shag was only topped by the gaudy artwork on the walls that was combined with the flower wallpaper and light blue comforters on each bed. Tori knew it was an older hotel, but the vanilla scented air freshener was a bit much.

"Well, unfortunately, many historic buildings closed in the eighties," Tori explained, as she placed her bag on the dresser. "I would have loved to have stayed in some of the historic hotels, but we just missed many of them closing."

"Well, maybe that's why they were going to Phoenix?" Tripp suggested. "Maybe they were moving out of the state?"

"Possibly. Maybe their moving truck went ahead of them, and it was easier for them to fly with the kids?"

"Not sure. We need more information. We have a few hours before the world wakes up. Want to catch some sleep?"

"Probably a good idea. We need to be a little more on our toes. Safety in downtown Detroit is not exactly on the high side here," Tori said. "We should probably figure out how to get them out of Detroit regardless of why they were on their way to Phoenix."

"Agreed."

Later that morning, around ten-thirty, the pair got up and left the hotel. "Okay," Tripp said, as they stood on the sidewalk outside of the hotel, "I checked to see what CAIT had. It said the dad, Sebastian, works at some plant."

"The GM plant?" Tori asked.

Tripp flipped through his notes. "Yes."

"Then, they *are* moving. The GM plant closes some time here in 1987."

"Really?"

"Yes. A *lot* of people lost their jobs. It was a seventy-something year old plant. Detroit is called the motor city for a reason," Tori explained.

"Got it. Maybe I could work at the plant?" Tripp suggested.

"It's huge. You may never run into him."

"We could go to their house?"

"It's Sunday. They're probably at church. If we had a car, it would be easier. We can't buy one until tomorrow."

"Okay. What about a taxicab?"

"There will be a record."

Tripp huffed, running his fingers through his hair. "The more we go forward in time, the more difficult it is to fix things due to technology."

"That's the irony. It's technology that brought us here, but it's technology that's also limiting us. Figuring out how to fit in is a challenge as well," Tori said, toying with the bottom of her ponytail. Then it hit her. "Church!"

Tripp shook his head.

"What church is near their house? Do we know what they look like?"

"Yes. Here's a picture. It was in a later story about those lost in the flight," he said, handing it to her.

"Geez! Our family has a certain look about it for sure!" she said, and then let out a low whistle. "These kids could be either of our kids."

"Our genes are obviously strong. This is definitely working. Each generation has three to four kids, who each have three to four of their own. Now, instead of a rogue ancestor having three or four, there are rogue ones who don't have any."

"Did you read their obituaries?" Tori asked.

"Yes. Why?"

"Where are their funerals?"

Tripp flipped through his notes again. Scanning the obituaries, he smiled and looked over at Tori. "You're a genius."

"At a church?"

"Yep!"

"Then, let's go!"

"You were going to get me in a church one way or another. Weren't you?" Tripp chuckled.

Tori ignored him, as she whistled and waved a taxi down to take them to the Baptist church listed in the article.

They arrived about ten minutes prior to church starting. Tori picked up a bulletin before the pair went into the sanctuary. They sat in the back row.

"Hi," the person in front of them said as she turned and looked at the pair behind her. "I'm Monica Smith. I haven't seen you here before. Are you new?"

"We are," Tori said, shaking her hand. "I'm Tori St. Claire, and this is my brother, Tripp."

As Tripp shook her hand, he mumbled, "Pleasure to meet you."

"How did you find our church?" Monica asked.

"Honestly?" Tori asked.

Tripp kicked her foot with his.

She ignored him. "We found it in the phone book."

"Oh! Wonderful!" Monica said with a wide smile. "Pastor James Phillips has been here for a few years. His wife is Sarah. They have three kids – John, James, jr, and Jenna."

"Nice," Tori said. Picking up the Bible in the pew, she asked, "Are these for anyone to use?"

"Use, or take with you if you need one," Monica explained. "Not everyone has one, so if you need it, feel free to take it with you."

"I have one," Tori said. "I just left it in my room. We were out when we decided to come check out the church."

"Fair enough," Monica said. Just then a man walked up and sat next to Monica. He had a six-year-old with him. "This is my husband Trent, and our son, Mike. Guys, this is Tori and her brother, Tripp. They're new."

"Nice to have you with us today." Trent shook both of their hands. "They're getting ready to start. Enjoy the service."

"Thank you," Tripp said.

Tori noticed Tripp's knee bouncing up and down, while he rubbed his hands together and looked around. "Nervous?" she whispered.

He shook his head. "Long story."

Just then, the music pastor got up and started the congregation singing hymns. Afterward, the choir sang a song, and then they went to their seats.

That's when the pastor got up for his message. Tori squinted to see him a little better. She shook her head and rubbed her eyes. Looking intently at him, she gulped. Grabbing the bulletin, she looked at his name. Monica told them, but it did not register until she saw him.

"What is wrong with you?" Tripp whispered. "You look like you've seen a ghost. Do we need to leave?"

"No. I'm…I'm one-hundred percent sure we're supposed to be here."

"Why?"

"Because I am also one-hundred percent sure *that* man is Pastor John Phillips relative from that church in North Carolina from 1922. His name was Pastor John Phillips, but that man could be his twin!"

"Oh!" Tripp said, taken aback.

"I don't believe in coincidences."

"I don't either."

"Let's see what he has to say," Tori said, opening her Bible to the reference the pastor gave – Ecclesiastes 3:1-11.

"Time," he said. Tori and Tripp looked at each other with raised eyebrows, before looking back to the pastor. "It's limited, but if you are a child of God's, it's eternal. Let's read verses one to eight: *There is a time for everything, and a season for every activity under the heavens: a time to be born and a time to die, a time to plant and a time to uproot, a time to kill and a time to heal, a time to tear down and a time to build, a time to weep and a time to laugh, a time to mourn and a time to dance, a time to scatter stones and a time to gather them, a time to embrace and a time to refrain from embracing, a time to search and a time to give up, a time to keep and a time to throw away, a time to tear and a time to mend, a time to be silent and a time to speak, a time to love and a time to hate, a time for war and a time for peace. What do workers gain from their toil? I have seen the burden God has laid on the human race. He has made everything beautiful in its time. He has also set eternity in the human heart; yet no one can fathom what God has done from begin-ning to end.'* Time. While it seems to go faster at times, and slower during others, it is still the same sixty seconds in a minute. The same sixty minutes in an hour. The same twenty-four hours in a day. The same seven days in a week. The same three to five weeks in a month. The same twelve months in a year. The same ten years in a decade. While it may seem to go on forever or that we don't have enough of it, we can take comfort in knowing God was there in the beginning and will be there in the end.

"In John 1:1, we are reminded that, *'In the beginning was the Word, and the Word was with God, and the Word was God.'* To Him, time is somewhat irrelevant, but for us it's important.

"This reminds me of a story in Second Kings. Please turn to Second Kings 20, verses 8-11. It reads, *'Hezekiah had asked Isaiah, "What will be the sign that the Lord will heal me and that I will go up to the temple of the Lord on the third day from now?" Isaiah answered, "This is the Lord's sign to you that the Lord will do what He has promised: Shall the shadow go forward ten steps, or shall it go back ten steps?" "It is a simple matter for the shadow to go forward ten steps," said Hezekiah. "Rather, have it go back ten steps.' Then the prophet Isaiah called on the Lord, and the Lord made the shadow go back the ten steps it had gone down on the stairway of Ahaz.'* In the last verse, the word *steps* translate as *degrees*. The *stairway of Ahaz* is what they used as a sundial. A sundial had degrees, which is how they measured astrological movement at the time. Hezekiah figured it would be easy to move time forward, but backward was a whole other story.

"People have tried to prove the Bible wrong, but found the missing time. Some scientists have tried to explain it, but they cannot. It's a God-thing," he said with a smile. "Our God can, has, and will do amazing things. Things we cannot explain. While we are concerned with tomorrow, He is already there.

"I know many in our congregation are concerned with the plant closing. You're wondering what's next? Where are you going to go? Some are biding their time while they look for alternative employment. I'm here to tell you to do your best and leave the rest up to God. He's got this. Something as small as a job may be big for us, but it's not for Him. Just have faith. I know you may not be able to see it right away, but trust Him.

"In Matthew 17:20, it says, *"Because you have so little faith. Truly I tell you, if you have faith as small as a mustard seed, you can say to this mountain, 'Move from here to there,' and it will move. Nothing will be impossible for you."* This is a mustard seed," he said holding it up. "Many of you cannot see it because it is so tiny. The Word says with a faith as small as this, you can move mountains!"

Putting it down, he looked back up and continued, "In Hebrews 11:1, we are reminded that, *"Faith is the confidence in what we hope for and assurance about what we do not see.'* Also, James 2:26 says, *"As the body without the spirit is dead, so faith without deeds is dead.'* That's not to be confused with Titus 3:5, *'Not by works of righteousness which we have done, but according to His mercy He saved us...'*

"Faith and time. You cannot touch either, but both are of vital importance. We have to have faith in the Lord. While we cannot see our path except for one step at a time, He can and does. We have to trust Him.

"Folks," he leaned on the pulpit, "this is a scary time for many in our church family. I'm not going to lie to you. If you look around this room, there are no less than three-quarters of the families directly affected by the closing of the plant. This is scary for all of us. There is not a family in here not touched by this one way or another. It's big. But guess what? Our God is bigger. Stay in prayer. Stay focused on Jesus. He will never leave you. Listen for the voice of the Holy Spirit. He will guide your steps. Where those steps take you, only He knows. You may be tossed out of your comfort zone, but I have a feeling He's got some big plans for everyone here – my wife and I included. I can't wait to see what He'll do!"

Coming around the pulpit, he got off the stage. "I know I don't normally come down here during the message, but as a family, we need to all understand we're on the same level. We are all in this together."

He went on to talk to the church family about changes coming and potentially what the church plans to do about the families moving out of the area. Tori tuned that portion out as she thought through his words on faith and trust. Both were critical. Both affected everyone on every level. While the plant closing did not directly affect them, it did affect their family. This could be the reason why that branch of the family chose to leave. They may have been following what The Spirit told them to do. *Would stopping them from getting on the plane go against The Spirit? Or did The Spirit send us here to stop that branch of the family from getting on the plane?* She did not have any answers, but she knew Who did. She would have to spend a lot of time in prayer. But first, she had to take care of one other thing before they left the church that day.

As church let out that morning, Tori leaned over to Tripp and whispered, "I have to talk to someone. Try to see if you can find Sebastian St. James and his family."

"Good plan. Meet just outside the front doors when you're ready?"

Tori nodded, keeping an eye on the pastor. While Tripp went one way, Tori went the other. She slid out of the pew, slowly making her way toward the pastor who was shaking hands with people as they left.

When it was her turn, she asked, "Do you or your wife have a little time to talk to me today?"

"Well, it is Sunday. Is it something that can wait?"

"Well, I'm sure it can, but I wanted to talk to someone about Jesus and accepting His offer," Tori explained.

His wife, Sarah, perked up. "I'll make time! Please get the kids and take them to McDonalds?"

"I can do that," Pastor agreed.

"Great! Come on," she said, taking Tori's wrist.

Together they went back into the sanctuary and took a seat in the front pew. Before Sarah sat down, she reached over the pew and pulled the Bible from that pew. "First off, I'm Sarah," she said, shaking Tori's hand.

"Tori. Thank you for taking some time out of your Sunday. I know family time is precious."

"Yes. It is. However, your eternal security takes precedence over everything. That's our mission. That takes priority."

Tori blushed. "Thank you."

"Okay, before I start, what do you know?"

"I know a lot. I've been talking to people for what feels like a hundred and fifty years." Tori smiled. "I know about Jesus, The Father, and The Holy Spirit. I know what I have to do. I was just trying to make the bridge between my head and what I know, and my heart and what I feel.

"Today, in hearing your husband's message, something connected," Tori explained. "What I was missing was faith. I was trying to force a connection. I was trying to put God in a human body to reconcile in my mind as to why He does things. The problem is He is not here. He's in Heaven. He is not bound by anything. He's not a white knight running in at the last minute to help. He's not just sitting back letting the world spin without Him. He actually has a plan for everyone. And He's not making plans, they're already made. I just have to listen to The Spirit's guidance."

Tori took a deep breath and slowly let it out. "My brother and I are on an assignment. In hearing your husband's message, I got to thinking. Were we messing with God's plan by fulfilling the assignment, or were we fulfilling it? I decided I would need to pray about it, and ask God to show me what His plan is. The more I thought about it, I realized He may not know who I am, because I wasn't one of His, so how could I listen to The Spirit if The Spirit isn't in me yet? That's when I knew I needed to follow Romans 10:9, but I've never prayed, so I don't know how to do it right."

Sarah smiled. She had a peace about her Tori felt with both Patrick, as well as the pastor from 1922. "There is no right or wrong when it comes to prayer," she said, setting the Bible aside. "I don't even need to read anything to you, since you already know it and know what you need to do. You see, God knows our hearts. Even if we don't have any words, or are so overwhelmed that we can't formulate a thought, He is there to let you know He understands. So, the words don't matter. It's your heart, and He understands your heart. You'll see us close our eyes and bow our heads. We close our eyes so there are no distractions. We bow our heads out of respect for the Lord God Almighty. The words that follow are from our hearts. We tend to end our prayers, *'In Jesus name,'* because Jesus is the go-between God and man. When He died on the cross, He took the place of us having to sacrifice animals to the Lord to earn forgiveness. Make sense?"

"Actually, it does. One thing I've learned in talking to those I've talked to, is that it's about our relationship with Jesus. It's actually about the relationship with all three of them, but Jesus is the One who walks with us daily. They all three crave a relationship with us, though."

"Very true," Sarah agreed.

"I've learned that through the years, the message of God, Jesus, and The Spirit has not changed. The method on how it is presented *has* changed, but the basic message is still there. We need to respect Their authority. They love us and want a relationship with us. They will all three help and direct us if we are willing to listen." She shook her head. "Sometimes I get frustrated when I read about the Israelites. They had God right there, and they still didn't do what they were told. However," she held her hand up when Sarah went to talk, "I also know I would probably do the same thing. People are people at their core. Again, our traditions may be changed, but people are still the same. The stories in this Bible," Tori said, holding it up, "may be hundreds of years old, but the stories still apply. Some people say this book is too old to be of any use, but from my perspective – the perspective of someone who just recently in the last few weeks started figuring this out – this book holds a lot more answers than people think."

"Sometimes people say they wish life came with an owner's manual," Sarah said. "I tell them that it does. Bible stands for: Basic Instructions Before Leaving Earth."

"I like that!" Tori grinned. "Basic Instructions Before Leaving Earth." She set the Bible on her lap. "An owner's manual on how to live life."

"Exactly. Well, since you seem to have a firm grasp on this. Do you want me to help you pray?"

"I think that would be good."

"Okay. You can either just pray from your heart, or you can repeat after me?"

"What if we start with repeating after you? If I feel like taking off with my heart, I'll squeeze your hands?" Tori suggested.

"This is your journey. If that's what you want to do, that's what we'll do."

Both Tori and Sarah joined hands, bowed their heads, and closed their eyes.

"Father, I come before You," Sarah started.

"Father, I come before You," Tori said, repeating after Sarah.

"A person in need of Your mercy."

"A person in need of Your mercy."

"Thank You for sending Your Son for me."

"Thank you for sending Your Son for me," Tori said, and then squeezed Sarah's hands before she continued. "Jesus, I cannot thank You enough for what You did for me. I don't fully understand why, but I don't have to. You do, and that's enough. Please forgive me for the sin that You took on your body for me. I cannot imagine what You went through, even though You knew it was coming." She shook her head as tears came to her eyes. "When they told me what all You went through, I could picture it in my mind, but I know it isn't even remotely close. There is nothing I can do to repay You for Your sacrifice. I know there is nothing I did that allowed me to get to be with

You for eternity, but through You giving Your life. However, I want to ask You to come in and take control of my life. Please guide my steps. Guide my heart. Please allow my life to be one that brings You joy. If I get the chance to bring others to You through it, whatever I go through will be worth it. Thank You for the confidence of knowing that if I ask You to come into my life, I know You will. So, please come into my life? Please be honored by my choices? Please allow The Spirit to come into my life and let me know what choices to make? Thank you. In Jesus name I pray."

"Amen," Sarah said, filling in what Tori needed to say.

"Amen," Tori said, and they opened their eyes.

"See," Sarah gently squeezed her hands, "you did it."

"As we were praying, those words just came out of my mouth. I don't even remember everything I said."

"That's okay. God does. You did beautifully," Sarah said, wiping the tears from her eyes. "Thank you for letting me be here with you to do this."

"Thank *you* for taking the time from your family to be with me today."

"That is my joy. Now, you do know you have another mission?"

"Yes. The other pastor told me about that. It's my job to spread the word about Jesus," Tori said.

"Exactly. Well, it sounds like the seeds were well planted and watered, and I got the privilege of harvesting." Sarah gave her a hug. "That's probably the fastest I've ever done this."

"Thank you. Now to figure out what God wants us to do," Tori said, nibbling on her nails.

"Is this something I can help you with?"

"No. This one's between my brother, God, and I, but thank you," Tori said as she stood. "Please go enjoy your time with your family."

"It was honestly my pleasure," Sarah said, as the pair walked out of the sanctuary into an empty foyer. "Hmm. Looks like we're locked up. Do you have everything? Once we leave, we cannot get back in. I don't have keys with me. Jimmy has them."

"I'm good."

As they walked into the bright sunlight, it took Tori's eyes a moment to adjust. "Wow! The church clears quick afterward," she remarked.

"I know. Sometimes that hurts my heart. I wish more would hang out a bit and talk or go out to lunch together," Sarah admitted. "Sometimes it is more of a check in for people, or check the box situation. If I had my way, it would be more of a family reunion type situation, where people hung around and talked afterward."

"Do you need me to wait?"

"No. My family is in that car," she said, pointing toward a station wagon. "Looks like your brother found some friends, though." She pointed toward Tripp, who was with a family of seven.

Tori's heart leapt. *He found them*! "Thank you so much for your time," Tori said. "I'm going to go catch up with my brother."

Sarah gave her a hug. "Welcome to the family."

"I cannot thank you enough for helping me."

Sarah rested her hands on Tori's shoulders, as she said, "It was honestly my pleasure."

With that, Tori jogged over to Tripp and the family.

"Tori!" Tripp smiled. "This is my sister, Tori. Tori, this is Sebastian and Heather St. James, and their children: Vicki, Seb, Scott, Sam, and Maggie."

"Pleasure to meet you," Tori said, shaking hands with Sebastian and Heather.

"Tripp's been telling us about how you just got here and were looking for work," Sebastian explained. "Since you're new, would you like to go out to lunch so we can talk?"

"We would love to," Tripp said. "We have to call for a taxi, though. We don't have a car yet."

"We have room," Heather volunteered.

"That would be great! Thank you!" Tori said.

They did have room. They had a conversion van as their family vehicle, so Tripp and Tori sat in the back seat with the oldest son, while the other kids shared two per captain's chairs in the middle on the way to the restaurant. It was a tight fit, but it worked for the drive to the restaurant.

The kids sung a song from their Sunday School, and they told their parents what they learned. Tripp and Tori got a mini lesson on how Moses got the Israelites from Pharoah via the ten plagues. And how God parted the Red Sea so they could escape. That took them all the way to the table.

"Okay," Sebastian said as they sat down, "you guys have monopolized enough of their time. Let us talk while you guys talk and color. Please behave," he said with a stern tone.

The kids had a mixture of reactions from nodding their heads to acknowledging what he said.

After the waitress took their order, Heather asked, "So, what actually brought you two to Detroit?"

"I'm a private detective. We are on a mission of sorts," Tripp explained.

"May we ask what it's in regard to?" Sebastian asked. "Maybe we can help?"

"Actually, you *can* help," Tripp said in a low voice so only the four of them could hear. "We are investigating a tip that there will be a plane bombing in about a week. Do you happen to have any connections into the airport?"

"My brother works there," Heather said. "We actually have a flight to Phoenix in about a week. We're moving."

"I am a manager at the plant," Sebastian explained, "but I know I will be laid off in a month or so, so I found another job. Our belongings, including our van, will be leaving next week. We take off in a plane the day after that."

"What if you adjust your plans?" Tori asked. "We know there is a threat out there. What if you follow the moving truck in your van, or leave a day or so before, and explore the country on the way down? Make it a learning experience for the kids."

"That *is* something to consider," Sebastian said, stroking his chin. "If we do that, we may be able to stop and see family on the way down. We have some family in Tennessee, and others in Texas."

"Spending time before starting a new job could be just what we need," Heather said to Sebastian.

"Can *they* handle the long hours?" Sebastian asked, nodding toward the kids.

"That's a good question," Heather said, glancing at her children.

"You could get them something they enjoy, and periodically add to it through the trip if they're good?" Tori suggested. "My mom used to do that. If we were not good, our siblings still got to open theirs, and the ones who were not good didn't get to open the new present. If it happened twice, two of their presents were split between the other siblings."

"That's pretty smart," Heather considered her words.

"Do you work?" Tori asked Heather.

"No. I have a job waiting for me in Phoenix at the high school."

"I'll tell you what," Tripp started, "since you are technically in between jobs, what if Tori and Heather go shopping and wrap the presents together? We'll get them for your young ones. We would much rather you were not in a possible line of fire with a threat toward planes right now. Would that work?"

Sebastian shook his head. "We couldn't ask you to pay for it."

"What if we still go shopping Heather? You and I could pick out the presents," Tori offered. "I'll take you out to lunch. A girl's day out."

"That sounds like fun!" Heather agreed. She turned to Sebastian, and asked, "What do you think?"

"I think we *may* regret it, *but* being able to see the family on the way down is a definite bonus," Sebastian said. "And with a possible threat against the airport, I don't want to chance our babies lives for sake of convenience."

"I think it's a wise choice," Heather said. "I have a feeling God led you into our lives for such a time as this."

"He brings people into our lives as a lesson or a blessing," Sebastian said. "I have a feeling you were here as a blessing."

"We've never been called that before, but thank you," Tripp said.

The group enjoyed getting to know each other more through the meal. In fact, they even stayed in the restaurant for a few hours. They left a good tip since they took the girl's table for so long. They also set up for Heather to pick up Tori at the hotel in the morning to go shopping before they dropped off the pair.

"Whew! That was easier than I thought it would be," Tripp said, as they went into their room.

"I think that was a God-thing," Tori said with a shrug.

"What does that mean?"

"Well, yes, we found them, but to connect with them so quickly, and being able to convince them to leave a few days earlier and drive, as opposed to taking a plane where the entire family perished has to be from God. Only He can make something like that happen. All we had to do was follow the path in front of us."

"While I am intrigued, I'm still not sure about this whole God thing," Tripp said, flopping onto his bed.

Tori locked the door before heading over to her bed. "Why are you so skeptical? With everything we've seen, the timing of it all, you're seriously going to tell me you think this is all by chance?"

"I *think* we picked the right timing."

"Oh really?" Tori crossed her arms. "Did we also make Commodore Perry assign you to Fred?"

"Well –"

"Did we make Warren show his true colors, pushing Maggie to make a decision?"

"No, but –"

"Did we make Pastor do that particular message the week we show up?"

"No, but what does his message have to do with timing?"

"Seriously?" Tori's eyebrows both raised. "Did you miss the whole 'Time and Faith' lesson? Time – we're bouncing through it. Faith – we have to have it to keep doing what we're doing. Faith as small as a mustard seed. Do you really understand how tiny that is?"

"No."

"Mini. Like seeds you would plant...and small ones at that. You have faith in CAIT and TORI to protect us and get us to the right time and place, but you can't have faith that God already knew we were going to do this? I've been studying God, Jesus, and The Holy Spirit. I kept my promise to Patrick and kept an open mind. It all clicked today. I saw what all God lined up to make our mission work. He could have not done it. He could have just let us flounder. As it is, He could still make it that the St. James family gets in a car accident on the way to Arizona. However, our goal of keeping them off the plane worked. The rest is between them and God. I feel like we are on a mission from God. He gave you the intelligence to create TORI and CAIT. He also gave you the knowledge to know which person to take with you. He gave me the faith to trust you and go on this journey with you. He also gave us both the guidance to find not only the right relative, but also ran into the right people I needed to hear from. I can honestly say that I love Patrick, but I know he's supposed to die in 1813. That's what makes the final push for Fred to change his ways. I heard Maggie say that. I understood at that moment that I was not supposed to be with Patrick. He did what he was supposed to do. He fulfilled his purpose, and then God took him home."

"How can you say that? He was a good man!" Tripp objected.

"He was. I will always have a place in my heart for him. He saved many lives on that day at the Battle of Lake Erie. I'm sure he would have saved many more, but in stopping the fight he saved generations of ours," Tori explained.

"But he died way too young!"

"For a man in the military back then, he lived longer than most. That's not the point. The point is God's hand is in it. Think about it! How did we end up in the perfect hotel where the concierges just happened to know about the *Charleston Confidential*, along with the password? You don't seriously think we're that lucky? Honestly! I was charged with murdering my best friend! You are the last in our bloodline! With luck like that, we were *definitely not* the people to go on this mission!"

Tripp chuckled as he crossed his arms. Tapping his finger on his chin, he nodded. "I see your point."

"There is sense to the chaos of this world. It is only through God Himself that things work out the way they do. I'm going out with Heather tomorrow to prepare them for a very long drive."

"Like almost two-thousand miles long," Tripp added.

"Exactly! If He protects them for the entire drive, then they were meant to survive this generation. If they don't, then they were not meant to survive, and God had a plan."

"Then, this trip would have been for nothing."

"*Not* nothing!" Tori snapped. Tripp looked taken aback as Tori said, "Look, there are too many things that lined up for it to have been pure coincidence. God had a plan. All we had to do was take the steps. His hand is in everything if you look hard enough."

"We haven't gone back to where Maggie said it started yet."

"That just means we have at least one more mission that we know of. Who knows?" She shrugged. "There may be more."

"I know. I just don't know how many more of these we have."

"At least one more," she said. "Once the family leaves for Phoenix, we can leave on our next mission."

"I have to admit that I am curious to visit the clan on Christmas in Ireland."

"Me too. However, right now we have to handle this time and place. We'll figure out where to go next once they're gone."

"Agreed," Tripp said. "Go get ready for bed."

With that, Tori went into the bathroom to take a shower. While she was showering, her mind still drifted back to Patrick. She understood and believed he was supposed to die on that day in 1813. He saved many generations of her family by doing so. Her heart broke, though, knowing he never truly found love. His talent regarding medicine was a gift from God taken from the Earth too soon.

"I know he's with you, Lord. Please take care of him, and let him know I think about him often!"

CHAPTER FIFTEEN

11AUG1987 (AM): A Time To Laugh

The next morning, while Tori got ready to go out with Heather, Tripp stayed in the room. As soon as Tori left, he grabbed her Bible off the nightstand between the tables, and started reading. Her note page was still in the Bible, marking the book of John, so that is where he started reading.

"Hi!" Tori said, greeting Heather as she got in the passenger's seat of the van.

"Morning!" Heather said. When Tori's seatbelt was buckled, Heather pulled away from the curb. As she drove, Heather admitted, "I'm kind of excited about the idea of driving to Arizona."

"Have you ever driven through the country before?"

"No. One of our missions is to go to AAA today and pick up the maps. He already called to get the trip-ticks this morning. Tonight, Sebastian and I will look through the route. And then tomorrow, the kids and I will go to the library to figure out what places we can stop to see along the way."

"Sounds like a solid plan."

"The kids are really excited too!"

"I can only imagine! So, where are we going?"

"We're heading to the Kresge store on Woodward."

"Never been."

"Really? It's great! We can even get lunch there."

"Really? That's incredible!"

"You will love it! Trust me!"

It took them several minutes to get there and find parking. What they walked into reminded Tori of a mini-mall. Heather was right, just about everything they would need was there, including a small diner!

"Okay, so what does each kid like? Preferably something that will keep them occupied, but not work the nerves of their siblings, which in turn will work your nerves," Tori said with a smirk. "Good line of thinking. Okay, let's start with Vicki. She loves to draw. She's phenomenal, and has won multiple awards for her art."

"That's easy! A sketch book, colored pencils, regular pencils, specialty pencils, etcetera," Tori said. "Next?"

"Seb loves sports," Heather said, writing Tori's suggestions down in a small notebook for shopping.

"Hmm. He may be a little more difficult. Does he like electronic games at all?"

"Not really sure."

"You know there are sports handheld games. Right?"

"I didn't," Heather admitted. "Do they make those?"

"They do," Tori said with a smile. "Write those down for Seb."

"Done," Heather said. "Scott loves to read."

"How old is he?"

"Ten."

"Does he read chapter books?"

"Oh yeah! He's been reading them since first grade."

"What about those choose your own adventure books?"

"What are those? Oh! I feel so out of touch!" Heather groaned. "No wonder we're struggling to connect with our kids!"

"Well, they're books where once they reach a certain point, they can choose to go to one page or the other, depending on which choice they make."

"That's awesome!" Heather nodded, writing them down.

"What about the Boxcar Children series?"

"Oh! He devoured those."

"Encyclopedia Brown?"

"Now, *those* he may also like," Heather said, writing them down. "Sam is Scott's twin, but they could not be more opposite. While Scott likes to read, Sam likes music and sports."

"Music!" Tori smiled. "Does he have a Walkman?"

"Yes."

"Does he have mixed tapes?"

"Oh yeah! Tapes them off his boombox all the time."

"What about batteries?"

"Ooo! Good point!" Heather wrote that down. "We'll also keep his tapes out of the boxes, and put them in the van."

"What does he like to do while listening to music?"

"Hmm. Sometimes he likes to read or draw."

"Easy. Looks like your kids do blend some. They can trade off. You can also get more supplies to add as you go across the states."

"I *really* like this plan!" Heather said. "Let's shop!"

They shopped for hours. Tori loved the eighties. She often felt like she was born in the wrong decade. Visiting the times they visited was something Tori would never forget!

As they were shopping, they stopped around noon to get some food in the small diner in Kresge's. While they ate, they chatted.

"You and your brother sound like a fun pair to be around! Do you have more family?"

"Feels like they're all over," Tori said.

"What about your parents? Where are they?"

"They're dead. They died in a car accident."

"So, what exactly do you two do?"

"We're private investigators."

"How did you find out about the plane issue?" Heather asked quietly.

"We stumbled onto it while investigating another case. We knew we had to get up here and figure it out. Lord willing, we can get it sorted before it happens."

"Agreed," Heather said, and then ate one of her fries. They both had a burger, fries, and a coke slush. "That's kind of scary. With everything else going on, that is *not* what Detroit needs. It needs something to hope for. There are ton of jobs that are going away when the plant closes. People are scattering, grabbing whatever job is available. That's why we chose to go out of state."

"You'll have better weather in Arizona."

"This is true!" Heather giggled.

"At least a couple hundred days of sunshine, and no snow."

"Well, not completely true," Heather countered. "The winters are much milder than Detroit. However, there are some days of snow once and a while."

"I didn't know that."

"Now, rain, that's a completely different story!"

"I'm sure!" Tori said with a smile. "Are you excited?"

"Actually, I am. I love everything we got for the kids so far as well. And the idea of stopping by to see the family as we go sounds perfect! We called them yesterday when we got home, and they're excited!"

"Sounds like an adventure!" Tori said, and they continued to chat while they ate.

Afterward, they finished shopping. Then they went to AAA to get the maps and trip-ticks before Heather dropped off Tori at the hotel.

"Whew!" Tori said, walking into the hotel room. "That was fun, but exhausting!"

Tripp set the Bible down and looked up at Tori.

Tori furrowed her brow. Locking the door, she then made her way to his bed and sat down next to him. "Are you okay?"

"Not really," he said with his legs stretched out in front of him and his arms crossed.

"What's going on?"

"Remember when I was really nervous in church yesterday?"

"Yes."

"You know how I'm kind of sarcastic when it comes to God and Jesus?"

"Yes. Care to explain why?"

"I'm working on it. I have watched you subtly change through these trips. Something Patrick said to you lit a fire under you. You were on mission with me, but also another mission...a personal one. You didn't let anything I said or did deter you from that mission. You were able to focus on both."

"Right."

"I'm having trouble with this whole God being in charge thing."

Tori did not say a word. She crossed her legs as she sat on the bed, resting her elbows on her knees. He needed to talk and sort through his feelings, and she would let him.

He sighed. Looking toward the ceiling, he took a moment, before he said, "Being the last one in a family line is a weird feeling." He looked down. "My parents are already dead. My mom died of cancer when I was eight, and my dad basically committed a long suicide. He drank himself to death. He died when I was twenty. I did have a sister, but she died at three years old when she drowned in a pool." Looking up at Tori, he confessed,

"Working with you these last few weeks, I've come to love you like a sister. It made me miss my family. That family feeling we experienced yesterday was foreign to me. I am honestly not sure I *want* to go back to my time. It was extremely lonely."

"I get it. Being in a jail cell wasn't exactly a walk in the park. I had my parents, though."

"What if I go back to my timeline and I'm still the only one?"

"Tripp," Tori set a hand on his ankle, which was beside her, "the world has changed. Our family line has changed. Regardless of whether or not you or I make it through this, we made a difference in our family line that created a chain reaction we will feel the effects of for generations to come! We did it, Tripp! Working together, we accomplished our mission. Regardless whether the St. James family makes it to Arizona or not, we saved them from dying in a fiery crash in a few days. We saved Maggie. We saved Fred. It seems, through the journals Maggie showed us, that we're going to go back in time to meet our clan in Ireland, and help shape generations before we even set foot in 1813! What we're doing is sending ripples through our family line! We did it!"

"But will we still be here when it's all said and done?"

"That, we will have to figure out for ourselves when we get back to our own timelines."

"God is supposedly in charge. I have been reading all day. I read John, Acts, and Romans. Then, I did some research on CAIT. How could He let His people get killed? Jesus's close friends were all murdered except John. He died on an island called Patmos. They gave their lives for something they could not see."

"That's faith. They had faith and trusted in Jesus and His word. They trusted God would welcome them regardless of how they died because He loved them. They took His message to the world. They taught others. They performed miracles. They had every right to feel all-powerful, but they chose to be servants to others. Their examples led many people to learn about Christ... me included," Tori said. "Just like Patrick and Pastor John told me about Jesus, His apostles told others as well. This led to Christianity.

"We are not supposed to 'be like' anyone but Jesus. Yes, there are different religions," she explained. "The only one that I am concerned with is Christianity. Even then, the only Ones I'm focused on are Jesus, God, and the Holy Spirit.

"The church is not a building. You should have learned that in Acts. It's the people in the building. Look," Tori said, thinking through her words, "God is, was, and always will be. As we went through time, despite hundreds of years, His basic message remained the same. He wants a relationship with us. He wants us to choose Him. Just like we cannot make our family members make the right choice, He does not *make* us choose Him. He does not *make* us worship Him. It has to be a choice. It has to be *your* choice. I cannot make it for you. Regardless of how things turn out, it's a choice only *you* can make. If we don't make it through the generations once everything shakes out, I know I will be with the Lord. You have to make the choice to do the same."

He leaned his head back as tears slowly crawled down his cheeks. "Going to all three members of my family's funerals in churches made me hate going into a church. You don't understand what it's like to bury your little sister. You don't know the feeling of seeing your own mother's and father's caskets in front of you. You don't know what it's like to shove the acidic vomit back down as looks of pity are on everyone's faces everywhere you go. The loneliness of walking into an empty house. Having to help box up your baby sister's belongings. Having to help put your mom's clothes into bags so your dad can donate her stuff. Watching as their lives were dwindled to boxes or bags was heartbreaking. Sorting through my dad's house after his death, I saw the records. I saw what happened to our family. Loading it all into CAIT, I saw the patterns. It was beyond frustrating to learn just how reckless our family was with their time! They let stupid stuff take their lives!"

"Not anymore. They have learned. When we go back, further than we ever thought we would go, we have a chance to make a bigger difference. Generations will remember us, whether we make it through this or not. The proof is in the family tree."

Tripp stared into her eyes for a moment, before he admitted, "I don't want to die."

Tori gulped. "I don't either. However, our family will live on. We have ensured that."

"What about me?"

"When we started, I was the one concerned with living through this. You helped me realize that really doesn't matter. What matters is what we did helped our family line to continue way past your generation."

Tripp shook his head. He looked up at her and asked, "How are *you* now the hopeful one in this?"

"Because I now know I am not the one in control. I have never been in control. I should have known that, but I didn't want to hear it, nor did I care. I lost my best friend and was accused of her murder. As far as I was concerned, my life was over.

"Then, you popped into my life – quite literally – and gave me a new life. You gave me hope! Then Patrick stepped in and gave me a different message of hope. A hope in Jesus. You read the Bible. You heard Pastor yesterday. Just like our mission of changing our family history has not changed, neither has Jesus's messages of love, purpose, or eternal life. Do you understand?"

"How do we know we are not messing with God's plans by doing this?"

"How do we know we are not fulfilling God's plan by doing this?" Tori countered.

Tripp breathed out a heavy breath of air. "Your reputation for being wise went through the generations. I had no idea what I was getting myself into by bringing you along."

Tori giggled. "Nope! You didn't!"

"Okay. I have some questions about what I read."

"Not sure if I can answer them, but I'll give it my best shot."

"That would be appreciated."

Tripp and Tori spoke way into the night. They ordered room service for their food, but continued to talk through it as well. They talked, laughed, cried, and even prayed. They shared stories from where and when they grew up. Some were sweet. Some were painful. Others were funny. While Tripp was grasping the concept of Jesus, he still struggled with losing all of his family at such a young age.

Finally, around three in the morning, Tori said, "Tripp we are not in control regarding what happened to us. We *can* control how we react to the situation. Just like you feel bad for everything that happened to me, you cannot change it. Now, circumstances may have changed since we made changes to our family's history, but those memories are still on my mind. You can continue to hold onto those feelings, or you can process them, pray, and move forward. You cannot be so stuck in the past that you cannot see your future."

"How am I supposed to even know if I *have* a future?"

"You said I had a baby with Sebastian Connor Hayden, right?"

"Yes."

"Then," she shrugged, "that's who I need to find when we return."

"If you're not in jail," Tripp pointed out.

"We don't know what we've done to our own timelines."

"That's the other concern. How do we get you back to yours and keep you safe? We cannot take you before I took you because you will create a paradox. Your timeline may implode."

Tori raised her eyebrows. "What? What are you saying? Are you saying I have to go back to jail?"

"Technically."

"Put me in a different time," Tori said firmly, her heart racing. "I mean it. Do *not* put me back in jail."

"You think you can control that?"

"If I die in another time, it shouldn't affect the timeline."

"If you do not meet my great-great-great grandfather, I don't exist," Tripp reminded her. "You met him *after* you got out of jail. You *have* to go back."

"Just take me to Sebastian when we're ready. I'll figure it out from there. Leave me a TORI to shift timelines. I'll make a choice from there."

"You're serious?" Tripp asked, wide-eyed.

"I *am not* going back to jail. I won't! You don't understand what it's like in there! I am willing to sacrifice my life for this family, but I *will never* go back to jail!"

"Tori," Tripp said, speaking softly to calm her, "you have given a lot for this family. You have a life you have to live from the point I took you. I have to put you back a minute after I took you to continue your lifeline. In order to do that, I cannot leave you with a TORI. I have to leave you the way I found you."

"Move me to a country without extradition, like Belize! Then, leave me with a TORI there."

"I can't. If I do that, you will *never* meet my great-great-great grandfather."

"And he will live. If I don't meet him, I won't shoot him."

"If I do exist, I won't be related to you. Doing what you are proposing will be messing with the timeline in ways you cannot imagine! We have to keep that minimal. That includes putting you back in jail."

"You're kidding!" Tori said, color draining from her face.

"We don't have a choice. If you do not go back where I left you, the family line after that will be messed up."

Tori dropped her head into her hands, shaking it. She took a deep breath and slowly let it out. "I'm exhausted, but my mind is buzzing. I don't know what to do with this."

In her mind, she heard, *'Trust Me.'*

"Did you say something?" Tori asked Tripp.

"No. I'm trying to figure out how to handle this," Tripp said. "Let me think."

In Tori's head, she heard Proverbs 3:5 and 6, *'Trust in the Lord with all thine heart; and lean not unto thine own understanding. In all thy ways acknowledge Him, and He shall direct thy paths.'*

In her mind, she prayed to God, saying, *'Father, this is not something I want to do. Jail is terrifying! And going back for something I didn't do...there has to be a better way.'*

In response, she heard Isaiah 43:2, *'When you pass through the waters, I will be with you; and when you pass through the rivers, they will not sweep over you. When you walk through the fire, you will not be burned; the flames will not set you ablaze.'*

She responded in her mind, *'If I go back, I go to jail. I will be trapped. How is this going to work?'*

She then heard Psalm 91:1 and 2, *'Whoever dwells in the shelter of the Most High will rest in the shadow of the Almighty. I will say of the Lord, "He is my refuge and my fortress, my God, in whom I trust."'*

'I do trust You. I do. But jail?'

Matthew 6:26 went through her mind, *'Look at the birds of the air; they do not sow, or reap, or store away in barns, and yet your heavenly Father feeds them. Are you not much more valuable than they?'* It was quickly followed by Jeremiah 17:7 and 8, *'But blessed is the one who trusts in the Lord, whose confidence is in Him. They will be like a tree planted by the water that sends out its roots by the stream. It does not fear when heat comes; its leaves are always green. It has no worries in a year of drought and never fails to bear fruit.'*

'So, You're saying You got this, regardless if I am in jail or not. You

will never leave me.' Tori nodded. Then she looked toward Heaven and whispered, "I trust You."

"What?" Tripp asked.

"I trust God. When it's time for me to go back, take me back to jail."

"Wait! What? You were adamant a little bit ago that you were not going to jail."

"I had a conversation with God," Tori explained. "He says for me to trust Him, and I am going to do that."

"What do you mean you had a conversation with God?"

"Remember when the pastor was talking about The Holy Spirit on Sunday?"

"Yes. He mentioned that."

"While you were talking to the St. James crew, I was praying with Sarah. I accepted Jesus's sacrifice for me. I gave control of my life over to Him that morning. In doing so, the Holy Spirit came to stay with me. When I was struggling, He brought verses to my mind. They applied to the situation, and He encouraged me to trust Him. I just told Him that I would trust Him in this situation as well. He will take care of me. I know it. When it's time, you can take me back to jail."

"I will, but I also have an idea. If it works, I will meet you at a later date with a TORI for you."

"Okay." Tori nodded. "I'm going to trust you both."

Tripp stretched and yawned. "Man! I'm tired."

"Well, it *is* three-thirty," Tori pointed out. "Do you want to go to bed?"

"Not yet. Let's play a game," he said, pulling out a deck of cards from his bag.

"What game?"

"We could play Texas Hold 'em with no pot. You know, just for fun. It may help us unwind so we can sleep."

"I think that's a great idea. Let me get a shower and in my pajamas first."

"Sounds like a plan," Tripp said, shuffling the cards.

They played until around six o'clock in the morning. They laughed and joked around during that time. Tori appreciated Tripp and his light-hearted attitude. With all of the stress they had been under lately, they needed the time to laugh and just relax.

That Friday, Tripp and Tori took a taxi to the St. James home. All morning and afternoon, they helped load the moving truck, along with several others from church. The family played a key role in the community. They would definitely be missed. However, they were also excited to start their life in Arizona.

After Sebastian pulled the door down and locked it, he turned toward everyone there and said, "We cannot thank you for all of the love and support you've shown our family. We're definitely going to miss all of you."

"I think I speak for everyone here when we say we'll miss all of you, too," Pastor said. "We'll see you in a few days to help unload."

Sebastian smiled. "Can't wait!"

"Let's join hands in prayer for a safe journey," Sarah said with her hands out.

Together, they joined hands and prayed over the family, their moving truck, their vehicle, and the vehicles around their van for safety in traveling. When they finished, the St. James family climbed into their van and started their drive. They chose to drive through the night in hopes that the kids would sleep for the first portion of the trip.

When Tripp and Tori got back to the hotel, Tripp closed the curtains while Tori locked the door and shoved a towel to block any light. Afterward, both sat on Tripp's bed with their legs stretched out in front of them.

"CAIT?" Tori asked.

"CAIT," Tripp agreed.

"I hope they made it," Tori said, nibbling on her nails while Tripp dug CAIT out of his bag next to his bed. "Either way, we did our best."

Tripp punched in the Detroit Free Press for August 17, 1987. The headline read, *'Metro Crash Kills 154,'* with a bi-line of, *'Northwest jet slams under I-94 overpass; fiery crash is Michigan's worst air disaster.'*

"Seven less than the original headline," Tripp pointed out. "The crash still happened. The four-year-old girl was still the only one who survived. However, Sebastian and his family were not in the plane."

"Okay," Tori said, taking a deep breath, "pull up the family tree. I need to know if they made it."

Tripp's heart raced as he punched in the family tree file. He looked over at Tori. "Everything we've done up until now rests on this moment. Did we do it, or did we fail? If they family made it, that's five children in just one branch that made it and filled the family tree. If not, we may still have other jumps to do."

"Not before we reach my generation. This generation we are dealing with in this time are the parents, aunts, and uncles of mine," Tori pointed out. "This is our last stop before my generation."

Tripp nodded. Then he pushed the button to bring up the family tree.

Tori's eyes watered. Tripp gulped. Sam and Maggie's names were black. She sniffed, trying to contain her emotions. "Wh-what happened?" Tori stammered.

Tripp punched on the keyboard. He could not read it aloud. So, together, they silently read the file. Sam died at fifteen years old in a car accident. He and several friends were coming home from a concert, when the driver lost control of the car and it went over an embankment, killing four, with one survivor. Sam was one of those who perished. For Maggie, when she was twenty, she was killed in a drive-by shooting. She was at a friend's house picking her up in a bad part of town. She was trying to get her friend out of that situation when the girl's boyfriend drove by and shot both Maggie and her friend.

"Oh, sweet Jesus!" Tori breathed out.

"They made it to Arizona," Tripp said. Sebastian, Heather, Vicki, Seb, and Scott made it through to old age. Tori, we did it! We actually did it!"

"What does the rest of the family tree look like?" Tori asked.

"Nope. You're going to have to learn that later," he said, changing the screen to the airplane crash.

She wiped the tears from her eyes as she said, "I need to know. Did it actually work? Did the family grow enough to extend beyond your generation?"

"If I look that up, will you look away? It's not good for you to know too much of your own future."

"Fine." Tori turned around and faced the wall. "Will this work?"

"Yes," he said and opened the family tree file again. A smile formed on his face as he looked beyond the current generation into the other generations. "For the record, even *your* name is now white."

"I'm not looking," she said in a sing-song voice as she

blocked the sides of her face with her hands so she would not be tempted.

"Just a minute. Let me check something," he said and began tapping away on the keyboard. Tori started whistling to tune him out. "Tori," he said, tapping her to get her to stop.

"Whaa-aat?" she moaned. "I'm not looking!"

"I think we can bend the time rules for just this once. We've already done the work. You need to reap the rewards. Look."

Tori slowly turned. Her eyes widened as she looked at her branch. Her eyes watered again. She sniffed and wiped her nose as she saw in her generation that she actually had siblings. She saw that she, herself, had four children. She reached forward and moved the screen up to see into Tripp's generation. She gasped. "You're not the last in our line!"

"I know. I even have multiple siblings now, too." He grinned. "Tori, my beautiful, smart, sarcastic, feisty, great-great-great-grandmother, we did it!"

They gave each other a high-five.

"We did it!" Tori squealed, clapping her hands. "It worked!"

"Okay. Now to get you back to your generation."

"I know. Can I ask one more favor before we do?"

"Anything."

"Patrick died on what date?"

"He died on September 14th, 1813."

"Can we go back to September 13th, 1813, so I can tell him how his challenge was fulfilled? That way when he dies, he knows I'll see him again when it's my time. I just want to do this one thing before going back to jail."

"I think that can be arranged," Tripp agreed. "What if we go back on the 14th, just in the early morning? I don't want Perry to see me or he could try to nail me for desertion."

"Good point. Thank you! I need you to get us some 1813 clothing. I think we should get a good night's sleep and then take off in the middle of the night tomorrow. What do you think?"

"I think that's a great plan," Tripp agreed. "Now, go get a shower."

"Will do!" Tori said and grabbed her nightgown before she headed into the bathroom.

When he heard the shower start, he took a few moments to make sure she was for sure in the shower, and then he punched in the date, time, and place he needed. He took a deep breath, pushed the button on his TORI, and disappeared from the room.

When he reappeared in 1813, he was in a dress shop. It was after closing, so he quietly made his way around the shop gathering what he needed. When he was about to leave, something caught the corner of his eye. He typed in the date, time, and location to get back into the hotel so he would only have to hit the button. Then, he went over to the window and looked out. There was a couple walking down the street arm-and-arm. He smiled. *Young love* now made him smile instead of sad.

He turned and grabbed one last item before disappearing in the shimmering light. As he was going, the store owner came downstairs with a candle in his hand. "Hello?" he called out, but Tripp was already gone.

CHAPTER SEVENTEEN

14SEP1813: A Time To Dance

Early the next morning, around three o'clock, Tori and Tripp were in their hotel room, dressed for 1813. "What are we going to do with all of these clothes?" Tori asked.

"My TORI's been charging all day. Give your bag to me," he said, putting his hand out.

When she gave him her bag, he disappeared. He returned only a moment later ready to go. "No bags. This is a one-day thing. He dies later in the day. You have to say everything you need to when we get there. He is going to die in the next twenty-four hours."

"Morbid." Tori shuddered.

"You are giving him the gift of peace," he said, squeezing her hand. "Now, here's the date, time, and location to put into your TORI."

Tori did what he said and input the information.

"Count of three?" Tripp asked. When Tori nodded, he said, "One...two...three..." and they hit the button on their TORIs at the same moment.

Tori watched as 1987 washed away in a waterfall of colors before it was replaced by darkness. She felt herself fall, but she did not feel like she was being torn apart. She hit the ground on her feet. It still took her breath away, but it was a much nicer trip than the first time.

"You okay?" Tripp asked quietly.

"Yes," she whispered. "Much easier travel with the TORI."

"Okay. As far as they know, we left three days ago," Tripp reminded her. "We left early on the morning of the 11th."

"Right," Tori said with a nod. She scanned the area to see if she could see Patrick. The men were mostly asleep, with only a few awake here or there.

"He's in the medical tent. He must have the night watch," Tripp whispered. "Here," he took her wrist and typed in March 3rd, 2022, for the date. The time was three-forty. Then, for the location, he typed in the Lyncher State Jail in Humble, Texas. He and Tori's eyes locked. She did a curt nod to let him know she was okay with it. "Take your time, but hurry up. We're not supposed to be here."

"I will. Thank you," she said and kissed his cheek before disappearing into the trees.

Her heart raced as soon as she saw him. She was alert but kept her eyes on Patrick.

At first, he was writing in his journal. Then he stopped. He put his pencil down and looked around.

Tori gasped. *He knew she was there. She knew they were connected!*

Coming out of the shadows near him, he looked right at her. "Tori?" he whispered. When she nodded, he got up from his table and ducked out of the tent. He ran up to her and gave her a hug. "I didn't think I would ever see you again."

"To be honest, I didn't think I would see you either," she admitted.

Taking a step back, he shook his head. "Beautiful as ever. You look like you have more peace in your eyes...in your soul."

"I do. I needed to come back to tell you something."

"What?" His face brightened. "That you're staying?"

"I wish. I have to go back and take care of something."

"What?"

"I have to go back to jail. They think I killed my best friend."

"I thought you said you were in the house when she was killed."

"I was. That's why they thought I did it, but I didn't."

"I don't think you did. It's not in you."

"It's not. I had to see you before I went back. I had to let you know something. I did a lot of research over the last few weeks, and –"

"Wait. Weeks?" He shook his head. "You've only been gone for a few days."

"Patrick, I'm going to trust you with something. You may think I'm crazy, but I need to be honest with you."

"What is it?"

"I'm not from this time. I am from the future."

He shook his head.

"I know this sounds confusing, but it's the truth."

"I can see in your eyes you are telling me the truth. I just do not understand."

She showed him the TORI on her arm.

"What is that?"

"This is how I travel through time. I'm showing you this so you will understand when I tell you that I have been through various times in our future and talked to many people. I kept my word to you and left my heart open to God. At a later date, I finally sat down with a preacher's wife, and I prayed and asked Jesus into my heart. It was important for me to –"

She was cut off when he grabbed her and hugged her tightly. "Praise the Lord!"

"Too tight!"

"Sorry," he said and released her. "I'm just so happy right now!"

"I wanted you to know," she said as he wiped away the tear in his eye. "I wanted you to know because of *you* I have Jesus in my life. It was important to me that you knew."

"Thank you," he said, breathless. "I still don't understand this, but I am grateful. How long can you stay?"

"Not too long. Perry cannot know we are here. I don't want Tripp to get into trouble. I'm in enough trouble for the both of us."

He shook his head. "I really don't understand this, but if you are a child of Christ, I am happy!"

"I know our time is short, but I also wanted you to know what you mean to me."

"What do you mean?"

She looked down for a moment before she looked up and admitted, "When we were talking on the rock, you said you liked me."

"I do! You make it sound like it was so long ago."

"For me, it was," she said. "For me, it's been weeks, not hours or days. I know this is confusing, and I'm sorry." She took his hands in hers, as she continued, "You have been in my heart, my thoughts, and my mind since we left. I like you...a *lot*. However, we are from two different times. Our future is not meant to be joined. As much as I want it too, we cannot be together."

He reached up and rested his hand on the side of her face. "If I am following you correctly, we do not have a future together, but we *do* have right now. Correct?"

"Yes. I don't know why you are not freaking out."

He shook his head. "Freaking out?"

"In a panic," she corrected.

"I am not freaking out, as you say, because I do not care how you are here, just that you are here. I know this is not proper, but would you take a few moments to dance with me?"

"Dance? There is no music."

"There is in my heart," he said and started humming. "May I?" He put his hands out. When she nodded, he continued to hum quietly so only the two of them could hear. They danced under the stars with no one else around but them.

Tripp watched the couple reunite from a distance. He knew there was no way for Patrick and Tori to be together. Patrick needed to die for Fred to realize the true error of his fighting ways. As much as it hurt his heart, he knew it had to happen.

Tori had to go back to jail. She had to get back there to where he found her. However, he made a choice right then and there while he watched the pair dance under the stars, to make something happen. She would have to behave as if she did not know anything different would happen, so he would not tell her. He would research and find out how to help her and fix it.

He went deeper into the woods before he typed in when and where he needed to go, and then disappeared in a shimmering light.

"If I am going to never see you again, I know it is not proper to ask, but may I kiss you?" Tori asked.

"If I am never going to see you again after tonight, I do not want to turn down any request you make of me, save one."

"I would never ask that," she said, knowing exactly what he meant.

He rested his hands on the sides of her face and then leaned down. The moment their lips touched, electricity shot through both of them lighting up their very souls! As they stood there, lost in each other's kiss, Tori started to cry.

Patrick pulled back ever so slightly. Rubbing his thumbs on her cheeks to brush the tears away, he whispered, "Why are you crying?"

"I know something, but I cannot tell you."

"What is it?"

"Please don't make me say it."

"It is breaking your heart. I can see it in your eyes."

She shook her head. He just wrapped his arms around her to hold her while she quietly cried.

After a few moments, she was able to pull herself together. "I'm sorry. I know I should tell you, but I cannot. I'm sorry." She shook her head.

"I wish I could take your hurt away."

"This is helping me more than you know. I needed to see you. I needed to tell you that I now know Jesus. I needed you to hear that from me."

"I hear you. I see you, too," he said in a low voice. "I know since both of us are God's children that if anything happens, we will be together in eternity."

"Stop," Tori said, her bottom lip trembling as she fought back the tears again.

"Stop what?"

"My heart is breaking."

"Why?"

"Because I know I will never see you again. It hurts."

"Tori," he said, taking her hands into his, "if this is the only time we have, I promise you that it will carry me into eternity."

Tori shook her head. "Me too, but −"

"No *buts*, Tori. If I were to die tomorrow, I would die a happy man."

Tori took a step back. Wiping her eyes, she said, "I-I need to go. I just needed to make sure you knew my decision."

"I-can you wait? Please? Just a little more time?" Patrick asked.

Tori smiled. "I cannot deny you."

"What are *you* doing here?" Commodore Perry's voice boomed. Both Tori and Patrick jumped. "Where is your brother?"

"He-he's not here," Tori stammered, heart racing. "I-I'm here by myself. I wanted to see Patrick."

"Young lady, this is not a place for you if your brother is not here. If your brother *is* here, I must speak with him post-haste."

"Sir?" Fred asked, coming out of the woods from sentry duty. "Tori? What are you doing here? I thought you guys left?"

Patrick stood in front of Tori and brushed her behind him. "She came to see me."

"Why?" Commodore Perry demanded.

"What's going on?" another guy by the fire sat up. He jostled the others near him.

Slowly, they made their way over to the medical tent to find out what was going on.

There were voices overlapping others with exclamations of, *'That's Tori! Where's Tripp? Why is she here? What's going on? Did something happen?'*

Tori rested her hand on Patrick's arm to stop him. "I came to talk to Patrick. I needed to tell him something."

"Where is your brother?" Commodore Perry pushed.

"I don't know," Tori said. "I came on my own."

"You did not! A woman on her own out here?" a man scoffed. "There is no way you came here alone!"

"I did!" Tori said. "Do not call me a liar!"

"You *are* lying!"

"How dare you insult her!" Patrick snapped.

Fred jumped in front of Patrick. "This woman gave her all for us! You have a lot of nerve! She is a lady! She fed you! She cared for many of you! She is stronger than she seems."

"What were you two doing out here in the dark?" a man challenged the couple. Then, under his breath, he added, "She will probably lead apes to hell!"

Both Patrick and Fred glared at the man while Fred flexed his hands open and closed.

"We were only talking," Patrick said through gritted teeth. "Take that back! NOW!"

"Why is her face so red?" another asked. "Were you caught? What were you doing? Do we get a turn, too?"

"Stop!" Patrick growled.

"I have this," Fred said with his hand out to stop Patrick.

"*I* will defend her honor," Patrick insisted.

"No. No one needs to defend my honor," Tori insisted. "We haven't done anything. We were only talking and dancing."

"Ah, so she's a two-bit whore!" another man shouted.

"Enough!" Patrick snapped.

"Shut your trap, Anthony!" Fred snarled.

"Oh, she's just the barque of frailty, that one!" another man shouted.

Patrick went to jump the man, but Fred shoved him away and went after the man himself. As soon as the first punch was thrown, everything broke loose! Fists started flying. They were quickly combined with the shouting and yelling.

"Gentlemen! Stop!" Perry roared. "ENOUGH!"

The fighting continued until someone yelled, "Gun!"

Tori looked up to see Patrick shove Fred out of the way just as the gun was fired. There was sudden silence...or an absence of sound. Tori could not determine which one. All she saw was Patrick crumple to the ground holding his chest. Her world collapsed around her in slow motion.

The man stood there in shock with a smoking gun in his hands. "I meant to shoot up, but Gregory ran into me!" he said in his defense.

"I did not!" Gregory shouted.

"It doesn't matter!" Tori finally collected herself enough to run to Patrick. She gathered him in her arms. "I'm so sorry! If I didn't come back, you wouldn't have gotten shot! Oh! This is all my fault! I'm so sorry!" she said, tears streaming down her face. Flashes of Chrissy's body ricocheted through her mind, as they intermingled with the horrific scene she just witnessed. While she rocked him, scenes from the Battle of Lake Erie rammed their way in as well.

"Hold me," Patrick whispered.

"I got you," Tori said, tears uncontrollably streaming down her face. "I'll never let you go." She kissed his forehead. "I'm sorry. I'm so sorry," she whispered.

Just then, a crackle shot across the sky, lighting up the entire island. Thunder rumbled and shook the ground around them.

"It has been threatening to rain for a few days," a man quietly said.

"Shut your mouth," another reprimanded him. "That's not important."

"Patrick, I'm so sorry. It's all my fault," Tori said in between sobs as she rocked Patrick in her arms. Stroking his hair with her fingers, she whispered, "I'm so sorry."

"No. It's my fault. I needed to control my temper, and I did not," Fred said. "Instead of feeding the anger, I should have diffused it."

Tori rested her blood-soaked hand on Patrick's cheek and shook her head. "I'm so sorry. How can I help you?"

"Where it is, you cannot," Patrick said and then winced. "You gave me many things in our short time. Memories that fill my heart. I will always remember dancing under the stars with you."

She nodded and sniffed, wiping her face with the back of her hand. "I will too."

"My heart is yours. When we come together again in Heaven, I will welcome you with open arms. Until then, find love again," he said and winced. "I love you, Tori."

"I love you, too," she said. She shook her head again. "I'm so sorry. I shouldn't have come."

"If you did not, I would not know about you and Jesus. Thank you for coming. Thank you for telling me." He rested his hand on her cheek. "Thank you for being you and for bringing love to my heart, my beautiful traveler."

The gunshot brought the remaining men in camp running. What they ran up to, they would never forget.

One of the men who took in the scene in front of him shouted, "Help him! Why are you all standing around?"

"He said we cannot," another somberly answered.

"I love you, Tori. You have made me a happy man," Patrick said to her. "You brought true love into my life."

"And you have shown me my heart. For that, I cannot thank you enough," Tori said. She smiled, but the tears continued to fall.

"See you in heaven. Remember, I will always love you," he said, and his hand dropped to the side only a moment before he took a staggered last breath. His eyes had a faraway look to them, but his face looked peaceful.

"No, no, no, no, noooo! Please no! Make it stop!" She looked around at the men. "Someone do something! Don't just stand there!" she shouted through her tears as she clutched him to herself. "Do something to help him! You cannot let him die! Patrick!" She looked back down. "Patrick! Come back! These men need you! I need you! Please! No!"

"Tori, lass, he's gone," Seamus said, kneeling next to her. He reached over and closed Patrick's eyes before crossing himself.

"No." She shook her head. "No. He can't."

"Lass, we need to let him go. He's not there anymore," Seamus said, pulling her hands from around Patrick's body.

Tori's body shook with uncontrollable sobs. She could not think. Her heart hurt. She felt like she would throw up. "H-he's gone."

"Yes, lass. He's gone. I'm sorry," Seamus said, crouching behind her. He rested his hand on her shoulder. "It will be okay. The men will come and take him to the tent. They need to bury him properly. He's gone, lass. Let him go."

"No! He can't!" she shouted, reaching for Patrick's body as a few men went to pick him up. Seamus wrapped his arms around her, holding her arms to her own body so the men could get Patrick. "Tori, he's dead. He's not there. We have buried many men these last few days. He is not alone in his journey to Heaven."

"No!" Tori cried. "No! It's all my fault!"

"It's not, lass."

"It is! If I didn't come back, the fight would not have started! It's my fault!"

Fred came and knelt in front of her. He rested his hands on the sides of her face, making her look at him. "Look at me, Tori," he demanded. When she did, he said, "This is more my fault. Your brother tried to tell me it would be better to learn to control my temper but I chose to fight. I make a vow to you on this day that I will choose peace when I return home. I will teach my children that there is another way. Patrick's loss will be felt for generations to come. Our family will know this story. Our family will know *his* story."

Tori fell back onto Seamus in tears. She heard Fred, but it did not register. She felt the loss of Patrick deeper than she ever thought possible. It took her over an hour of sobbing before she finally passed out in Seamus's arms.

He gathered her up and moved her to the medical tent. She barely opened her eyes to see them digging a grave next to the officers.

"What are you doing?" one of the men shouted. "That space is for officers only!"

"This man worked day and night to make sure you survived the battle. He deserves a place of honor. Only the men here will know where we laid him. His family will know he is in a place of honor," another man who was digging snapped. "Now, go back to what you were doing! Leave us be!"

Tori shuddered. She slowly got up. No one was paying attention to her, so she ducked into the trees. The tears still flowed down her cheeks, but she continued to wipe them away as she went deeper into the woods.

Hearing men calling for her, she ran faster. She did not want to see anyone. She did not want to be there anymore if Patrick was not there. She ran for what felt like miles until her legs felt like rubber, and she collapsed onto the ground in tears.

Right before her, Tripp shimmered as he appeared. "You need these," he said, handing her the prison outfit.

She dragged herself off the ground and crawled behind a tree. She stripped off her 1813 clothing and got dressed in her prison garb. Knowing Patrick was dead and that it was her fault, she felt like she deserved whatever she had coming to her.

Coming around the tree, she handed Tripp her clothes.

"What happened?" Tripp asked.

"He's dead," Tori said. She felt numb. "It's my fault. If I didn't come back, he would be alive. He died this day, protecting my honor. I deserve to go to prison."

Before he could say another word, she hit the button on her TORI. She looked up to see him working feverishly on his TORI as she shimmered away.

Reappearing in her jail cell, she collapsed on the ground in tears. She tried to stay quiet, knowing the women would give her a hard time if she woke them. Her heart was shattered into a million pieces.

Tripp appeared in her cell only a few moments after her. Kneeling in front of her, he asked, "Do you trust me?"

She only nodded in response.

"Then, I'm going to take this with me," he said, taking the TORI off her wrist. "Trust me on this, Tori. I will give it to you at a later date. Please just trust me."

She nodded again as she wiped her face.

"I love you, Tori. I know you're hurting deeply right now," he said, resting his hand on her shoulder. "I'm sorry. Know I am with you in spirit."

"*When you pass through the waters, I will be with you; and when you pass through the rivers, they will not sweep over you. When you walk through the fire, you will not be burned; the flames will not set you ablaze.'* He is here. I am not alone. He will not let me drown."

Tripp tucked a portion of Tori's hair behind her ear as he crouched in front of her. "I don't want to leave you in this vulnerable and fragile state."

"No." She shook her head. "I deserve this. I deserve to be here. It's my fault Patrick was killed. He and Fred were defending my honor. Had I not been there, he would have lived through that day."

"You don't know that."

"I do," she whispered. "The fight was started because of me."

"Tori, you're breaking my heart." Tripp let out a slow breath of air. "Here," he said, shoving a book under her pillow, "it's a journal I got in 1813. I drew a picture of Patrick in the back for you when you're ready." When she did not respond, he said, "Look, I have to go. I can't let them see me here. I'm sorry." He kissed her head and then shimmered into the night.

Once he was gone, she sat in the darkness of the concrete cell that would be her home for at least the next several years. While she did not kill Chrissy, it was her fault Patrick was dead. As far as she was concerned, she deserved every bit of this. She felt like she robbed the world of Patrick's love and kindness – his gift of medicine and heart.

She climbed onto her bed and rolled over, facing the wall. Her mind was filled with thoughts of Patrick...and her heart shattered into a million pieces all over again.

CHAPTER EIGHTEEN

03MAR2022 (AM): A Time To Mourn

Tori got woken up the next morning by the lights turning on around the cell block and the cells unlocking. She heard the voices of those in the jail with her, but she did not want to get up and face a world without Patrick. She stayed in bed, lost in thoughts of him.

In fact, she stayed in her bed all day. She did not eat. She did not talk to anyone. She did not want to feel. She did not want to do anything.

This went on for a few days until Sharice, Carla, and Talia came into her cell around noon on the second day.

"Leave me alone," Tori groaned, rolling back toward the wall. "I didn't do anything to you. Just leave me be."

Talia knelt next to Tori's bed. When Tori rolled over to face her, Talia said, "We know it sucks in here, but you have to eat. You were just sentenced a few days ago. You can't just starve yourself to death. or they'll win."

"It's been longer than that for me. I don't care about the sentence. I don't even care that I'm in here. I deserve it," Tori said, wiping the continuous tear stream off her face that would not stop.

"Then, why are you cryin'?" Sharice asked. "You don't eat.

You don't sleep. And don't tell me you do because I know that ain't the truth! I hear you cryin' every night...all night."

"I deserve everything that is happening to me," Tori said quietly.

Sharice crossed her arms. "Why? You say you didn't do it."

Tori looked over at Sharice. "I did *not* kill Chrissy. Patrick's dead, and that *is* my fault."

"Wait," Carla said, holding her hands in the air, "*who* is Patrick? What does he have to do with Chrissy? I'm lost!"

"He was killed because of me," Tori explained.

"Patrick?" Sharice asked. When Tori nodded, she said, "I don't understand."

Tori slowly sat up. Due to a lack of food and water over the last few days, her head spun uncontrollably. She dropped her head back onto the wall and took slow deep breaths until her head stopped spinning. "I...um...he died, and it's my fault."

Brows drawn, Talia asked, "What do you mean? I am *so* lost!"

"He was defending my honor when he –"

"Your honor?" Sharice cackled. "What you talkin' about defending your honor? Patrick was defending her honor. Y'all hear that? Girl! You done lost your mind!"

Tori's eyes snapped up as she glared at Sharice. In a cool tone, she said, "He died defending me. I do *not* want to hear his name come out of your mouth...*ever*."

Sharice put her hands in front of her. "Ooo! The sister's got attitude now."

"Leave!" Tori growled.

"You know what, I don't need this," Sharice said and left.

"I'm gonna..." Carla pointed toward Sharice and left after her.

When they were gone, Talia sat down next to Tori on her bed. She took Tori's hand into hers and said, "I know we don't really know each other. In here, you kind of can't get to fully know someone. We have to put up walls of toughness regardless of who we are at our core."

"Ain't that the truth!" Tori said on a sigh.

"Look, I can see that whatever happened with you and this Patrick hurt you deeply. I'm sorry. But he's not here, and *you* are. You need to eat. You also need to drink. We're going to be doing this for a long time. If you need someone to make you eat and drink, I'll do that for you."

Tori shook her head. "I don't know."

"I do. Now, it's lunchtime. Come with me and ignore Sharice and Carla for now. Sharice can be a pill when she wants to. Carla does whatever Sharice wants her to do. You look like you need a friend. I want to be there for you."

"You cannot trust anyone in here."

"Oh! I get it!" Talia chuckled. "I've been here for five years."

"Why *are* you in here?"

"Honestly?"

"I thought we *were* talking honestly, or are you not?" Tori challenged.

"I am." Talia took a deep breath and slowly let it out before she continued. "I was eighteen and at a party. There was a lot of drinking and even a little drug activity going on. There was also this guy I really liked. Like, he was the hottest guy in the school as far as I was concerned."

"Uh-oh. This sounds like a recipe for disaster."

"Oh! It was! He actually saw me that night...or at least I thought he did." She looked down for a moment before looking up to continue. "He and I, well...yeah. Then, he invited his friends to come in and take part. I fought them as much as I could, but it didn't go well."

"Sweet Jesus!" Tori whispered as her heart broke for Talia.

"Yeah. Well, I got my revenge. I slit the cretin's throat!"

"Talia!"

"I know! But what he did to me was unspeakable! At least I thought it was, but he and his friends made sure everyone in the school knew just what kind of person I was."

"That's horrific!"

"You're telling me! So, I slit his throat. No one knew for sure that it was me, but people suspected. So, I had to get more creative for the other five."

Tori gasped. "Five?!"

"Yes. Five, well, six total. So, I researched various poisons. Some worked faster than others. I would slip it into their food when they came to torment me at the restaurant where I worked. They thought it was funny, but I got the last laugh. Watching them get sicker over the weeks, watching them see their friends die, knowing they could be next...yeah. That makes this all worth it."

"Talia!"

"Here's the thing: they knew what they did. I tried to take them to court, but it was their word against mine. Who would believe an alcoholic teenage girl who had social issues over a pack of jocks? They were the stars of the school. It didn't matter what I did; they kept at it."

Tori shook her head. "I can see why you took out vengeance. I'm not saying it's right."

"Neither am I. I'm paying for my crime. They paid for theirs. What I *am* saying is I did it. I owned it in court. They sentenced me accordingly. You won't hear that a lot in here. Most people, like you, say they are innocent. Whether they are or not is known only to them. I don't think you did either of what you're saying. Your spirit is too pure."

"Thank you. I appreciate you saying that, but –"

"But nothing! Most of the people here are dark. You are not. Anyone with a pair of eyes can see that. There's a light and peace about you."

"Sharice doesn't see it."

"Ha! Yes, she does. Why do you think she keeps giving you grief?" When Tori shrugged, Talia explained, "The brightness of your spirit invades the darkness she wants to keep around her. She sees your innocence as weakness. I see it as a strength. If you can maintain that purity for the entire year you've been here, you're stronger than any of us! When you first came, it wasn't as bright. Even though you've been withdrawn over the last few days, you're brighter. Some people will love you for it. Others will hate you for it. We all crave that light, but we all cannot find it, and some cannot handle it."

"You *can* all find it."

"How?"

Tori looked toward Heaven, praying for the right words. "The light is not my own. It's Jesus. There is no way I would have the strength to do any of this without Him."

Talia scoffed. "Great. A Jesus freak. I was hoping for something with a little more substance."

"What does that mean?"

"Jesus...the Bible...it's all past. It's all subjective," Talia said, waving her off. "It's old as dirt!"

Tori's heart skipped a beat. When Talia went to get off Tori's bed, Tori grabbed her arm. "Wait."

"What?"

"Please. Sit for a moment?" When Talia sat back down, Tori explained, "There *is* a difference. It's taken me a long time to see it, but that difference is Jesus."

"I don't –"

"Just bear with me a moment?"

She huffed, crossing her arms. "Fine!"

"Life is unpredictable. Chaos is often laced throughout all history. However, there is one constant – the message of Jesus. He came to earth with a mission. He came to show God's love to the world, ultimately through His own sacrifice. I've searched Him out. I have listened through the ages, and His message has stayed the same. Even in this dark environment," she said, gesturing around the jail, "He is still here, bringing His light to the world."

"How can you say that? This place is as dark as it gets."

"What if we could bring the light to everyone here? Then, what would happen?"

Talia raised an eyebrow. "How would that work?"

"We bring His message of love to this place, one person at a time."

"Many in here don't feel they deserve love of any kind – me included. I've killed men. Pretty sure that's a big one on that ten-commandment list."

"Here's the thing: sin, is sin, is sin. It's all sin in the eyes of God – the little and the big. He paid the penalty for all of them on that day. He died carrying all that sin into hell. However, He overcame all of it, bringing with Him the keys to eternal security in Heaven with Him. We can all live for eternity with Him in the light."

"Not gonna lie. It sounds interesting but impossible at the same time."

"I thought so, too. So, I'm going to challenge you the way Patrick challenged me. He asked me to keep an open mind. He asked me to look to see where Jesus was throughout my story. I searched Him out. I found Him. I could have just broken my word and set it aside, never thinking of it again. Patrick would have never known."

"What happened to Patrick?"

"When I went back and told him that I found Jesus thanks to him, a fight broke out. He was honestly defending my honor. I was serious when I said that. He and a relative of mine were defending me against several men. When they did, fists started flying, and then a shot rang out. To me, it happened in slow motion, but in reality, it was a matter of seconds. I remember every second of that morning. I play it in my mind over and over. Had I not been there, Patrick would not have died."

"Why *were* you there?"

"I felt that I had to tell him about me and Jesus. He needed to know I accepted Christ as my Savior."

"Wait. Savior? Savior from what?"

"From Hell. Like, literal Hell. You see, sin rules this world.

Because of that, we are born into sin. We have to make a choice to make a change. That change includes Jesus. Without Him, there is no light. Without Him, there is no hope. Without Him, I would never see Patrick again. However, with His goodness and mercy, and ultimately His sacrifice, I *know* I will see him again."

"You seem pretty sure of this."

"I am."

"I'll tell you what," Talia said, processing Tori's words, "it's lunchtime. Let's go eat lunch. Afterward, we can talk again. I'm not shutting you out. I just want you to eat. I don't want the light that is in you to go away. We need you here. Sharice even thinks so; otherwise, she wouldn't have come with me in the first place."

"What about Carla?"

"She's Sharice's lapdog. She'll do anything Sharice wants her to. Sharice protects her."

"Who protects you?"

"Hopefully, *we* can protect each other," Talia said, watching her reaction.

Tori slowly nodded. "In here, we need friends. You haven't made fun of me yet, so going to assume you're being honest. If not, I'll learn soon enough."

"You watch my back, and I'll watch yours," Talia said, putting her hand out.

"Agreed," Tori said, shaking her hand.

09AUG2022

Over the next few months, Tori and Talia talked a lot. Whenever they were together, Talia asked questions. Soon, others were joining in their meal discussions. Tori did her best to answer the questions. For the ones she could not, she wrote them down and did some research in the library.

One day while she was doing her research, a thought struck her. When she and Tripp helped load Sebastian and Heather's moving truck, Pastor mentioned meeting them down there in a few days. She looked up the Detroit Free Press, starting on August 17, 1987. She quietly read aloud to make sure she was reading it correctly, *"On the way to Phoenix, AZ from Detroit MI. Northwest Airlines flight 255 clears the runway at 8:46 PM. It tilted slightly, clipping a light pole. The damaged plane sheared the roof off a car rental building in Romulus, MI. Left a half-mile trail of bodies, charred wreckage, magazines, and trays of food along Middle Belt Road. The plane's crew failed to set the wing flaps properly for takeoff. Cockpit warning system did not alert the crew."* Good Lord, have mercy!"

The photos were horrific. Pieces and parts of luggage and airplane were strewn about the highway. She shook her head. "I cannot imagine!"

As she read the rest of the article, she got a sick feeling in her stomach. She knew her family was not on the plane. *That was already established, but what if...*

She searched until she found the list of the victims. She gasped when she reached them. Quietly reading aloud, she said, "Pastor James Phillips of First Baptist Church in downtown Detroit was on the plane with his family. His wife, Sarah, and children: John, James, jr., and Jenna all perished in the crash. Services will be held at the First Baptist Church of –"

Tori dropped her head in her hands. Her body shook as tears crawled down her cheeks. "We saved our family, but they lost theirs."

"What's going on?" Talia asked, walking up to Tori in the library. Seeing Tori crying, her face softened. She crouched next to her with her hand on Tori's back. "What happened? You're shaking."

"The pastor's wife who led me to the Lord, along with her entire family, died in a plane crash."

"Wow! I'm so sorry!" She reached up and hugged her. "Is there anything I can do?"

"No. I-it's too late. I can't believe they all died."

Talia looked at the screen. She furrowed her brow as she read the article and then the date. "Tori, this says they died in 1987. How did she lead you to the Lord if she was dead before you were born?"

Tori sniffed, wiping her nose. "They're in Heaven. They're at peace."

"Tori?"

"What? Huh?"

"They died in 1987. How is that possible?"

"If I told you, you wouldn't believe me."

"Try me. You and I have talked a lot over these last few months, but this?" She gestured toward the computer. "How is *this* possible?"

"I traveled through time."

Talia laughed. Slow at first before gaining loudness. "You've officially lost it!"

"Nope. Remember the pastor who talked to me in 1922?"

She raised an eyebrow. "In 1922?"

"Here," Tori said, typing on the computer. "Remember when I said his name was Pastor John Phillips?"

"That article said his name was James."

"No. The pastor I talked to in Charleston...the one who told me more details about Jesus, was Pastor John Phillips."

"Oh! Right!"

"*This* is Pastor John Phillips," Tori said, pointing to the article about when Pastor Phillips took over the church in Charleston in 1920.

"How is this possible? Wait. He looks like the dad in that other family."

"That was his great-grandson."

"I don't-Tori, I don't get this."

"You don't need to. Just know I feel horrible."

"Wait a minute. You said God was in control of everything, right?"

"Right."

"Well, we need to find the good that came out of that family dying."

"What do you mean?"

"You preach all the time about finding the good. Show me the good here."

Tori sighed. Then, rubbing her chin she nodded. "All right. Let's find it."

She typed away on her computer for any and all articles regarding the family. Multiple ones popped up as memorials to the family. Some were testimonials of people who came to Christ through the loss. Some were prisoners who he used to talk to in the jail who made life-changing choices for Christ after his loss.

"The good," Talia said, wiping a tear from her eye. "You were right. There is good that comes out of bad when God's hand is in it."

"Tori?" the librarian called to her.

"Yes?"

"Warden wants to see you in his office right away."

"Yes, ma'am. I gotta go," Tori said.

"See you for dinner," Talia said, standing up. She gave her a hug. "I know there was good that came out of it. I'm sorry you lost your friends. I don't completely understand how all this works, but I'm still sorry."

"Thank you, sister," Tori said and then left for the warden's office.

"As you can see, you are not at fault for the death of Christine Bell."

"Chrissy."

"What?" the warden asked.

"Chrissy. Her name was Chrissy."

"Okay. You are still not at fault for the death of Chrissy Bell. You're being released."

"When?"

"Now."

"What?" Tori sat up in shock.

"Now. You are leaving now."

"But –"

"No buts. Officer Burkes!" he shouted.

The officer who accompanied her walked into the office. "Yes, sir?"

"Ms. St. James, you are released with apologies from the State of Texas."

"I want to say goodbye," Tori protested.

"You are released," the warden said firmly. Turning to the officer, he said, "Make sure she leaves. Do not let her go back to her cell. Give her her belongings. She gets one phone call to have someone pick her up."

"Yes, sir," he said, pulling Tori up by her arm. "C'mon."

"Wait!" Tori said, trying to pull away.

"Now!" the officer said impatiently.

Despite her objections, the officer gave her the bag with her clothing and what she had on her the day she was arrested. As she got dressed, she had flashes of the day of Chrissy's death. She grabbed her head in pain.

"C'mon! Move it, or I'm sending in a female officer after you!"

"I'm coming!" Tori called back. "Mmm!" She groaned as her head pounded. "I'm coming!"

She finished getting dressed. After a few more moments, she finally got control of the flashes and was able to continue.

"You have one phone call," the officer said.

"I don't have anyone *to* call."

"So be it," the officer said and led her through the halls and checkpoints out of the jail.

She walked through the gate. It slammed behind her. Turning, she looked back to see the officer walking away. Her nightmare was over.

When she turned back around, she gasped. Tripp was leaning on a car with his arms crossed. She ran up to him and threw her arms around his neck. "Tripp! I'm so glad to see you!"

"Me too, Tori! I have a confession to make."

Tori took a step back. "What?"

"I got ahold of my great-great-great-grandfather, and told him how to find the evidence to get you out. Here," he said, handing her the TORI he took from her.

"What? I don't understand."

"You couldn't have it in jail, but you can now. You can choose to do with it what you want. However, I need to caution you not to mess with the timeline more than we did."

"I get it. Thank you for this, by the way," she said holding up the journal. "It took me awhile before I could look at it, but when I could, I was grateful for his picture. I also started journaling all of my feelings in it, along with any stories from inside. Who knows? Some day I may write a book about it."

"I'm sure it will be a best seller."

"It could be."

"Anyway, here is Private Investigator Sebastian Hayden's card. It has his address and phone number. Please reach out to him. He's invested a few months into looking into your life. He's interested in talking with you."

"What do you mean?"

"He may be looking for some help. I would recommend we visit your family first. To them, I'm just a friend. Okay?"

"Um, okay. So, I know my parents," she said, getting into the car with him. Once inside, Tripp took off. "Who is in the rest of my family?"

"Well, you have one sister and three brothers."

"Really? I remember I had siblings from the family tree, but I don't remember much."

"Your siblings are: Sebastian Fredrick, who is twenty-seven; Richard Scott, called Rick, who is twenty-five; Elizabeth Joy, or Beth, who is twenty-one; and Benjamin James, called Ben, is twenty."

"Oh boy! I'm going to need a chart!"

"No. It's okay. Just remember the order: Seb, Rick, Beth, and Ben. Seb and Rick are older than you by a year each. Then Beth and Ben are a couple years younger. Now, as far as they are concerned, you were innocent the entire time."

"Good."

"So, do you want to meet you family first, or your saving grace?"

"Saving grace?"

"The private investigator."

"Oh! Well, I have a feeling I won't be able to get out of the house if we go to the family first. What about the private investigator?"

"Sebastian Hayden."

"Right."

"Okay," Tripp said, and he turned right down a road.

T ori walked into the office with Tripp right behind her. "Hello?" she called out.

A man about Tripp's height walked in. He had medium-length wavy black hair, and dark-brown eyes. His skin was cocoa colored, almost like he had a permanent tan. To Tori, he looked exotic.

"Uh, hi. I-I mean, hey, Tripp," he said, not taking his eyes off Tori.

"Sebastian, this is my friend. She's the one you saved from

jail. She just got out and wanted to come to say thank you," Tripp said, nudging her forward a few steps.

"Hi," Tori said, her eyes locked on his as well.

Sebastian took a few steps forward so he was standing right in front of her. "Hi."

When no one said anything for a few moments, Tripp said, "Sebastian, I understand you may need some help. Since she just gotten out of jail, I'm sure she could use a job."

"Are you available?" Sebastian asked.

Tori simply nodded.

"Okay. I'm going to leave you two to it for a bit. What if I come back in about an hour to take you to your family?" Tripp asked.

Tori nodded again, still not taking her eyes off Sebastian.

"I can see I'm just in the way now," Tripp said and left.

"So, you're Tori?" Sebastian asked.

"Yes. And you're Sebastian?"

"Come. Let's sit and talk," he said, gesturing toward the couch in the reception area. "I know so much about you from the investigation that I feel like I know you. I want to hear it from you now. I want to get to know the woman behind the stories."

About an hour later, Tripp came back to find the pair still deep in discussion.

"Hi," he said, walking into the office.

"Hey," Sebastian said, still not taking his eyes off Tori. "Seems I have a new hire."

"Yep," Tori said with a smile as she tucked a portion of her hair behind her ear.

"Want to go see the rest of your family?" Tripp asked Tori.

"I do, but..." her voice faded.

"That requires you to get up from the couch," Tripp hinted.

"What if I come with you?" Sebastian asked. "You know, since I came up with the evidence and all?"

Tori grinned. "I think that's a *great* idea!"

With that, they left in Sebastian's car for her parents' house. When they arrived, only her parents and two younger siblings were there, but the reception Tori received was something she was not expecting. Growing up, her parents were not affectionate at all. When she got there, she was given hugs and kisses. At first, Tori was taken aback, but then she soaked it all in. It was the loving family she always wanted!

After everyone got over the shock of seeing her standing there, they called her brothers, who came over about an hour later.

They ordered pizza and talked way into the night. Tori soaked in the stories her siblings and parents told. She memorized each one of them. She knew she would journal everything she learned that night. She wanted to remember it all.

14SEP2022 (AM): Put-In-Bay

Tori worked with Sebastian. She gave him all of her time. She only asked for one day off.

On September 14th, she went to Put-In-Bay. She got on the ferry in Port Clinton, Ohio with butterflies in her stomach. The last time she saw the island was the day Patrick died.

The ferry took ten minutes before it pulled up to the island. As the ferry neared the island the three-hundred-and-fifty-two-foot Greek column stood out to her. She gasped. *That was where the willow tree once stood. Patrick!*

Getting off the ferry, she made a beeline for the monument.

She walked up the path toward the massive structure in awe. "No more willow tree," she said aloud to herself.

As she stood in front of it, she read the plaque. It said, *'This single column commemorates the end of a battle and the heralding of a lasting era of peace between Canada and the United States – two neighbors dedicated to brotherhood and progress within the family of free nations throughout the world. It provides lasting testimony that our common values of freedom and diversity can be attained and strengthened through mutual respect and regard." – John F. Kennedy, White House, 1963.'*

Looking toward the top of the monument, she shielded her eyes from the sun. She stepped onto the concrete and made her way to the top of the monument. "I am the only one alive who knows you are below my feet," Tori said quietly to herself as she made her way to the elevator to ride to the top.

When she reached the top, she was blown away! From the top of the monument, she could see the entire island chain. She could actually see portions of Canada, Michigan, and Ohio. She took a few photos with her phone camera, but it did not do the spectacular view justice. "Next time I'm bringing my good camera," she whispered. "This is amazing!"

Afterward, she headed back down. She did not want to visit the attractions. She *lived* the battle! Maybe someday she would venture onto the mini-golf course where people could get history lessons along the way, or *Perry's Cave*, but not today. Today was about remembering Patrick.

She pulled the rose from her bag and hid it at the base of one of the trees around the monument. "This is the best I can do for now," she said and walked away, back to wait for the ferry.

As she walked away, a man stood in the distance. He squinted to see better. Looking at the back of the journal, he then looked back up at the woman in shock. She was a dead ringer for the woman in the drawing!

Before he could get to her, the ferry pulled away from the dock. He would return every day in hopes of seeing her again.

Tori's life was finally working out! On New Year's Eve, she and Sebastian were at a beach for the weekend. They got there on Friday. They wanted to already be in Florida for New Year's Eve on Saturday. Saturday night, they went to the beach around eleven, so they would have their spot reserved long before midnight.

Their blanket was laid out about five miles down the beach from where the fireworks would go off. Tori loved it, because there was hardly anyone else where they were. She felt like it was *their* beach.

She soaked in the slight breeze coming off the ocean, and the roar of the ocean. They were a good twenty feet from where the waves stopped, so there was no chance of the waves hitting their spot. She had a true sense of utter freedom.

There were lights from the hotels and condos up and down the beach, but their main source of light was granted to them by the bright moon that hung above. With the mist from the ocean, the brightness of the moon, and the clouds that tried to obscure the moon, the rays of moonlight were nothing short of spectacular.

She closed her eyes and inhaled the scents from around them. She picked up the faint hydrogen sulfide from the sea weed and odor other various saltwater sea creatures. The breeze blowing through the grass and inkberry plants brought an earthy scent to the mix. As the wind rushed past Sebastian, she caught his cologne, and it stirred her insides. "Smells wonderful, and the waves are absolutely peaceful."

"Agreed."

While they sat on the blanket, Sebastian poured them champagne to get ready to bring in the New Year together. Tori wrapped her arms around her legs, watching down the shoreline to where the fireworks were supposed to be in a little while.

Sebastian scooted next to Tori with the glasses in his hands. He handed her one. She absentmindedly held the glass in her fingers while still keeping an eye in the distance.

"Tori?"

"Hm? Yeah?" she asked, turning toward him.

"You are an incredible woman. I feel so honored to have you in my life. The idea that you could still be sitting in prison blows my mind."

"Mine too. I actually made friends in there. I know it sounds weird but true. Talia probably saved my life."

"From what you've told me, they may have saved your life, but you saved their souls by introducing them to Jesus."

"True." She nodded. "I didn't even want to live at one point. I was ready to check out."

"I'm glad you didn't. I'm also grateful to Tripp for bringing me into your case to get you out."

"Me too! I cannot thank you enough for that."

"I cannot thank him enough for bringing you into my life. I'm sorry he had to leave so quickly afterward, but I'm grateful for the time he gave to bring you to me."

She looked over at him and smiled. "Me too."

Just then, they could hear the people shouting a countdown in the distance. "10, 9..."

"Tori, I love you," Sebastian said.

"I love you, too."

"...5, 4..."

"Will you make me the happiest man alive and marry me?"

Sebastian asked, producing a ring in a small box from behind his back.

"...I!"

"Yes!" Tori said as the fireworks went off in the distance.

Sebastian slid the ring, which fit perfectly, onto her ring finger. Then he looked up at her, wiped the tears off her face, and kissed her.

Tori's body exploded in electricity. The romance of the moment and the fireworks in the distance were only topped by the love she felt for Sebastian.

CHAPTER NINETEEN

2023: He Made Everything Beautiful In Its Time

The lives she lived all seemed so long ago. Tori and Sebastian got married on Valentine's Day that year. It was one of the happiest days of her life up to that point! The day was absolutely perfect! They got married on the beach in Florida – a destination wedding. Her siblings were at the wedding, as were his two sisters and brother.

The only thing missing was that Tripp was not there. He popped in one night a few days before the wedding while she was asleep in her apartment. He scared her and nearly gave her a heart attack!

"What is wrong with you?" Tori snapped, her hand to her chest while she tried to catch her breath. "Don't you believe in normal times?"

"I'm sorry. I just wanted to tell you congratulations. I know you're getting married in a few days. I cannot be there. Try to come up with some excuse for me?" He asked, pulling over the chair at her desk to the bed.

"Already taken care of. I told him you were on a trip to Europe that you had planned for years. He tried to convince me to change the date, but I wanted to keep it on Valentine's Day.

So, to *what* do I owe this pleasure?" she asked, sitting cross-legged on her bed.

He rubbed the back of his neck as he let out a slow breath of air.

Tori raised an eyebrow. "It's that bad?"

"I need you to know something."

"What?"

"Everything is still on target."

"That's a good thing...right?"

"Yes."

"Then why am I waiting for the other shoe to drop?"

"You're not...yet. I'll be back on the 20th of June. Okay?"

"Okay," she said, uneasy.

"Just remember that. It's important for you to remember that I will find you on June 20th. Understand?"

"Sure. Can I know why?"

"Not yet. In the meantime, I want you to enjoy everything this life is giving you. You are getting married to an incredible man who loves you, and you will get pregnant with my great-great-grandfather pretty soon afterward. So, have fun!"

Her face flushed bright red.

"Oh, come on! It's not like I don't know where I came from," Tripp said amongst his laughter.

"I know, but..."

"It's okay. I know where I came from. I'll still be born. You two are getting married in a few days, and the timeline will continue to stay on track. He'll just be born a few years before he was supposed to from the other timeline. That leaves you more time to have more kids."

"Oh. Okay." She nodded. "Why do I feel like there's something you're not telling me?"

"There is. I'll tell you on June 20th." He turned the chair around to lean on the back with his arms crossed. "Now, I want to know the details of the engagement! Don't spare a thing!"

Tori giggled. "I feel like I'm talking to my best friend."

"Hey! We literally went through time together. I consider you a good friend. Quite honestly, probably my best friend. You put up with some of my vague details, and we still ended up fixing everything."

"We did it together," Tori pointed out. "And, I wouldn't want to have done it with anyone else."

"Agreed!"

The wedding was a day Tori would always remember. They got married just as the sun was setting, creating spectacular photos to commemorate the event.

However, that event was quickly topped when Tori found out she was pregnant on April 15th! She went to the doctor because she thought she had the flu. When the doctor told her she was pregnant, she just about passed out. She was around two weeks pregnant by that point. Tori found it amusing that her target date of getting pregnant was April 1st.

When she told Sebastian and the family, cheers could be heard around the world! Tori was the first of her siblings to get married and pregnant. She would have the first of the next generation. She already knew what his name would be: Sebastian Connor Hayden, the third. She would nickname him *Tripp*.

Tori was in the office on June 19th doing billing when two police officers walked in with her brother, Seb. "Hey, Seb, guys. What's going on?" Tori asked.

Seb did not say a word. He simply went around the desk and wrapped his arms around Tori from behind in a hug. "I love you, sis."

Tori's heart raced. "Why are they here?" she asked, fearing they had come to take her back to jail.

"Ma'am, this is one of those things we do not like to do, but it is a necessary portion of our job as servants of the community," Officer Williams (according to his nametag) said. "At ten-thirty this morning in Grace Dunne Richardson Park, there was a shooting involving Addison Grayson and Sebastian Hayden."

Tori gasped, grabbing Seb's arms.

"I'm here," Seb whispered. "You are not alone. I'm here."

Tori nodded as tears formed in her eyes. Her body shook. She tried to catch her breath, but it was not easy.

"In...and out. C'mon, sis. In...and out," Seb coaxed. "I'm here."

"Ma'am," Officer Williams started. He and the other officer both took off their hats. "I regret to inform you that Sebastian Hayden was killed this morning due to the shooting. Addison Grayson has been arrested for his murder."

Tori gulped, her mind reeling.

"Ma'am," the other officer, Officer Marshall, said, "there were multiple witnesses who stated your husband was not at fault and that Addison Grayson shot him. There is no way he is getting away with this."

"You-you can't promise that," Tori stammered.

"Yes. We can," Officer Williams said. "He was like one of us. Sebastian helped us out on multiple cases. We owe him this. Everything was by the book. There is no doubt in the prosecutor's mind. We've already talked to him. He's going after Addison with everything he can."

Tori nodded.

"Are you okay?" Seb asked.

Tori shook her head.

"Do you guys mind if I take her to my parents' house?" Seb asked the officers.

"Of course. I'm sure there will be questions as to what he was doing there," Officer Marshall said. "We'll look for her there."

"Ma'am, we will need you to come down to the morgue in the next few hours to identify the body," Officer Williams explained. "We don't mean to traumatize you further, but we need to follow procedure."

"Rick and I will make sure to be with her," Seb assured them.

Just then, Tori remembered Tripp's words, *I'll be back on the 20th of June.*

She glanced at the desktop calendar. It was the 19th of June. She felt her worlds collide – time traveling and her new life. She threw her hand over her mouth and ran for the bathroom. She barely made it in time before she threw up her breakfast.

"Tori!" Seb said, running in after her. He crouched behind her, resting his hands on her shoulders. "Calm down. You need to stay calm for the baby."

"I-I know," she groaned, resting her head on her arm on the toilet seat. "This baby has to live."

"It's a piece of Sebastian that will live on."

"...In his son," Tori finished.

"How do you know it's a boy? It's too soon to tell."

"It's a boy," she said. "And," she pushed herself up off the ground, with a little help from Seb, "he *has* to be born. Please take me back to my house...our house. I want to sleep in our bed. I want to smell his scent on his pillow. It won't be real if I don't go home and see it for myself."

"Tori, I can't." He shook his head. "That's not a good situation to leave you in."

"I will be fine," she said, brushing her pants off from sitting on the ground.

"Let one of us stay with you."

"No. I need to do this myself."

"Fine. Then Rick and I will be in a car outside in case you need us."

"You don't need to do that."

"You can't stop us."

Tori rolled her eyes as she crossed her arms. "You guys can sleep in the house."

"Knew you would see it my way."

"Okay. Take me home, and then get Rick."

"You're in my charge at the moment. We're going to get Rick, come back for your car, and then go home."

Tori shook her head as she wiped the tears from her eyes. "I can't believe he's gone. I feel numb. I feel like this is some weird event that isn't real. We should probably go to the morgue and get it over with. I need to see him for myself."

"Are you sure?"

"If I don't, then I'll just convince myself he's on a stakeout. I need to see him. I need to see what that man did to my husband, to my love, my heart. Then, I need to go home...to our room. If I don't see it all for myself, it won't be real."

"Okay. Let's go, sis," he agreed. Putting his arm over her shoulder, they left the office.

That night, most of her family stayed in the house with her. She refused to have any of them sleep in the room with her, but she let them sleep in the other rooms and on the couches in the house.

When she went to sleep, she remembered Tripp's words again, *"I'll be back on the 20th of June."*

"Tori," Tripp gently shook her. "Tori!"

"Wha-shhh! My family is here," she hissed.

He looked around to listen and see if anyone heard them. Not hearing a sound, he sat on the side of the bed. "Sorry," he whispered.

"While I know part of that is for the noise you made, I also know you well enough to know that *you* know what happened yesterday," Tori said quietly.

"I do."

"This *is* a boy. Right?" she asked, resting her hand on her stomach.

"It is. And, yes, you name him after my great-great-great-grandfather. He's born a little early on Christmas Eve."

"What triggered that?"

"It seems you have all your little ones a bit early," he pointed out.

"So, he'll be okay?"

"More than okay. The doctor actually thinks he may have gotten the date wrong. He's only a few days early when the doctor readjusts the date."

"I see," Tori said, rubbing her stomach.

"Tori," he rested his hand on her shin, "I'm sorry. I didn't wish this on you, but I knew it was coming."

"I don't understand why you didn't tell me?" Tori asked. "I could have gotten us out of town or something. We could have stopped it."

"We've changed enough of the timeline already. Trust me. This needed to happen. You know that theory of yours when you say that God makes all things work together for good?"

"Yes," she groaned, knowing her words were coming back to haunt her.

"Trust me when I say that your journey is far from over. Just keep your chin up. Mourn your husband, but keep it in balance so your baby lives."

"I know. My family makes sure I eat and drink. My brothers took me to my doctor today to make sure I was okay. He told me to try to get some rest and drink plenty of water to prevent early contractions."

"Have you had any?"

"I had one in the doctor's office. That's why he was concerned. My family have his personal cell phone in theirs. He told them to call if they need him."

"Good. Sounds like you're in good hands here."

Tori looked down for a moment, rubbing circles around her stomach. With tears in her eyes, she asked Tripp, "Why do I keep falling in love with men who die on me? How can I possibly ever fall in love with another man again without feeling like he'll die on me?"

"Look, Patrick was out of your time. There was no way that was going to work. I know it broke your heart, but you have to know deep down he was only going to be in your life for a season."

"I do. It still hurts, but I do."

"As for Sebastian, he was meant to die in any timeline. He was never to know what his child looked like. Only in this timeline, *you* weren't the one to kill him."

"I couldn't!"

"I know. I also know it's heartbreaking to know you are going through this yet again, and there is still not a thing I can do about it. As much as I want to go back and change things, we cannot."

"Why not?" Tori asked. "Isn't that why we have the TORIs?"

"No."

"No? Why not?" Tori crossed her arms. "Isn't that what we have them for? To change time?"

"No. We had them to correct it. We *did* correct it."

"Then, why do I still have it?"

"We'll talk about that on another day. Today, we will mourn your husband together."

She looked over at his pillow and ran her hand over it. "I can't believe he's gone. It doesn't seem real. I feel like I'm in a fog. I feel like things are not real. I feel like with all the time traveling we have done that there *has* to be something we can do." She looked up at him. "If it were *your* wife, what would you do?"

"It's not. It's your husband. However, I *do* know our family's history. I need you to hold on and focus on the little one inside you."

"Why can't we change this?"

"There is something better coming. Trust me. When things get dark, and they will, I want you to remember this phrase, *'He made everything beautiful in its time.'* It's important that you remember that phrase."

"Why?"

"That phrase will carry you on days you don't want to go on. You still have to face making arrangements for his burial. You still have to face his actual funeral. You still have to face packing up his belongings while getting ready to bring his child into this world. You have many choices to make – including whether or not to continue the investigation business. When things pile up and you feel like you're drowning, remember, *He made everything beautiful in its time*. That phrase will save your sanity. It has also saved the sanity of many in our family, even through to my generation."

"That is a verse," Tori said. "How can you hold onto a verse when you are not a Christian?"

"Who says I'm not?"

Tori's eyebrows raised in surprise. "Are you?"

"This is a gift we will give our ancestors at a later date, but yes. I accepted Jesus as my Savior when I got back. Everyone in my family is Christian. When I got back, they talked to me. What they said matched exactly what you said. I know Jesus is real. I know God is real. I know the Holy Spirit is real. I know this world is so much bigger than any of us ever imagined! We have only scratched the surface in traveling the way we did. You and I both know we still have one more trip as well," he said with a wink. "However, to God, it has all happened in the blink of an eye. He sees it all. He knows everything that will happen. He has plans that we are to follow."

Tori processed his words. "So," she looked up at him, "this is something I have to go through?"

"Unfortunately, you do. You will be stronger for it. You will be an incredible mom! You are bringing in the first of the next generation, and you will do a spectacular job.”

“I can do that and still mourn for both Patrick and Sebastian?”

“Yes. You will even fall in love again. I won’t tell you when, or that may ruin the magic. Just know this is not how your story ends. You are not destined to become a black widow of some kind. Love is still in your future, as well as more children.”

“So, what we saw on the family tree still happens?”

“It does. Just not in the way you think. You will make it through. Trust me. Trust God.”

“I will,” Tori assured him.

“Stay focused on God. You will cry. Your heart will shatter over and over again. You will go through pain and agony. You think you will drown, but stay focused on God during the storms life will send you through.”

“How? How do I do that?”

“You found the light in that jail.”

“According to Talia, I *was* the light.”

“The light came from Jesus. And He’s still here. Even though your heart is shattered into a million pieces, He is still here. He was with you when you found Chrissy so long ago. He was with you on the day Patrick was shot. He was with you when you found yourself in jail once again, trusting in Him. He was even with you on the day you got out and the day you met your husband. He was there on the day you got engaged, and He knew when you got pregnant. He will be there with you on the day you bury your husband and on the day you have his son. He always was, is, and always will be. He is here, Tori. He will never leave you. Trust Him.”

Tori wiped a few tears from her face, as she asked, “How?”

“Imagine God is like a lighthouse. The storm is raging all around you like you’ve never seen before. You are worried about getting back to shore safely. The rain is pelting you from every direction, and you don't know where to turn. Then you see the light from the lighthouse. You turn the boat toward the lighthouse, focused on the light. Despite the rain, wind, and waves that threaten to kick you out of the boat, you still focus on the light. As you near the shore, the light shows you the dangers of the shoreline. You are able to get your boat back to the shore safely. But you're still in the storm. So, you look up at the lighthouse and start climbing the rocks. They're slick from years of being beaten by the water. However, you stay focused on that light. You slip a couple times, sometimes falling a few feet, but you keep your focus on the lighthouse. You finally climb over the edge, and the lighthouse is only several yards away. The light is lighting up the entire area. You are exhausted, but you stay focused on the lighthouse. Finally, you make it. You knock on the door. Jesus answers the door with a blanket in His arms to wrap around you. He saw you coming. He knew what you would need when you got there. He sits you in front of the woodstove, which is kicking off some serious heat to warm you to your bones. He brings you a cup of hot cocoa with marshmallows."

Tori smiled.

"He knows what you want and need. He knows you are in the storms. All you have to do is focus on the lighthouse. Stay focused on that light. Even though those storms are still raging around you, you are in the safety of the lighthouse. Let Jesus keep your heart and mind safe."

"Thank you," Tori said and gave Tripp a hug. "Thank you."

"You have gone through a lot in your young life. You're not done yet. Each day brings new things. You have to make a choice about how to respond to each situation. Leave both Patrick and Sebastian a place in your heart. Your heart is big enough to hold them. It's also big enough for more. Trust me on this."

Tori nodded.

"Mourn your husband. Bury your husband. Get ready for his son to join the world, knowing *you* will get to raise him. Leave your heart open to love. Let your son feel that love, so he can pass it on to the next generation. It will not do him any good for you to turn your heart to stone. Keep it open."

"I will," Tori promised.

"Know you are loved, and remember, *'He made everything beautiful in its time.'* It will carry you through a lot!"

"I will. I'll write it down in my journal today."

Tripp got up and got her journal from the desk, along with a pen. "Write it now. You *need* to remember those words."

"Yes, sir," Tori said and wrote it down.

"Good. Now, I need to go. Know I will see you at a later date. We still have a date in 1650 Ireland."

"How do you know the date?" Tori asked.

Tripp wiggled his eyebrows. "The journal of Fredrick's that Maggie had is still in the archives. It seems Christmas was supposedly canceled during that time. We are going to bring them Christmas."

"So, it was the Christmas that almost wasn't?"

"That sounds accurate. That is until we got there."

"Awesome," Tori said with a smile.

"Finally! A smile," Tripp said. "I missed that. Listen, things will get darker before you see the light. Seek the lighthouse, and the Lighthouse Keeper, Jesus."

"I will. I promise."

"Good. We've pushed our luck for now. I've gotta go. Know I will always love you and will see you in the future. We still have one more mission, but I need you in a better headspace to do it."

"Love you, too," Tori said. "I have my words to look at when I can't see straight."

"You got this," Tripp said and gave her a hug. "Take care of my great-great-grandfather."

"I will." Tori shook her head. "This is so messed up!"

They both snickered as Tripp input the date, time, and place into his TORI. "Love you."

"I love you, too!" Tori said, and he shimmered away.

Tori tucked herself under the covers, her mind racing. There was so much in such a short conversation. She understood what was coming. She knew there was a lot she would have to take care of. She sat up and made lists all night so she would not forget, including a trip to Put-In-Bay in September.

22JUN2023

On June 22nd, Tori said goodbye to her husband. The funeral was brutal. She cried for hours. During the time of making arrangements and the funeral itself, she clung to her journal. They carried the words she needed to stay focused on as much for herself as for her baby. On the inside of the front cover, Tori had written, 'He made everything beautiful in its time.' Tripp was correct that those words carried her through her darkest days. That included today.

"He was a savior to many," the pastor continued. He had been talking for thirty minutes by that point. "Including to his wife. Their story is one of triumph and now tragedy. When I married them, I asked them a question. I asked them what would happen if one of them were to pass before the others. Tori's response was that she had the heartfelt knowledge that she would see Sebastian in Heaven, and that she would rest in that comfort. Sebastian's response was similar, but added that his heart would be shattered. For this couple, it was love at first sight. It was a whirlwind romance that matched them together perfectly. God had a plan. He needed them both to be at a certain point in their lives before He brought them together. Even now, Sebastian is sitting there, probably talking to Jesus about Tori. I'm sure, knowing him, that Sebastian already has plans lined up for her. Folks, we never know what tomorrow will bring. I know most of you here, so I can say with confidence that while we may not know what the future holds, we certainly know Who holds the future! I invite anyone who wishes to share a story or two to come forward. Afterward, I will close us in prayer. Then, all who want to join us in the celebration of the life of Sebastian Hayden, are welcome to come over to the church. We'll meet in the reception hall."

Tori's brother, Rick, got up to speak. "Sebastian came into our lives when we needed him the most. Many of you know Tori's story. You know she was accused of killing her best friend. We all knew she was innocent, but we did not have the proof. It was one of those situations where she was guilty until proven innocent. When Tori's friend Tripp went to Sebastian with her story, along with the beginnings of a case for her innocence, Sebastian attacked her case with a vengeance. He thought it was unjust what happened to her, and he was going to prove it. And prove it he did! He got her released in a matter of months. Tripp and Sebastian are two people we cannot thank enough for saving our sister. We gained another brother from the venture in Sebastian. When he joined the family, there was no shortness of laughter and fun. He could be a prankster when he wanted," he said to several snickers. "Yet, he would turn around and listen to someone who needed him. He would give anything to make sure justice was served. He often helped the police by going where they could not. He often took on cases that people thought were unwinnable and came out on top. He was one in a million...and he will be missed," Rick said, and then sat down.

Seb got up after him. "I wholeheartedly agree with Rick. The family met Seb after Tripp contacted him, but I knew him in college. You see, part of what made him an excellent private detective was that he knew exactly what to look for. He went to school for criminal law. He actually had a law degree – even passed the boards. His struggle came in to play when he saw things he could not use to prove innocence or guilt, because they would not be able to be inadmissible in court. Being a lawyer myself, I have to agree with his frustration. So, we got together and tried to figure out what could be done. His private investigative service idea took shape. I'm not the only one grateful for his services. While most private investigators are looking for cheating spouses, he was working with lawyers and the police department. His heart propelled him to go deeper than the norm. He was certain if they were innocent, the evidence would tell the story. Making sure true justice was served were his passion and heart. I know me and my family are grateful for the direction he chose in life."

When Rick sat down, Beth grabbed Tori's hand, and whispered, "If you want to go up, I will stand beside you and hold your hand."

"Thank you," Tori said, and stood, not letting Beth's hand go. Together, they went up front with Tori still clutching the journal. It was the journal Tripp gave her in jail that he got from 1813. It also contained the words Tripp had her write down on the front cover.

She could not stop the tears from flowing, but she would be strong and do this for him. She could not say any final words over Patrick's grave, however she could for Sebastian. Setting the journal down on the podium, she opened the cover to see the words, *'He made everything beautiful in its time.'* She nervously cleared her throat. Wiping the tears off her face, she started, "Sebastian was a lover, a fighter, a warrior, and my true love. Sometimes we are blessed to find this in life. I found it twice. With Sebastian's love and zest for life, he breathed into a portion of my heart I thought was dead. He showed me that life is worth living, one spectacular day at a time. We traveled. We worked together. We were so close, Mom even said we had our own language," she said with a nervous chuckle. "He was the one who finally found the evidence needed to release me. He saved more than my life that day, though. He saved my heart. God has my soul, but Sebastian had my heart. I have the utmost confidence that when he passed, he made sure God gave his heart to the little one growing inside me right now. It brings me joy to know his heart will live on in him." She rested her hand on her stomach. "While I cannot bring him back, I do know others will make sure this little one knows about his dad. Sebastian was taken too soon. He was taken in an incident where he was utilizing that passion Seb talked about earlier. He was helping someone, and then everything went wrong. Many will miss his smiling face, his infectious laughter, his massive heart, and the light in his soul that lit up every room he walked into. To you, Sebastian was a friend, a savior, a neighbor, a fellow church family member, but to me he was my life. If you have any funny stories about him, please share. He wouldn't want all of this crying going on during a celebration of his life. Here. I'll start. He *was* a prankster. He knows just how much snakes terrify me. In the morning hours of April Fool's Day, and yes, I should have known," she said, and a few more snickers were heard, "I got up to get him breakfast. When I went into the kitchen, he had already placed one of those spiders that have motion sensors on the floor. I saw it scurry across the floor and just about had heart failure. He came running in. He was laughing, but trying to comfort me. Of course, I slapped his arm. My adrenaline was on over drive. Once he got me calmed down, he went to the living room with his cup of coffee. I got into the fridge to make scrambled eggs. As I pulled out the egg container, I dropped it on the floor and screamed. He had placed a rubber snake in the egg container." Some people groaned; others laughed. "After I literally punched his arm for that one, he hugged me, but I was not having it. To make it up to me, he took me on a beautiful day away from the world and any further pranks. So, you see, while he was mischievous, he was also tenderhearted. And I cannot thank God enough for bringing that man into my life!"

With that, she and Beth sat down, still holding hands. One after another got up to talk about funny stories regarding Sebastian. Most were hysterical, but others had the same twist Tori's did, solidifying her perception of his fully balanced life – in both his professional and personal. She cherished each memory shared, and that night, she wrote each one down in her journal so she would never forget.

As she wrote down the memories, she cried. Her journal was becoming more of a safety blanket these days. During the time of making arrangements and the funeral itself, she clung to her journal. They carried the words she needed to stay focused on as much for herself as for her baby. On the inside of the front cover, Tori had written, *'He made everything beautiful in its time.'* Tripp was correct that those words carried her through her darkest days. That included today.

14SEP2023

Tori made her way to Port Clinton the previous night. She lay in her bed all night deep in thought. Now five months pregnant, it was obvious she was pregnant. She got to see little Sebastian about a week ago, and it was confirmed he was a boy. She did not need a machine to tell her what she already knew, but it was a nice confirmation.

She got out of bed, packed up her room, and took her luggage to the car. Then she drove to the dock and got on the first ferry of the day. Seeing the memorial in the distance, she held her journal with a rose inside to her chest. She would keep her promise to honor both Patrick and Sebastian.

She did not know if Patrick's family really knew where he was buried, but she did. She would mark off September 14th and June 22nd every year to mourn the loss of two incredible men. These men showed her love, even when she did not feel that she deserved it. Both saw something in her. They believed in her. They both cherished her heart and had faith in her, bringing out a love she never knew. For that, she would never be able to thank them enough. Patrick gave her spirit freedom in Jesus, and Sebastian gave her freedom from jail and a son.

Walking up the sidewalk toward the monument, she could not help the tears that slowly trickled down her cheeks. She was alone but she was not. She had a baby growing inside her who would bring light into her life. The Spirit was with her, providing light from inside her heart. Jesus walked beside her every day. And the Lord God watched over her every step.

Reaching the monument early, there was no one else in the area. She read the inscription again. Afterward, she went over to the tree where she had left a rose the previous year.

Gently finagling her way to the ground, she set the flower down at the base of the tree. "There's no marker to mark your body, but I know. This monument is a symbol used to unite us, but it also contains the remains of six officers, and a man who had the heart of a warrior and the soul of a healer. Patrick, you will always be missed by me. The name for this first one is already claimed by history, after the wonderful man who gave him to me. But the next male I have will bear your name – the name of the man who gave me Jesus."

"What are you doing?"

Tori heard a voice behind her and jumped. She gulped. Not turning around, she said, "I-I'm leaving this here in memoriam."

"The anniversary is on September 10th. Why are you here today? You're four days late."

"Listen. This is a pub –" Tori stopped as she turned and stared...*into the eyes of Patrick*!

She gulped. Standing, she used the tree to brace herself. "W-who...how?"

The man crossed his arms. A journal hung from his fingers. "Who are you?"

"I-who are you?"

"I asked you first."

She gulped again, struggling to slow her heart that was racing beyond control. "I-I'm Tori."

"Tori...*who?*

"Tori Hayden."

He opened the journal and flipped to the back. Showing her the drawing, he said, "According to this, you are Tori St. Claire. How is this possible?"

Tori dropped her journal and snatched his before he had a chance to react. "How do you have this?" she demanded. Seeing Patrick's handwriting at the beginning of the journal, and the dates from 1813, the color drained from her face. "How is this possible?"

"That's what *I* want to know."

"Who *are* you?" Tori asked, narrowing her eyes.

"I'm Liam."

"Liam...*who?*"

"Liam St. James. Why?"

Tori flipped to the back of the journal and looked at the drawings of both she and Tripp. "How do you have this?"

"It's from one of my ancestors."

"Explain!" she pushed. "You look like Patrick. You even look the same age. But you're not him. Explain this to me!" She showed him the pictures in the journal. "How do you have these?"

"What? Do you want my family history?"

"Yes."

"You cannot be serious. Give me my family's journal back."

"Tell me!" Tori pressed.

Liam crossed his arms. "Feisty little thing, aren't you?"

"Being little is something I have *never* been accused of."

"Well, you're tall, but you're shorter than me."

He was right. He looked to be at least several inches taller than she. Her guess was around six-foot-three or four. He had Patrick's blond hair and blue eyes. He may have been taller than Patrick was, but he was still the spitting image of him.

"Whose journal is this?" Tori asked.

Liam let out a frustrated sigh. "If I tell you, can I have it back?"

"Yes."

"Fine. Let's go sit on the bench over there. Nothing personal, but you look like you're pregnant, and you also look like you're going to pass out."

She let him usher her to the bench. He went back and got her journal. "For collateral, in case you don't give me mine back," he said with a smirk.

He was cute; she would give him that, so she let him keep her journal. "Now. That's my family's journal," he started. "Through the years, it's been passed down to a member of the family to keep the tradition of honoring a relative who is buried here."

"Who is buried here?"

"His name was Patrick Shawn St. James. He was from my family. He didn't die in the Battle of Lake Erie but a few days afterward. The story goes that he stopped a fight, and was shot doing it. There was a man. Here, let me see that a minute," he asked, handing her the journal while he had his hand out for his. When she traded, he skimmed through the pages until he found the name. "Here. There was a man named Fred Collins. After the war, he brought this journal to my family, along with a story."

"What was the story?"

"He said that one night, there was a woman, this woman," he said, pointing toward the drawing of Tori. "You see, she and her brother, this man," he said, pointing toward Tripp, "came to the island the day before the battle. The brother was placed under Fred's care, and the woman did the cooking and helped my relative, Patrick, with the medical during the battle. The following early morning after the battle, they both disappeared. Patrick asked Fred to draw them, so he could remember them. You see, Patrick loved this woman. In his journal, he talks about how much she opened his heart. She had something in her he clung onto. Then, a few days later, on the 14th, she came back. He said their love brought her back to him. Unfortunately, things got out of hand quickly once people realized she was there. They said things about her that angered both Patrick and Fred, and a fight broke out over her honor."

Tears formed in Tori's eyes as she remembered every detail of that night so long ago. To her, it only felt like a year or so. In reality, it was over two hundred years ago.

"Long story short, someone pulled out a gun and fired. They meant to fire into the air, but the bullet went into Patrick. He died in her arms. It's a love story that's been passed down to each generation, along with this journal. He told the family that the men buried there were six officers," he said, pointing toward the monument. "When Patrick died, they placed him in a place of honor for the lives he saved during the battle. Unfortunately, with them being officers, it was against the norm, and they couldn't mark his grave, but he felt the family had a right to know. He also wrote the story so every generation would know. Since that day, every September 14th, the family member with the journal comes here to honor his memory. Now, last year, I saw you, and I saw this picture. I've been here every day for a year, keeping an eye out for you. I find it unique that you were here last year on the 14th of September, leaving a rose, and again this year on September 14th leaving a rose. I've shared my story. Now tell me yours."

Tori took a deep breath, and then slowly let the air out. "You may not believe me."

"You could tell me you time traveled and I would believe you," he said on a chuckle.

She stared at him.

He furrowed his brow. "No. Really. How are you in this? Did you have a relative then, too?"

"Not exactly. Well, sort of yes, I did, and sort of not."

"Explain, please?"

That," she said, pointing toward her own picture, "is me. That," she pointed toward the picture of Tripp, "is my relative."

He narrowed his eyes at her. "I don't...I tell you the truth, and you give me a line of crap."

"That *is* me. And *that is* my great-great-great-grandson, Tripp. We told people we were brother and sister because it was easier. We also used his last name of St. Claire because it was easier. My real last name at the time was St. James."

"Stop it."

"It's true."

"You are *so* full of it!"

"Let me guess what this journal says about me. If I'm right, you can shove that attitude where the sun don't shine. If I'm wrong, you can call me a liar."

Liam rubbed his chin a moment before he finally nodded. "Okay, tell me something I haven't told you that's in here?"

"Early in the morning after the Battle of Lake Erie, when we were sitting on the rock next to the shore, he told me about Jesus. He asked me to keep an open mind and to look for Jesus. He took time after a bloody battle to share Christ with me. That man changed my life forever. *That* is the reason why I went back on the morning of the 14th. I knew he was going to die that day, and I wanted him to know the impact he had on me. How was I supposed to know that my returning is what caused his death?"

"The predestination paradox," Liam said with a nod.

"The what?"

"It's where the person traveling back in time becomes a part of past events, to the point that they may actually cause the event they were trying to stop. In this case, you knew he was supposed to die, so you went back in time to stop it, or at least let him know your decision so he knows before he dies, and therefore you caused the incident."

"That makes sense. So, do you believe me?"

"I've had this journal for five years. I got it when I turned twenty-one. This is my fourth year coming here. I am a history teacher and have what some people would call a history fetish. It fascinates me beyond imagination. If I ever had the chance to go back in time, I would do it in a heartbeat! I have memorized this journal forward and backward. While he cared for those still healing from the war, still losing one or two after, he took time to pour out his heart. It struck me how much he loved a woman he only knew for about twenty-four hours. However, if you *are* the same woman, I can now see how he felt that way. You are opinionated, stubborn, feisty, and the spitting image of this woman. It looks like you are beautiful in any time period."

"I *am* that woman."

"I know. You were right in what he wrote about you."

"He actually asked to court me that night."

"I know," he said, holding up the journal. "No one but those who have had the journal know that. Only those who have had the journal know he told you about Jesus. Only the woman and those who buried him know where he was buried. You did. You knew the date and place."

"I do," she said, looking toward the monument. At first, it was a willow tree," she said, lost in her thoughts.

"How did you know?" he breathed out.

"I was there. It was a weeping willow. That irony of placing their bodies there was not lost on me. The six officers – three from their side, three from ours – were buried there. Our medical tent was set up near the willow tree. The blood and gore were –" She shuddered. Closing her eyes for a moment, she pushed the memory away. "That night, the night he died, there was a lot less blood than I thought there should be. He was shot in the chest. It didn't take him long to die. He was..." she made a circle with her arms as she said, "right here. I held him close to me. I wanted him to know I was there. I wanted him to know he was not alone. I held him as his life drained from his body. He asked me to hold him close, and I did." She wiped the tears off her face. "He was there one moment, telling me that he loved me, and gone the next. No one did anything to help. No one could."

Liam took her hand into his. "I'm sorry you had to go

through that."

She sniffed as she wiped her face again. "If that wasn't bad enough, I had to bury my husband in June."

"What?"

"My husband. He died in June. This is his baby, but he's gone. Here, I have time at my fingertips, and there was no way to help either of the men I loved with all my heart. Some people only find true love once. I found it twice...and I lost it twice."

"I'm so sorry."

"So am I. *But* Tripp gave me these words to hold onto. Here, look," she said and opened her journal. "It says, '*He made everything beautiful in its time.*' Despite it all, I have to trust in God. I have to trust in His timing. I have to have faith and trust in His grace and kindness...in His mercy. I will trust in Him every day."

Liam smiled.

"What?"

"Look," he said, opening the cover of Patrick's journal. In Patrick's handwriting were the words, '*He made everything beautiful in its time.*'

Tori shook her head. "Sometimes things amaze me that shouldn't."

"Do you want to go to breakfast with me? We don't even have to leave the island. It's right over there. We can go to the upper deck."

"Okay. I feel too drained to go home right now anyway."

"I can see that. Come on."

They talked long into the day and night. Tori filled him in on her and Tripp's time travel adventures. He had a thousand questions. She was able to answer just about all of them regarding the times they went to for adventures. He told her about himself, and she told him about herself. Tori went for a memorial, and came away with a good friend. She half-wondered if Patrick had a hand in their meeting.

They both caught the last ferry back to Port Clinton, where Tori got a hotel for the night. During their talk, Tori finally figured out what she was going to do. After the baby was born, she would go to school to be a nurse. Until then, she would work on shutting the investigation service down and get ready for baby Sebastian to come.

She had help with shutting everything down and building Sebastian's room. Liam got a job as a professor at the local college teaching history. He moved at the beginning of October. Normally a college did not let the professor come in part way, but their history professor got sick and had to leave, so his timing was fortuitous. Tori fully believed this was a God-thing. She did not believe in coincidence or luck – she believed in God and His timing.

History was Liam's passion, and the way in which he shared it allowed his students to catch the fire. Tori would sit in his class once and a while just to listen. She was amazed at how drawn in the students were to his speaking.

Finally, the time came for Tori to deliver. The family was sitting in her parents' house on Christmas Eve, sharing stories with Liam as a guest when her water broke.

"No! It's too early!" her mom panicked.

"No, Mom. It's going to be okay," Tori promised. "I knew he would come early."

She and Liam shared a look that both understood how she knew.

Rushing her to the hospital, the family was nervous. Tori continued to hold onto the hope of Tripp's words that the baby would be perfectly fine.

When she heard the bellowing wails of her new little boy, her heart leapt.

"It's a healthy baby boy," the doctor announced as he handed the baby off to the nurse to clean up. "Not sure how, but this baby does not look like a preemie."

"Maybe you got the original date incorrect?" Tori suggested.

"Maybe. After all, who wants to own conceiving on April Fool's Day," he said with a smile. "Got a name yet?"

"Actually, I do," she said to the surprise of her mother, who was sitting with her. "I'm going to name him after his dad: Sebastian Connor Hayden, the third. We'll nickname him *Tripp*."

"Love that idea," her mother gushed.

"It's how it was meant to be," Tori said confidently. "After all, He made everything beautiful in its time."

19 DEC 2026

"Tori!" Tripp jostled Tori, as she slept with her husband, Liam, in their deep east Texas home. Their children rested in their own rooms on either side of the master suite.

"Who are you? What's going on?" Liam demanded. He and Tori had been married for two years by that point. Liam rubbed his eyes and looked again.

"What?" Tori asked, sitting up. "Tripp? Tripp!" she squealed, throwing her arms around him. "I've missed you!"

"Who is that, and what is he doing in our bedroom in the middle of the night?" Liam growled. "As a matter of fact, how did you get in here?"

"I'm her great-great-great-grandson," Tripp said with a smirk.

Liam furrowed his brow. "Tori?" he asked.

"He's telling the truth," Tori said. "He's the one I traveled through time with to fix the family."

Liam gestured toward him. "He's Tripp?"

"Yes. I am," Tripp said. "Congratulations on your daughter. She's what? A year old now?"

"Yes," Tori said. "Little Elizabeth Victoria turned a year last week. And Tripp is three now."

"Elizabeth Victoria & Tripp – both good choices. You have sufficiently carried on the family names with your little ones. You've even got your nursing degree. Now, we need to make a new tradition in our family, starting in 1650."

Tori nodded, remembering the journal their relative Maggie told them about in 1922. "The Christmas that almost wasn't."

"Here are your clothes," Tripp said, handing her a bag of clothing for women from 1650 Ireland.

Liam turned on the light and looked at Tripp's clothes for the first time. "Wow! Those look authentic."

"They are," Tripp said. "I went back and got both of us a couple outfits."

"Can I come too?" Liam asked.

"No," Tripp said. "If something happens you need to be here for the babies."

"I'm a history professor. I could be of great use," Liam offered.

"Who will look after the little ones, sweetheart?" Tori asked.
Liam frowned. "Fine."

"Maybe we can take a trip when I get back," Tori suggested to his delight.

"When will you be back?" Liam asked as Tori slid out of bed and went into the bathroom to change.

"It will seem like moments to you," Tripp explained. "I will protect her and bring her back."

"You'd better or there is no time you can escape to in order to stop me from finding you," Liam threatened. "That woman has been through enough. Do *not* get her hurt!"

"I won't. I promise. I will put myself in front of her before that happens. If it helps, Maggie said we were fine. Well, the journal said we were fine. It said travelers came during Christmas to the clans and brought with them a message of hope."

"Is that all it said?" Liam asked.

"That, and that we brought Christmas to the village, and Christianity to their family. There were also pictures of both of us in the journal."

Liam whistled as he looked beyond Tripp to see Tori come out of the bathroom. "You look amazing! Good thing you are dressing warm. It's going to be cold," he pointed out. "Oh! I have something for you," he said, jumping out of bed.

"What is it?" Tori asked.

"This," he said, pulling out a bag from the back of the closet. "It's a medical bag. You don't know what will happen when you go back. You have the medical training now."

"She cannot take back anything that is not from that time," Tripp warned.

"It is, but it isn't," Liam said with a twinkle in his eyes. "Tori told me eventually you would be going back to 1650 Ireland. Since then, I have been researching medical things from that time period and area. I looked up herbal remedies from back then and stocked a bag. I also added some things you may need, Tori, at the bottom, like antibiotic ointment, but put it in an unlabeled container. No one but you will know what it is. I tore strips for bandages. I also put in some tools should you need to do any type of surgery. They are sterilized. In another container, there is alcohol for sterilizing. Those are the only things that are from this time. Everything else is from 1650...at least the plants exist there. People may not know what to use them for, but *you* do. You studied herbology in school during your nursing as an elective. Right?"

"I did," Tori agreed. "Thank you," she said and kissed him as she took the bag from him. "I don't know what I would do without you."

"I aim to never let you find out," he said, hugging her.

"Ready?" Tripp asked, typing the date, time, and location into his TORI.

Tori went to her desk and pulled her TORI out. "Still charged," she said with a smile. She handed it to Tripp to type in the information while she hugged Liam. "You, my love, I will miss!"

"Only for a few minutes on his side," Tripp pointed out.

Tori rolled her eyes. "Semantics."

Tripp chuckled. "We're going on Thursday, December 23rd, 1650," Tripp said. "We're going to go in about three in the morning."

"You *really* need to time that better. This early morning stuff stinks," Tori complained. Tripp chuckled at her remark.

"You got this, babe," Liam said. "I'll be waiting for you right here."

"I'll be right back as far as you're concerned," she said and they shared a kiss.

"Remember, He made everything beautiful in its time," Liam encouraged. "See you when you get back. I have the little ones."

"I love you."

"I love you, too."

With her bag on her shoulder, Tori went over to Tripp and looped her arm through his. "On three?" she asked.

"On three," he agreed. "One...two...three..."

To be continued in the short story: *The Christmas That Almost Wasn't.*

This story will appear in the Texas Sisters Press 2022 Holiday Anthology in the fall of 2022. You can find it on the specials page: https://texassisterspress.com/specials

BOOKS BY C.J. PETERSON

Grace Restored Series can be found: https://cjpetersonwrites.com/team-angel-series-books

Holy Flame Trilogy can be found: https://cjpetersonwrites.com/team-angel-series-books

Divine Legacy Series can be found: https://cjpetersonwrites.com/team-angel-series-books

Sands of Time Trilogy

Sands of Time Trilogy can be found: https://cjpetersonwrites.com/sands-of-time-trilogy

Stand Alone Books

C.J.'s Stand Alone Books can be found: https://cjpetersonwrites.com/stand-alone-books

Anthologies Where C.J. Peterson Is A Participating Author:

Anthologies where C.J. Peterson is a participating author can be found: https://cjpetersonwrites.com/anthologies

The Adventures of Chief and Sarge Children's Books can be found:

https://cjpetersonwrites.com/chief-and-sarge

www.ingramcontent.com/pod-product-compliance
Lightning Source LLC
Chambersburg PA
CBHW060923190726

48286CB00002B/617